Praise for
MYSTERIA

"Splitting the difference between *Desperate Housewives* and *The X-Files*, this paranormal romance brings magic and monsters to the steamy suburbs in four satisfying novellas about the town of Mysteria . . . There's magic, heat, and lots of laughs."
— *Publishers Weekly*

"Charming, funny, and quite offbeat, this collection highlights the vast talents of these authors. The perfect escape read!"
— *Romantic Times*

"This [anthology] has all of the elements that I just love to read about . . . I had such fun reading this book. I really didn't want these stories to end. I loved the town of Mysteria and hope these authors see fit to visit the townspeople . . . again!"
— *The Best Reviews*

"*Desperate Housewives* meets *Charmed*, this collection of novellas is as varied in its content as the authors who've written them. From sweet and passionate to dark and sexy, the werewolves, vampires, demons, witches, fairies, and humans of *Mysteria* are as engaging and fun as they are diverse and compelling."
— *Fresh Fiction*

MYSTERIA LANE

MaryJanice Davidson

Susan Grant

Gena Showalter

P. C. Cast

BERKLEY SENSATION, NEW YORK

THE BERKLEY PUBLISHING GROUP
Published by the Penguin Group
Penguin Group (USA) Inc.
375 Hudson Street, New York, New York 10014, USA
Penguin Group (Canada), 90 Eglinton Avenue East, Suite 700, Toronto, Ontario M4P 2Y3, Canada
(a division of Pearson Penguin Canada Inc.)
Penguin Books Ltd., 80 Strand, London WC2R 0RL, England
Penguin Group Ireland, 25 St. Stephen's Green, Dublin 2, Ireland (a division of Penguin Books Ltd.)
Penguin Group (Australia), 250 Camberwell Road, Camberwell, Victoria 3124, Australia
(a division of Pearson Australia Group Pty. Ltd.)
Penguin Books India Pvt. Ltd., 11 Community Centre, Panchsheel Park, New Delhi—110 017, India
Penguin Group (NZ), 67 Apollo Drive, Rosedale, North Shore 0632, New Zealand
(a division of Pearson New Zealand Ltd.)
Penguin Books (South Africa) (Pty.) Ltd., 24 Sturdee Avenue, Rosebank, Johannesburg 2196, South Africa

Penguin Books Ltd., Registered Offices: 80 Strand, London WC2R 0RL, England

This is a work of fiction. Names, characters, places, and incidents either are the product of the authors'
imagination or are used fictitiously, and any resemblance to actual persons, living or dead, business
establishments, events, or locales is entirely coincidental. The publisher does not have any control over
and does not assume any responsibility for author or third-party websites or their content.

MYSTERIA LANE

A Berkley Sensation Book / published by arrangement with the authors

PRINTING HISTORY
Berkley Sensation mass-market edition / October 2008

ISBN: 978-0-425-22294-2

BERKLEY® SENSATION
Berkley Sensation Books are published by The Berkley Publishing Group,
a division of Penguin Group (USA) Inc.,
375 Hudson Street, New York, New York 10014.
BERKLEY SENSATION and the "B" design are trademarks belonging to Penguin Group (USA) Inc.

PRINTED IN THE UNITED STATES OF AMERICA

10 9 8 7 6 5 4 3 2 1

CONTENTS

The Town of Mysteria . . .

Hundreds of years ago, in the mountains of Colorado, the small town of Mysteria was "accidentally" founded by a random act of demonic kindness. Over time, it has become a veritable magnet for the supernatural—a place where magic has quietly coexisted with the mundane world.

It's a town like any other town, where the high school's Fighting Fairies give fans something to cheer about, where everyone knows your name—if not exactly *what* you are—at the local bar, and where the wishing well actually lives up to its name. Strange occurrences happen every day, but now the ladies of Mysteria are about to unleash a tempest of seduction that will have tongues wagging for centuries to come . . .

DISDAINING
TROUBLE

MaryJanice Davidson

This is for the girls, who know who they are (if you want to know who they are, check the dedication page from Mysteria). They turn these projects into an awfully good time. Who said writing was work? Okay, my grandpa. And Jenny Hildebrandt. And Jessica Growette. And my sister. And my sister-in-law. And—well, I like it, anyway.

Acknowledgments

I owe many people thanks for this story, primarily all the readers who bought *Mysteria* without which, natch, there would be no sequel. So thanks for unlimbering the credit cards, y'all!

Thanks also are due to my long-suffering editor, Cindy Hwang, and my agent, Ethan Ellenberg, who really didn't suffer much at all.

Triplet: One of three children born at one birth.

—*The American Heritage Dictionary of the English Language*

Too good for mere wit. It contains a deep practical truth, this triplet.

—Herbert J. C. Grierson, *The Good Morrow*

Prologue

When the Desdaine triplets were born on a frigid February night (Withering came first, then Derisive, then Scornful, all sunny-side up and staring with big blue eyes at the ceiling), the doctor and attending nurse screamed and screamed. This startled Mrs. Desdaine, who started doing quite a bit of screaming herself, despite the epidural. Two other nurses and a resident also came running, and so did a custodian, wielding a mop like a lance.

The doctor was screaming because the nurse had dropped a tray full of sterilized instruments on his foot, and a scalpel was sticking out of his little toe. The nurse was screaming because he knew his clumsiness was going to cost him his job. Derisive, Scornful, and Withering just stared at the hysteria greeting their first moments out of the womb, then obligingly yowled when the cold air bit their fair skin and they were poked and prodded and (finally) swaddled in warm blankets. (The janitor went away, presumably to mop something; ditto the superfluous personnel.)

Of course, even in a town like Mysteria, natural triplets (that is, triplets born without the aid of artificial means like

IVF or a really good splitting spell) were rare, and triplets that brought about screaming fits from qualified medical personnel were rarer still.

So it wasn't long before stories began to spring up about the Desdaine triplets. The why behind the stories became blurred over time, but the plain truth behind the stories—the triplets were weird—never shaded much one way or the other.

On their second birthday, the girls discovered they could do magic.

On their third birthday, they discovered if they cooperated, they could do *more* magic.

On their fifth birthday, they decided being good guys was for suckers.

And on their sixth, they decided they could count on no one but themselves, but that was perfectly all right. Mom was scolding and loving and superb at not noticing things; Dad had died a month before they were born.

And so time passed, probably the only magic those who don't live in Mysteria are aware of or care about. And the triplets grew older, but not fast enough to suit them or their mother.

One

"Ho-ho," Derisive chortled. "Here he comes."

The triplets were sunning themselves by the wishing well, a charming stone well shaded by trees in the center of town. They had chased the nightmare away for the sixth night in a row with a combination of charms and spit spells and were celebrating by torturing the mailman, who was a drunk, a kicker of cats, and unpleasant besides.

The girls, who were beautiful and knew it (bad) but attached no importance to it (not so bad), were identically dressed in denim shorts, red tank tops, and white flip-flops. Although most twins and triplets outgrew the dressing-in-the-same-outfit stage by, oh, sixteen months, the Desdaines liked it. The better to fool you with, my dear.

"Mom alert?" Withering asked, squinting. Their mother, thank all the devils, was nowhere in sight.

Scornful waved her hand in the direction of the Begorra Irish Emporium. "Still looking at those tacky little leprechauns."

"Not so tacky," Withering reminded her sister. "They do grant one wish."

"Yawn," Scornful replied. "Little silly wishes, like not over-doing the turkey. Nothing significant."

"Do-gooder alert?"

Derisive also waved a hand. "Do-gooder" encompassed three-fourths of the town; there were so few really *evil* people around these days. That would change when they grew up. As it was, at fourteen, they were formidable. If a Mysteria resident wasn't a do-gooder, they were neutral, and stayed out of things. This suited the triplets fine. "No problems. Everybody's at lunch."

"Here he comes," Withering said, her nails sinking into Scornful's arm like talons. She ignored her sister's yelp of pain. Her conscience was clear, but then, it usually was. Besides, Mr. Raggle, the postal carrier, wouldn't be the focus of their wrath if he hadn't called their mother That Name. And in front of the whole pizza parlor, too. "Jerkweed," she added.

"Now," Derisive said, and all three girls made the sign of a *V* with their fingers, spat through the *V*s, then stomped on the spit. They visualized Mr. Raggle coming to harm and, before the thought had barely formed in their treacherous teenaged minds—

"Hey! Help! Aaaagggghhh!"

"Scared of heights," Scornful said thoughtfully, eyeing the postal carrier who had been picked up by unseen forces and flung into the highest branch of the closest maple tree.

"Probably shouldn't have mentioned that where you could hear," Withering said, smiling with approval. She rarely smiled, and both her sisters took it as a gift, and not without astonishment.

"Teach him to call our mother names," Derisive added, and spat again for good measure.

"Girls!"

"Uh-oh."

Derisive craned to look. "Must have run out of leprechauns to look at."

"You girls!" Their mother was running toward them at full speed, black curly hair bobbing all over the place. The triplets knew they took after their late father; their mother was petite, while they already had two inches on her; she was dark-eyed, while their eyes were sky-colored; and they had straight blond hair that hardly moved in gale-force winds. "Girls! I swear, I can't turn my back on you for five seconds!"

"That's true," Withering said. "You can't."

"Get him down! Right . . . *now!*"

The triplets studied their mother, whom they loved but did not like, and tried to gauge the seriousness of her mood. A grounding, they did not need. Not with Halloween only three months away.

"Girls!" Panting, shoving her hair out of her eyes, even wheezing a little, Giselle Desdaine staggered up to her girls and glared at them so hard her eyeballs actually bulged. That was enough for the triplets who, as one, made the *V* with their fingers, said, *"Extant,"* in unison, and spat.

Mr. Raggle shot out of the tree just as their mother said, "Why don't you just *grow up*?!?" He plowed into Withering, knocking them both back into the wishing well.

Two

Thad Wilson was back in Mysteria, and not at all happy about it. Unfortunately, he had been born here, lived the first twelve years of his life here, and had taken fifteen years to realize that Mysteria got into your blood like a poison. The kind that wouldn't kill you but just kept you generally miserable.

An air force brat, his father had re-upped the spring he was in seventh grade (Thad, not his father), and around and around the country they went: Boston, Minot, Ellsworth, San Antonio, Vance, Nellis, Cannon. No wishing wells that really worked, no werewolves who disappeared during the full moon. No witches, no horses that brought nightmares. No wish-granting knickknacks. Just missile silos and PXs.

He'd been so bored he thought he'd puke. And as if bouncing around with his folks hadn't been enough, once he was of legal age, he'd moved to six cities in five years. Finally, he'd given up and come back to Mysteria. He'd had no doubts about finding it. Once you lived there, you could always get back.

As it happened, the local river nymph (what had her name been? Pat? Pit?) had sold the building, and he'd bought it, turning it into a pizza place. Living in Chicago and Boston had taught him what real pizza was supposed to taste like, and by God, he'd show the other Mysteria residents just what—

He heard shrieking, dropped the dough, and bolted out the door. Lettering in track in both high school and college stood him in good stead now; his long legs took him to the scene of the crime (because, since the Desdaine triplets were involved, what else could it be?) in no time.

"You girls!" Mrs. Desdaine was yelling. The girls—whom Thad had very studiously avoided since getting back to town, they just *reeked* of trouble and were way too cute for jailbait— looked uncomfortable and unrepentant. "Get him down right now! *Girls!*"

That's when he noticed the mailman, an unpleasant drunk named—what? Ragman? Raggle?—come sailing out of the tree and slam one of the triplets into the wishing well.

"Oh, shit," he said, screeching to a halt before he could topple into the well himself.

Three

Mrs. Desdaine had helped the wet and enraged postal employee out of the fountain, and the man had run off without so much as a thank-you, which surprised Thad not at all.

Almost immediately after that, a creature shockingly ugly popped up out of the fountain. It smelled, if possible, worse than it looked: like rotten eggs marinating in vomit. It was about five feet tall, squat, with four arms and a long, balancing tail. It was poison green and had what appeared to be a thousand teeth.

Then Thad noticed that the creature turned the exact same shade of gray as the blocks making up the well. Ugly as hell, and a chameleon, too. Terrific.

Mrs. Desdaine was screaming. The two (dry) triplets were screaming. People were starting to come out of their stores, much too slowly, and he put on speed.

He was, in the language of the fey, *naragai*, which literally translated to "no will."

What it actually meant was that he had inherited nothing from his fairy mother: not the immortality, not the strength, not the wings, not even the height (at six feet four inches, his mother was five inches taller than he was). Human genes, he had decided long ago, must be super dominant, because he took after his father in every way.

But he could run like a bastard, which he did now.

"Watch out, watch out!" he yelled, nearly toppling into the fountain himself as he tried to put on the brakes.

"That thing ate Withering!" one of the triplets wailed.

"My baby!" Mrs. Desdaine yowled.

The thing—it looked like a cross between a man and a velociraptor—climbed out of the fountain and stood on the brick walk, dripping and growling and slashing its tail back and forth like a whip.

Thad had no idea what he was going to do to it. Kick it? Breathe on it? Try to drown it without getting his face bitten off?

Then another figure rose from the water, this one a tall, luscious blonde dressed in tattered leathers and armed to the teeth; he counted two daggers and one sword, and those were just the ones he could immediately see.

"Wha?" was all he could manage.

She looked like she was in her early twenties, and he was amazed she'd come out of the fountain, which was only eighteen inches deep. Of course, the lizard man had come out of the fountain, too.

She smiled at Lizard Guy. "This will not end well for you."

Lizard Guy snapped and snarled and wiggled all four arms at her. Its thighs were as big as tree trunks.

The gorgeous blonde did something with her sword; she was so quick he didn't quite catch it. It was almost like she'd flipped it out of her back sheath and was now holding it easily in her left hand. She saluted the monster with it, smiling a little. *Great* smile.

"Dakan eei verdant," she said, trilling her *r*. *"Compara denara."*

Lizard Guy lunged at her. She ducked easily under the swing and parried with one of her own. "I've chased you across three worlds and ten years," she said, almost conversationally. "Did you think I would let you get away now?"

Thad wasn't sure if this was in addition to what she had said, or if she was translating what she had said. What was interesting was that she wasn't out of breath, didn't look excited or flushed . . . just businesslike.

Her backswing lopped off Lizard Guy's head.

"*Cantaka et nu,*" she said, saluting the headless (gushing . . . purple blood, ech!) body. "*Deren va.*"

The other two girls had stopped screaming, and Scornful (or was it Derisive?) kicked Lizard Guy's head out of the way. Thad had to give her props for her rapid recovery. He was still having trouble following the events of the last forty seconds.

"Are you—are you Withering?" Scornful asked in a tentative voice Thad would not have believed any of the triplets capable of.

The grown woman looked around and frowned. "*Cander va iee*—I just left, did I not?"

"I—I wished you'd grow up," Mrs. Desdaine said faintly, looking like she might swoon into the water. "And then you were gone. But you came right back."

At once the woman went to Mrs. Desdaine and knelt, the point of her sword hitting the bricks with a clunk and actually chipping off a piece. "O my mother, when this woman was a girl, she caused you many trials. This woman would ask forgiveness and would spend her life making things right for thee."

"What?" the other three Desdaines gasped in unison.

"Please, this woman asks most humbly," the tall blonde said, her gaze fixed on the bricks.

"That's not Withering," the other two said in unison.

"This woman certainly is."

"Honey, get up off the ground," Mrs. Desdaine said, pushing back matted dark curls. "It's fine, everything's fine. I'm just glad you're—you're back." She choked a bit on that last, but Thad thought she did a fine job of pretending she didn't mind missing the entire adolescence of one of her children.

"Hi," Thad said, utterly dazzled. "I'm Thad Wilson; I run the pizza place across the street."

Slowly, she rose until she was at exact eye level. Her blond hair was matted to her head, and she was dripping all over everything; her sword was stained purple, and he still couldn't take his eyes off her. "Sir, this woman is pleased to meet you."

"Look at you!" Derisive (or was it Scornful?) said, circling the woman. "You're all grown-up and bulgy. And you're talking with a seriously weird accent."

"It took many years to find my way back."

"Let's talk about it," Thad suggested, "over a pizza."

The woman—Withcring—cracked a grin. "This woman has not had a pizza in some time. This woman would be delighted."

And so they trooped across the street.

Four

✳

Withering ate as if someone was going to take it away from her. Given the state of her clothing (clearly homemade from animal skins) and the way her collarbones jutted, Thad guessed her meals were hard to come by.

And where had she been in the five seconds—fifteen years?—she'd been gone? Someplace demanding . . . even unforgiving.

Scornful and Derisive weren't at all happy with the new development, it was obvious to see. Normally you couldn't shut them up. But now the girls picked at their lunch and couldn't stop staring at their sister, then at each other, then at Withering.

Thad couldn't help staring at Withering, either, but for an entirely different reason.

"Honey, I'm so sorry," Mrs. Desdaine was saying, mournfully sprinkling red pepper flakes on her pizza slice. "I never should have said something like that around the wishing well. I've lived in this town my entire life, and I can't believe I was so careless—and at my own daughter's expense!"

"You meant no harm. And, if this woman's memory is correct, we were causing trouble in the first place."

"Traitor," Scornful muttered, picking another slice of pepperoni off her pizza.

"Wicked tall traitor," Derisive added, pushing her plate away.

"I don't care!" their mother cried. "You obviously were sent somewhere awful and forced to grow up there. Your clothes—and your weapons—and you're so *thin*."

Withering looked surprised, as if she wasn't used to anyone worrying about her. Probably she wasn't. "This woman adapted."

"Can you use some pronouns now?" Derisive snapped. "The whole 'this woman' bit is getting real old."

"You shush, Derisive," their mother ordered. "Tell me, Withering, dear. How long were you—were you wherever you were?"

Withering shrugged. "This wom—I didn't keep count. Long enough to survive and take over the realm."

"Realm?" Thad said, speaking for the first time.

"The demonic realm I fell into. I learned to fight by killing demons. And when the time was right, I killed the leader and took over. The one you saw in the water—that was someone trying to snatch back the crown."

"So you're like a queen in that other place?" Scornful said, finally sounding a little—just a little—impressed.

Withering shrugged. "I lead. But now . . ." She looked around the nearly deserted pizza parlor. "I know not where my place is."

"It's with your family, of course," her mother said firmly.

"Perhaps, O my mother," she replied, but she looked doubtful.

"Well, why not?" Thad asked.

Withering looked uncomfortable. "It may not be . . . safe. For me to remain here."

"Of course you're going to remain here," her mother said sharply.

"Yes," Scornful added, then giggled. "This woman will stay."

"You don't have to decide anything right this minute," Thad pointed out and was rewarded with one of her rare, rich smiles.

Five

Withering landed in black dust with a skull-rattling thud. The breath whooshed out of her lungs, and for a moment she just lay there, gasping and inhaling that strange dust.

She painfully climbed to her feet, looking around in bewilderment. She was in an utterly strange, utterly *alien* place. The colors and textures were all wrong; they actually hurt her eyes. She was in a large circle of black dust, beyond which was bright blue grass. It appeared to be an oasis of some kind, because beyond the grass was a waterfall gushing purple water over green rocks.

What had happened? Where the hell was she?

She remembered her mother shouting, she remembered that nasty postal worker knocking her into the—

Oh, no.

No, no, no.

"Mother! Please come get me!" In her extremity of terror, she was screaming. "Please don't *leave* me here!"

"This man . . . is pleased . . . to see this girl."

Her head snapped around, and she saw a grievously wounded man lying about ten feet away, on the edge of the blue grass. He had blood all over him, and every time he gasped for breath, blood bubbles foamed across his lips.

She scrambled over to him. "Where am I? What happened to you?"

His pupils were blown, actually bleeding into the whites of his eyes. She was awfully afraid she was going to barf. Never had she seen someone so hurt. And everything was happening so *fast*, she couldn't—

"Kellmannd Dimension," he groaned. "Demons . . . this man is done. This girl will take over."

"I don't understand. Do you know how I can get back?"

"Nobody gets back. We . . . fight. And die. And someone new comes."

"Fight? Fight who?"

The man managed a nod over her shoulder and coughed. She spared a glance . . . and nearly screamed. The ugliest creature she had ever seen was inching toward her, making its way across the blue grass, thick tail dragging, wrathful growls ripping out of its lungs.

"Take these." He pulled a knife and a sword from somewhere and handed them to her; they were so slick with gore she nearly dropped them. "And fight. Do not . . . fear. We are . . . the forces for good."

Withering had been called many things in her fourteen years, but a force for good wasn't one of them.

"Find . . . the others . . . of this man's kind. And . . . lead."

"But I don't—"

"Behind . . . you . . ."

She stood, holding the sword straight out, and the monster, which had been coming fast, couldn't slow in time and impaled itself on the point.

Not too bright, then. That's something.

She yanked the sword free, gagging at all the purple gore, and neatly sidestepped as the thing fell to the ground. She turned back to the man and discovered he had died during the brief fight.

She stood, looking around the odd landscape, sword

dripping, panting slightly from the adrenaline rush. For good or ill, she was stuck here indefinitely. Apparently strangers dropping in out of nowhere was quite the common occurrence around here.

So. She would fight. She would defend.

She would *live*.

Oh, but her mother and her sisters . . . how could she turn her back on her family? It was too awful, resigning herself to never seeing them again. She'd give anything—anything—to hear her mother scolding her again.

She resolved to put them out of her mind and to keep them there.

A solitary tear trickled down one cheek; she wiped her face, wiped the sword on the grass, and went to look for other people.

Six

Withering obediently followed her mother and sisters out of
the food place (restaurant? Gods and devils, how long since
she had been in a restaurant?), leaving Thad behind to make
more pizza pies. She was still having trouble following the
events of the last hour. One minute she'd been chasing that
horrid Katai, the next there was a crash of light and sound and
normal-colored water (except the clear water seemed wrong
to her, after all the years of purple water) and she was back
with her honored mother and sisters.

And that strange man! Thick dark hair, wonderful chocolate
(ahhh, chocolate! How long since she'd had some?) colored
eyes. Lean, muscular body, and very quick on his feet. Spook-
ily quick.

She had been impressed at how he had rushed over to help;
she could sense no magic in him, nothing especially extraordi-
nary. And yet he had jumped into the fray without hesitation

And how long since she had looked at a man as a potential

mate instead of a fighting partner? Back in the demonic realm, her couplings had been quick and very nearly emotionless; two people trying to snatch a little warmth because one or both would very likely die the next day. Now that she was back, perhaps there would be time for . . .

No. She had responsibilities. She had to keep the portal between Earth Prime and Secondary Earth closed; Mysteria was a wonderful place and did not deserve demonic infestation. She had to get back, and quickly.

But why? It isn't fair! I'm home now, I belong here, not Earth Prime.

But did she? Did she really? She knew now, as she had not many years ago, that special people fell into the demonic realm every few years, that they were charged with keeping the demons in their place.

She had been the first to wrest power from the demons and take over the entire realm. But her position would always be precarious; the demons wouldn't stand for her leadership. Now that she was back—now that her mother's wish had been granted—did that mean she had to put aside any chance for happiness?

She did not know.

"And you remember the home place, Withering, dear." Her mother was leading her into the old house. Strange how small everything looked! "And we'll just—ah—your bedroom is—you remember."

She did. She looked around the master bedroom (her mother had taken the guest room and had given the triplets the largest bedroom), eyeing the bunk beds and the twin bed against the opposite wall. She looked at the dressers and closet, which would be filled with clothes that were too small, not to mention age-inappropriate.

Her sisters said nothing, only watched her.

And suddenly, she felt like crying.

Seven

※

Janameides knocked on the door of the red house with black shingles. He was on a mission from his queen, Potameides, a river nymph whose territory encompassed the entire Mississippi River.

After a moment, the door opened, and a short, chubby brunette stood in the doorway.

"Hey!" she said by way of greeting. "You look like my friend Pot!"

"It is my honor," he said, "to be her subject. I am Janameides."

"Well, come in, come in. My husband's not here right now, but I—"

"I am here to see you, madam."

"Okeydokey." She stepped back and let him in. The house was all right (he preferred open water), with wooden floors and cream-colored walls.

"Who the hell is that?" a rude voice said out of nowhere.

"It's Janameides. He's a friend of Pot's."

"Well, what the hell is he doing here?"

"I dunno. I'm Charlene," she said to him, "but I imagine you knew that."

"Yes, ma'am. Is that the ghost?" he asked in a near whisper.

"I can hear you," the ghost snapped.

"Sorry. Who is she?"

"I can *still* hear you. If you must know, I was a roofer and got my stupid self killed patching a hole."

"And had the bad manners to stick around," Charlene said cheerfully. "Now. What can we do for you, Janameides?"

"My queen asked me to check on her friends. As you may know, she became very attached to some of Mysteria's residents during her exile here."

Charlene nodded. Pot—Potameides—had been exiled from her beloved river and had only been able to go back last year, when a coup returned her to power. Since then, there hadn't been a word.

"You know my name, ma'am," Janameides said politely to the ghost. "Might I have yours?"

"Mind your own damned business."

"It's Rae," Charlene said helpfully.

"Traitor!"

"Oh, hush up." She turned back to a bemused Janameides. "As you can see, we're doing just fine. Please give Pot our warmest regards."

"Don't give her my regards," Rae bitched. "She took off, so she's dead to me."

"Says the dead woman," Charlene muttered.

"I heard that!"

"What are you still doing here, Rae?" Janameides asked.

"Why do you care?"

"I do not know," he admitted. His queen had told him about the ghost, not glossing over her unpleasant personality, but he was intrigued despite his queen's well-meant warning. He felt sorry for Rae, stuck in this house for almost a century. "But I am interested."

"I'm the handyman."

"It's true," Charlene piped up. "She keeps the furnace running, she keeps everything up to code. I never have to so much as call a plumber."

"Flattery will get you nowhere," the ghost said sourly.

"But do you not wish to—to move on?"

"Move on *where*?"

"Wherever people go when they die."

"Rae will never admit it," Charlene said, "but she loves it here. And she loved Potameides."

"Didn't!"

"Without a house to take care of and my husband and me to nag, she'd be lost."

"Lies!"

From down the hall, they heard a baby start to cry. "Oh, nice going," Charlene said, exasperated. "You woke the baby."

"Oh, like that's a big trick. That thing doesn't sleep; it cat-naps for thirty seconds at a time."

"That thing," she said sternly, "is my daughter, and that's quite enough of your attitude, miss."

"Mmmph," the ghost said.

"Excuse me," Charlene said, and hurried out of the room.

"So, Jan," the ghost said, "anybody ever tell you, you smell like the deep end of a swimming pool?"

"No."

"Not that it's a bad smell," she added hastily. "It's just different. Pot smelled the same way, that abandoning cow."

"I must ask you not to speak so about my queen."

"Ask away, pal, and see where that gets you."

"She did warn me about you," he admitted.

"What? That jerk was talking about me? What'd she say? Ooooh, I'll kill her!"

"How can you, if you're discorporated?"

"Just never mind. What'd she say?"

"She said you were unpleasant and rude as a defensive mechanism because you're really quite lonely."

"Lies!"

"Well," he said, drumming his long fingers on the kitchen table, "perhaps we can discuss that."

Eight

Thad managed to stay away from Withering Desdaine for a whole day, until he gave in and brought a pizza to her house. He was knocking on the door when he felt cold steel slip around his throat. This was disconcerting, to put it mildly.

"Uh . . ." He coughed. Cripes, he hadn't heard her move, much less get the drop on him. "Lunch?"

"Oh! This woman apologizes. Old habits, you know." He turned and saw Withering sheathe her knife. She had obviously been taken shopping, because she was wearing jeans and a T-shirt, both of which fit snugly. Also, she had on her sword and both knives. It was startlingly sexy.

"And you brought food!" She greedily snatched the pizza box from him. "This woman is so grateful."

"This man says it's no sweat. Invite me in?"

She blinked at him with those big baby blues. "Why?"

"Uh . . . so we can share the pizza?"

"Oh. Oh! Of course. Yes, indeed, please come in. My honored mother is at her job, but my sisters are here."

"Terrific," he muttered, following her inside.

"Oh," Scornful said, eyeing him in a distinctly unfriendly way. "It's you."

"It's me," he agreed. "Want some pizza?"

"No."

"Please excuse me for a moment," Withering said. "I was just about to urinate when you came."

"Oh. No problem."

Withering was barely out of the room when Scornful started in. "Look, pal, I know what you're up to."

"You do?" It was downright unnerving, looking at a much younger version of Withering. Same blond hair, same riveting blue eyes. "Odd, because I hardly know myself."

"You're sniffing around my sister like some kind of speed freak dog."

"A speed freak d—'?"

"Leave her alone! She's still adjusting to being back. And we're still adjusting to her being—ugh—a grown-up."

"It's just a pizza," he huffed, offended.

"Suuuuuure, McHorny, whatever you say." She was seated at the kitchen table, flipping through a book that was not written in English but instead covered in runes and various squigglings. She slammed the book shut and added, "Look, you think we don't know she's a knockout? That whole polite/tough/vulnerable thing prob'ly works on you like a hormone shot."

"We are not," he decided, "having this conversation."

"Look, we get it. But she's got enough on her mind right now. Not to mention she's trying to find a way *back*. Or, at least, we think she is," Scornful added in a barely audible mutter. "It's hard for us to tell *what* she's up to; she sure keeps her cards close to the vest."

"Wants to go back? Why in the hell—"

"We don't know, nimrod! She's not talking."

"All right, calm down, don't have a stroke and *don't* cast a spell on me. I hate that shit. Can't she just hop back in the wishing well?"

"You know how capricious that thing is. There's no guarantee she'd end up exactly where she wanted to be."

"Why would she even want to—" He shut up as Withering entered the room. "Have a slice of pepperoni?" he finished.

Scornful looked amused but said nothing.

"Do you think Derisive would like some food?" Withering asked.

"No. She's deep in the Web right now, trying to research your weirdo demon kingdom."

"She's in a web?" Withering looked alarmed. "That doesn't sound safe at all."

Scornful stifled a groan. "Never mind."

"How could she search for another dimension on our Web?" Thad asked.

"Magic, dummy."

"Scornful," Withering said sharply.

"Hey, you're technically the same age as me, so back off."

"I certainly am not; I am your elder, if not necessarily your better, and you will treat our honored guest with respect."

Scornful made a retching sound. "Honored guest? Withering, what the Christ *happened* to you over there?"

"Several things," Withering said dryly. "Watch your language. Now eat, dear one, or begone."

"Can't I do both?" she griped, snatching a piece and flouncing out of the room, her book of runes tucked under one arm.

"I trust you will overlook my dear sister's rudeness. This is a difficult time for her."

"For *her*?" He couldn't believe the mature, supercool Withering was sticking up for *that* brat. If nothing else, being stuck in that hell dimension had sure improved her people skills. He guessed fighting for her life most days and eventually taking over as queen of all demons was almost as good as charm school. "How about for you?"

Withering shrugged, took her own piece, and chewed. "It is . . . difficult for my family. Seeing me as a grown woman after being gone—how long was I gone?"

"About five seconds our time."

"Interesting. And yet it explains much. You can imagine their difficulty."

"Actually, I was a lot more worried about yours."

Withering shrugged again.

"What's this I hear about you going back?"

"That, good sir, is none of yours and all of mine."

Thad mulled that one over for a moment. "Listen. I normally don't thrust myself into other people's lives—"

She nearly choked on her pizza. "No?"

"—but I made an exception in your case. You must have missed your family all these years. Now you're back. Why the hell would you leave again?"

Withering stared at her pizza slice, then put it down as if she had suddenly lost her appetite. "It's complicated, good sir."

"Thad."

"Yes. Thad. I have many responsibilities. And it is not in me to hide in this lovely town while—while things happen that I must prevent."

"Don't you at least deserve a vacation?"

"Vacation?" she asked blankly.

"Or a date?"

"Date?" she asked, just as mystified.

"Do you like bowling?"

"I—I don't quite remember what that is. Is it like hunting?"

"Sure, except with balls and pins instead of swords and slings."

She brightened. "Then I might be good at it!"

"So. We'll go. Tonight. Hey, if you have to go back, I respect that—and like you said, it's none of my business." This was a rather large lie, as he felt (unreasonably, he knew) everything about Withering was his business. Was there another woman in the world—worlds—like her? He thought not. Was he going to let her go so easily? No damned way. "But before you take off, don't you deserve some fun?"

"I—I did not consider that."

"So. I'll pick you up tonight."

"You didn't listen," Scornful yelled from the living room, "to a word I said, McHorny!"

Withering glanced in that direction and frowned. "Please overlook my sister's rudeness."

"I could care less about *that* sister."

"Eh?"

"So," he added brightly. "Pick you up at seven?"

Nine

The late Rae Camille, former roofer and current spirit, watched with interest as Jan the river guy poked around the outside of the house. First he'd knocked on the front door for a good five minutes, but he was shit out of luck. Charlene had taken her smelly baby to a playdate with another drooling, incontinent infant and wouldn't be back until three. And Char's werewolf husband was visiting the Cape on Pack business.

Now he was futzing around in the back garden, and now he was trying the back door. What the hell? Was he some sort of river-nymph thief guy? Yeek.

Now he was—was he? Yes! He was actually kicking the back door with his long, squishy, pale feet. In fact, he looked a great deal like her old friend Pot, Jan's queen: ridiculously tall and too thin.

She could see the skull beneath his face, see the bones stretching through all the limbs. His hair was a sort of greenish blond, like he spent too much time in a chlorinated pool (which, for all she knew, he did). And his eyes were a pale, swimmy green, like a summer pond filled with algae. His eyebrows and lashes were so pale, they actually seemed to disappear. His fingers and toes were weirdly long; his voice low and bubbling, like he was always speaking through water. It should have been creepy, but it was sort of—what? Interesting? Yeah. Even soothing.

"Rae?" he called in that odd, bubbling voice. "Rae? May I enter?"

He was here to see *her*? Yeesh, when was the last time *that* happened?

She made the back door unlock itself, and in he came.

"Hello, Rae," he burbled cheerfully.

"Hello yourself, you big, wet weirdo. What's on your squishy mind today?"

"You," he said baldly.

She laughed, the sound echoing throughout the empty (well, not anymore) house. "Then you got problems, squishy."

"Perhaps. How may you be released?"

"Eh?"

He was pacing in the kitchen, every step a squish. Charlene was going to *freak* when she saw the mess. "Released. Freed from this prison of a house."

"Hey, this *prison* has a fixed mortgage rate of six point nine. Not to mention authentic hardwood floors and all the original woodwork. And, if I do say so myself, the place runs like a frickin' top."

"But your immortal soul is trapped on this plane. We must release you."

" 'We,' huh? Why all the weird, creepy concern, Jan, Jan, the river man?"

"I have never met anyone like you before," he said simply. "It distresses me to think of your imprisonment."

"Imprisonment!" she hooted. "Ho-ho! Let me explain something about the afterlife to you, chumly. It's all about free will. Sure, you see the bright light and all, you see Grandma and your dog Ralph—"

"I never had a dog named—"

"—you feel like reaching out to it and being warm forever and ever. But you don't *have* to go. Especially if you feel bad because you left the house a mess."

"Left the house a—?"

"Stop interrupting, squishy! So, like I said. You don't have to follow the light. Especially if you like the town you've been in and want to find out—oh, I dunno. It's like walking out in the middle of a great movie. You feel cheated. You want to see how it ends."

"And have you seen how it ends, Rae?"

"Here? In *this* town? Not even close, chumly. Not even a little bit close." She paused. What came next went against her nature, and she could hardly believe she was thinking it, much less saying it. "But it's really nice of you to be concerned. I, uh—" She was struck with a sudden coughing fit, recovered, and finished, "I appreciate it."

"But you cannot remain stuck here for—for a lifetime!"

"Says the guy whose people live for centuries. You ever thought about what it's like to be human? With a life span of maybe sixty years? Well. It was sixty years in my day. It's more like eighty-some now."

"At eighty-some," he admitted, "we have barely attained maturity."

"Right. So why would I want to check out early? Huh? Huh?"

"But are you not lonely? Do not lie. I know you are."

"You don't know shit, chumly."

"I do indeed know shit, Rae."

"How so?"

"Because," he replied, "I am lonely, also."

"You?" She couldn't hide her surprise. Also her irritation at his incessant probing. "But you've got a zillion river nymphs to hang out with. You've got your queen back after she was exiled here for—what? A hundred years? You've got the whole Mississippi River to run around in. And you're *lonely*?"

"Yes," he said simply.

"Well, jeez." She paused, chewing on that one. "That's the saddest damned thing I've ever heard. And I saw the Depression."

Ten

Withering whipped the ball down the lane, envisioning the pins as a pack of Daniir demons, and watched with total satisfaction as they scattered and disappeared. She threw her arms over her head in triumph. "Die! Die, you filthy, unearthly scum! Die, die, *die*! Yessssss!"

"Uh, okay, that's another strike." Thad was eyeing the other bowlers, who were eyeing Withering. "Just simmer down, okay?"

"This is a battle like any other," she said grimly, snatching up another ball, testing its heft, and readying herself to hurl it down the lane. All strength, no finesse—which had always worked fine for her. "And I will win it."

"That's the spirit," he muttered, marking down her score.

"Although I detest wearing group shoes."

"Hey, they spray 'em every night with a disinfectant."

"This woman is not comforted."

"This woman," he sighed, "is kicking my ass at a game she barely remembered and has never played before. If I can put up with that humiliation, you can wear the bowling shoes without bitching."

"The man has a point." Kuh-clank, *Bam!* "Die, die, *die*! Ar-rrrghh! There's one still alive."

"It's a pin, Withering. It's never been alive, not once."

Hmph. Although she found him disturbingly attractive, *distractingly* attractive, he didn't have much in the way of a competitive spirit. Did the man not know that everything, every single thing, must be won? No matter how long it took, no matter the cost? Even a silly game of pins and balls? You could never know who was watching, weighing, judging. Deciding the manner of attack based on her most recent actions.

"I think," he was blathering, "you could stand to, uh, lighten up a little bit. You're not fighting demons tonight. Tonight is about taking a break, remember?"

"This woman does not understand this man."

"Well, that makes two of us," he said, and got up for his turn. Without hardly looking, he tossed the ball down the lane, and it went into the small alley—what was it called? Gutterball. A shameful, humiliating gutterball.

He cheerfully marked down a zero—how could he stand it? He hadn't even tried. He didn't even care. "Like we were talking about earlier," he continued. "You deserve a break. You've spent as much time at war as you spent in Mysteria raising hell with your sisters. I can't think of anyone who deserves a break more than you."

"It is difficult—and unworthy—to take a break from one's responsibilities. It pleases some on Earth Prime," she admitted, "to call me queen. But does a queen ever get a vacation from royalty?"

"But you're not on Earth Prime. You're back home. And while we're on the subject, I think *this* ought to be Earth Prime. What'd you say this was? Secondary Earth? Jeez. How many are there?"

"Thousands," she replied simply.

"Well, from what you've told me, Earth Prime is all weird grass and demons and only a few humans. *This* Earth has Mysteria and tons of humans and almost no demons. Ergo, we're Prime."

"I," she said, amused, "did not name the parallel universes."

"No, you only rule one."

"Hardly that," she said, laughing a little to hide her discomfort. Why was he looking at her like that? So intently, as if everything she said was exceedingly important? "This woman keeps it safe for those who cannot protect themselves. If it pleases some to call this woman queen, this woman has other things to worry about."

"See, see?" He threw another gutter ball, ignoring her groan. "This is what I'm talking about. You won't even take the spoils of war—a royal title! It's just kill, kill, kill and work, work, work with you."

"And bowl, bowl, bowl," she said, snatching up another ball. "Now watch this, Thad. You have to *look* at where the ball goes. Visualize the enemy lying dead and bloody. Then throw." She hurled the ball; the pins split apart so hard, one actually flew into the next lane. "Then, victory."

"Psycho," he sang under his breath, marking down her score.

"This woman is unfamiliar with that word."

"It means terrifying warrior queen."

She narrowed her eyes at him. "Your face does not match your words; this woman thinks you lie."

"Well, you're a pretty smart psycho. We'll add that to the list of your very fine qualities."

"You seem oddly cheerful."

"Why not? I'm on a date with a gorgeous warrior queen who bowls like a fiend and can eat half a large pizza by herself."

She laughed in spite of herself. "You may blame yourself for that last, sir; you make an excellent pizza pie."

"It's true," he said without a trace of modesty. "I do."

"But you cannot bowl," she teased, then remembered one of Scornful's favorite epithets, "for shit."

"Ouch, nasty! Gorgeous, there's hope for you yet."

Eleven

✳

They walked outside the bowling alley, to Thad's serial killer gray van (which his employees occasionally used for deliveries; thus, the logo WILSON'S PIES: YOU COULD DO BETTER, BUT WHY BOTHER? plastered on the sides in bright red paint). Thad was still fumbling with his seat belt when Withering seized him by the shirt and hauled him toward her. His elbow hit the horn, which let out a resonant *brronk!* and then her mouth was on his.

"What am I?" he asked, managing to wrench free and gasp for breath, "the spoils of war?"

"No. I wish to mate. Right now."

"Well, I'm sorry," he huffed, straightening his shirt and hair, "but I'm not that kind of guy. I need wooing and romance. I need flowers and dinner. I—oh, fuck it, come back here."

They climbed into the back of the van, which was empty, carpeted, and smelled strongly of garlic and pizza sauce. They rolled around the strong-smelling floor, tugging and yanking at each other's clothes, Thad marveling at her smoothly muscled body: not an ounce of fat anywhere, but my God, the scars!

They didn't detract from her beauty; they deepened it,

made her seem more like a real woman and less like a goddess. The one arcing across her abdomen was so long and twisted, he wondered how she'd survived the original wound.

She wrapped her legs around his waist and urged him forward—well, yanked him forward was more like it. He was concerned; he normally liked to give a partner more than eight seconds of foreplay. But she was having none of it, pulling him forward, her fingers digging into his shoulders, her hips rising off the carpet to meet his.

"I don't want to hur—whoa!" Sex with Withering wasn't unlike being caught in a rowing machine. A hot, limber, blond rowing machine. Used to being the aggressor in sex, Thad just closed his eyes and tried to hang on for the ride. In less than a minute he was spasming inside her and shaking so hard he wondered if the van was rocking.

"Gah," he said as she gently pushed him off her. He flopped on his side next to her, trying to catch his breath. "Well. That. Ah. That was—"

"Very quick," she said, sounding indecently satisfied. She was rapidly rearranging her clothes, tying her long hair back with a ponytail holder. "Thank you."

"I guess it's all right," he said slowly, "that swiftness impresses you."

"How else would you do it? This way we can clothe ourselves and be ready to face danger."

Oh my God.

"Uh. There are lots of other ways to 'do it.' In fact—"

"Oh, no. No, no, no. Much too dangerous."

"But did you even come?"

"Come where?"

Oh my God. Please let me teach her the many ways two people can pleasure each other. Please let her stay *so I can teach her, please God.*

"I guess," he said slowly, buckling his belt, "I'd better drive you home."

Twelve

He dropped a cheerful Withering at her front door and began the walk back to the van, when suddenly the sidewalk turned to glue (or so it felt) and he was stuck fast.

"Cut it out, you two!" he said loudly, struggling to extricate himself.

Scornful and Derisive peered down at him from their tree house. The town knew the girls were too old for it, as they also knew that was where the triplets (when they *were* triplets) retreated to work on their more diabolical plans.

"You'd better explain," Scornful said.

"And right now, before the sidewalk ends up over your head."

"Unnnf!" he replied. "Nnnnnfff! Mmmmmff!" One foot moved a whole inch.

"So talk," Derisive added.

"Mind—nnf!—your own—mmfff!—damned—argh!—business," he panted.

"Our sister *is* our business. She might look like a hottie grown-up, but she's a little naive in some areas, like you haven't noticed."

His feet were moving slightly easier. "You can't—nnff!—do the magic—rrggh!—you could when—mrrgg!—you were the Desdaine triplets."

"We can do enough," Scornful said shortly, and he knew he had touched on a sore spot. He wondered what had happened to Withcring's magic. Out of practice, probably, from the years of fighting. "So what are you doing with her?"

"None of your damned—ha!—business." One foot was free. He set to work on the other.

"It is, too! Is this why you came back to Mysteria? To score on the new girl?"

"No. And *that* is none of *your* business."

"We can do a lot more than stick you in cement up to your ankles," Derisive threatened.

"Think I don't know? But what's between your sister and me is private."

"Guess he doesn't kiss and tell," Scornful said to her sister.

"Prob'ly just as well; who needs to puke after that good supper Mom cooked?"

He knelt to get better leverage as he tugged on his left foot. "You two are a menace!"

"Tell us something we haven't heard since we were two. Look, all we want to know is, are you sticking around this time?"

"This time?"

"We looked you up in the archives. Your whole family picked up and left when you were a kid. Now you're back, and you're sniffing around our sister. So are you in it for the long haul, or just a slap and tickle before you vanish?"

"I'm—never—leaving—again. God *damn* it, what'd you turn the sidewalk into, rubber cement?"

"Oh."

"Huh," Scornful added. "Never leaving again?"

He temporarily abandoned his efforts to escape. "I came back because I thought Mysteria had gotten into my blood. There's nowhere else like it in the world, kids, but I guess you know that."

"So?" they asked in unison.

"So. Your sister grew up in five seconds, and now I'm here for her. I'll always be here for her. I'm trying to get her to stay.

I'm trying to get her to relax and not be ready to fight all the time. Now get me out of this shit!"

The girls made identical gestures, as if they were pulling invisible taffy, and his foot popped free, and the sidewalk was solid again. He nearly toppled backward but righted himself in time.

"I guess that's all right, then," Scornful said.

"We can't watch her twenty-four/seven," Derisive added.

"So nice to have your permission," he snapped.

"Don't kid yourself, Thad. You did need our permission. Unless you like the idea of getting stuck in every sidewalk, driveway, and linoleum floor between here and the shooting range."

"Oh, and Thad?" Scornful added sweetly as he stomped down the sidewalk. "Break her heart, and we'll break your spine."

"Among other things," Derisive added.

Great, he thought, climbing into his van, *teenage mob enforcers.* Just what the town needed.

Thirteen

✳

"Pardon me," Janameides said politely, "but do any of you know where I might find an exorcist?"

He was standing in the Desdaine living room, having been ushered in by Mrs. Desdaine, who had been headed out the door for work. Shrugging at the sight of the river nymph (but not at all worried for her daughters' safety—she hadn't been *before* Withering grew up in an alternate dimension)—Mrs. Desdaine had made herself scarce.

"This woman would know why the—the man needs an exorcist," Withering said. She was the only one fully dressed at 7:45 a.m.; the other two girls were in the shorts and T-shirt sets they used as pajamas.

"Yes, what *are* you?" Scornful asked. "You look like Pot . . . she's the lady who used to—"

"She is my queen. I am her subject."

"River nymph!" Derisive said, snapping her fingers and pointing at him.

"Just so. And I require an exorcist, please. I was told you three might help." Jan frowned, the expression much more dour than it could be on a human face. "I was also told you are the same age."

"Technically, we are," Derisive said.

"But it's a long story," Scornful added.

"Actually, it's not," Derisive said, "but who cares? What's the exorcist for?"

"A haunted house. But perhaps the three of you could handle the task. I was told your power as triplets—"

"Is no longer a resource to be tapped," Withering said.

Scornful turned to her tall sister. "Yeah? And why is that? Did you forget the spells? Because we can get you books and stuff."

"I did not forget. I merely submerged my share of our magic into my fighting skills, an essential component to my survival. As such, I am faster and stronger than most; I also heal from wounds very quickly."

"So, you made yourself bionic?" Scornful snorted.

"I did what I had to," Withering said simply, "to live."

The two girls were, shockingly, shamed into silence. It was only temporary, though. "I think we can help you," Derisive said. She turned to her younger sister. "The new guy? Not Thad, the other new guy."

"The witch doctor?"

"You're only assuming that because he's Jamaican."

"Yeah, but he might—"

"He might."

"So we should—"

"We should."

"What my sisters are saying," Withering explained to an increasingly bewildered Jan, "is that we may be able to assist you. If you will come with us, please?"

"This has nothing to do with you, gigantic big sister."

"This woman will see the girls safe."

"Oh, barf," Scornful said, stomping toward her bedroom to get dressed.

Fourteen

✳

The witch doctor shook various homemade implements at various appliances in the kitchen. He had multiple piercings (including four gold rings in each eyebrow), but was dressed in street clothes and carried a blue backpack, from which he pulled various odd things.

He refused to tell them his name, so Scornful christened him Dr. Demento. As in, "Hey, Dr. Demento! You gonna keep shaking stuff at the toaster, or are we actually going to get to work, here?"

"Dis house, she's evil, mahn."

"Evil, my big butt," the ghost said out of nowhere. The two younger girls jumped; Withering had her knife in her hand by the word *my*. The witch doctor shook harder. "You realize, I only let you idiots in because nobody's home, and I'm bored out of my tits. Right?"

"Now, Rae," Jan said in his bubbling, oddly soothing voice, "just cooperate, and soon your essence will be set free."

"Sounds nauseating. I think I'll stay put."

Dr. Demento reached into his backpack and withdrew a

second mysterious object (a good trick, with the backpack strapped behind him as it was), and shook both at the fridge.

"I can't believe we've never been here before," Scornful whispered to her younger sister.

"I heard that, you little brat. And you don't have to get your perky little noses into *everything* in this town."

"You do not belong here, ghost," Withering said, the knife point never wavering. "Begone at once."

"Look who's talking! Don't you have a demonic realm to be ruling? Instead, you're nosing around in *my* house and poking around in *my* business."

"How did you—"

"Ha! The whole damned town is talking about it, that's how I knew."

"Then if this woman may so inquire, what is it like to be displaced?"

"If I didn't like it, I wouldn't be here, get it? So buzz off, and take the witch doctor with you. Better than him have tried and failed."

Jan protested as Withering sheathed her knife. "But he will set you free, Rae!"

"Aw, that's super. No sale."

"Hey, Dr. Demento. Can I shake something at the television?" Scornful tried to get at his backpack, but he whirled and backed away from her, still shaking various homemade tools. "Aw, come on. How come you get to have all the fun?"

"You call this fun?" Rae grumped. "Will you people get lost before the fridge accidentally falls on one of you? Two or three times?"

"Yeesh," Derisive said.

"You say it's been tried before? Was that John Harding, by any chance?"

"Sure."

"But he was alive when *you* were alive. The way I heard it, his heart wasn't in it, and that's why he couldn't banish you. Dr. Demento here doesn't care how you got here or where you go."

"Jan, you got a lot of nerve, bringing the psycho triplets and a witch doctor—a *witch doctor* of all things!—into this house."

"But Rae, I wish only to—"

"—be an enormous pain in my ass. At which you're succeeding beautifully."

"There is little we can do here," Withering told her sisters. "I suggest we take our leave."

"And take Dr. Demento with you!" Rae called.

"No." Jan actually stomped his foot, which squished. "He will set you free, and you will no longer be imprisoned."

The refrigerator slid all the way across the room, the yanked plug trailing behind it like a tail.

"We're out of here," the younger girls said in unison as Withering grabbed the witch doctor by the elbow and started hauling him toward the front door.

"I'd vamoose, too, if I were you, River Nymph."

"That's good advice from the kid," Rae warned. "Whichever one it was."

"Thank you," Jan called as all four made their way to the doorway, "for your assistance."

"Yeah, and next time, take your damned shoes off in the entryway!" Rae hollered as the front door slammed.

Fifteen

✳

"You tried to get rid of me!"

Jan ducked as the toaster sailed over his head. "It was my dearest wish to see you free, yes."

"Tossing me like a dead Easter chick!" The small board that normally held car keys soared toward him; he backpedaled on his long feet and handily avoided it.

"Rae, you are reading this entirely the wrong way."

"If *I* showed up in the Mississippi River with antinymph spray, how would *you* take it?"

"Anti what?"

"Oh, never mind. Just get out of here."

"I will not." He stood his ground stubbornly, even when Stephen King's *The Stand* (hardcover edition, which weighed approximately twenty-seven pounds) hit him in the chest. "You need my help, and I will not leave until you have it."

"I'll bet Pot will have something to say about that, Squishy."

"My queen has given me leave to stay. In fact, she was pleased that one of her people will watch over the town she so loves."

"Pot said torturing me with witch doctors who wear

Dockers is okay? What the blue hell is the world coming to?"

"I do not know. I do know I cannot bear to see you trapped when I have unlimited freedom of movement."

"But Jan—" Rae's tone softened, and he tried not to display his surprise. "Jan, by staying here, you're restricting your own movement. You said it yourself, your home is a long way away from here."

"My home," he said firmly, "is wherever you are."

There was a long, long silence. When she broke it, it sounded like—but of course he must be mistaken—but it sounded like she was crying softly. "You mean it? You want to stay here with me?"

"Yes. I never lie, Rae, and I certainly would not start with you, even if I did."

"But why?"

"I do not know," he said simply.

"Because if it's because you feel sorry for me, I'll throw the door at your head right now."

"I did at first pity you. But even in my pity, I greatly admired your fortitude in a difficult situation. And when my queen's business was finished, I was unable to leave town. Because of you, Rae, I was unable to go back to my people. That is not pity. That is—something else."

"Something else," she mused.

"If you will not leave this silly red house and move to the next plane, I have no choice but to also remain."

"I could build an extension," she said eagerly. "I could give you your own bathroom and everything. A *big* hot tub for you to soak in whenever you want!"

"So you do not mind if I remain?"

"Like I can do anything about it?"

"You cannot," he said smugly.

"Char and her husband might have something to say about it—oh, who am I kidding? They're always looking for babysitters for the Thing That Poops. And they've been reaping the benefits of my free handiwork for ages. Okay, for a few months. But I'll ramp up the value of the house if I build on another bed and bath. Of course, they'll have to buy the supplies, but it's still cheaper than—"

"Rae, do be quiet."

"Better get used to it, pal. Anybody nutty enough to fall for a ghost—*my* ghost—and give up his river for Mysteria had better be resigned to everyday chatter. But I'm betting there are compensations."

"Compensations?" he asked, then gasped as he felt her essence rush through him like a cool wind, raising goose bumps on his arms and causing him to rock backward on his heels. He could feel cool, ghostly hands on him, touching, caressing, stroking, and oh, the sensation was delightful, the coolness was delightful; living humans were just too *warm*.

He heard her laugh in his ear, and that raised more pleasurable goose bumps, heard her sigh and felt her grip tighten, except it seemed as though she had four hands, ten, a dozen, and they were everywhere, everywhere, touching and cuddling and making him hard and making him shudder and making him spasm all over until he realized he was flat on his back on the kitchen tile.

"Oh," he gasped, thinking he needed five or six bottles of water. Right now.

"Hmmm," Rae replied, sounding like she was lying beside him.

"That was—that was—" What? Supremely satisfying? Sublime? Out of this world?

"Fun!"

"For you as well?" He was unable to hide his surprise.

"Whoo, yeah! First orgasm I've had in—what century is this again? Never mind. When I went into your body, I could feel everything you were feeling, which made me feel even better, which I projected onto you, which made me feel better—you get the picture."

"Oh, my," he gasped. "So you can do that whenever you wish?"

"Apparently so."

"I may never walk again."

"So who's asking you to?" she said and laughed in his ear, the sound a warm caress.

Sixteen

✳

It came from the wishing well and found it was dark in this place; the moon was high, and the stars were bright—and the stars were wrong. It followed the hated woman's scent through the small park, down the oddly flat lane (the blacktop felt strange beneath its feet and claws) and toward the small red house, her scent getting stronger with every step.

And with every step, it became angrier.

It would find the usurper, the dire queen, and pull her throat out with its teeth until it was gulping her blood and picking its teeth with her vertebrae. Then the land would once again belong to its people, the Krakeen, and this land, too, this ridiculous land of soft pink things. This land with no demons, this land that had spawned the dire queen and foisted her on its people.

It charged up the walk, already drooling at the prospect of chewing on the usurper, and easily pushed down the door, barely noticing the astounding crash the wood made as it hit the floor.

It walked into the house, still following the trail, which was stronger here; she had spent some time here, at any rate. But one of the soft pink things wasn't so soft, because it was standing protectively in front of a female and a baby, and it was baring its teeth at the demon.

"Cole, don't!" someone without a scent said. "Get Char and get the baby and get the hell out of here!"

The man paid no notice; the man growled and came closer, his eyes seemed almost lit from within, and the Krakeen licked its lips and wondered how the man's liver might taste.

"Cole!" the voice screamed. "Get your wife and get your kid and *get the fuck out of here*! Find Withering! Go now!"

The voice seemed to penetrate this time; the man remembered his responsibilities and fled with the female and infant. The Krakeen let them; they were not its rightful prey. This time. Instead, it looked around for the voice—and staggered as some strange, hard object smashed into the back of its head, followed by a rain of smaller objects.

"There's more drawers, and there's more silverware," the voice warned him, "so get lost."

It growled, dribbling saliva on the floor, and swiped at the air, reaching for the voice.

"Not the brightest bulb, are you?" the voice said, this time from behind him. It whirled in time to catch another heavy object in the face, and it staggered. "How'd the toaster taste? Hey, stand still, so I can crush you underneath the washing machine."

It roared, infuriated at something it could not see or smell, still wanting the dire queen's blood but not at all happy at shedding its own—*its* blood, for like all Krakeen, it had both male and female genitalia.

"Boy, did *you* pick the wrong house," the voice remarked, and something smashed into the back of its head and shattered, something that smelled sweet and crumbly.

"Char's gonna kill me; she made that stupid cookie jar in her pottery class. Eh, easy come, easy smash."

It stepped across the shards, its hide far too tough to be cut or even scratched. The dread queen's scent was strong here, but then seemed to backtrack, so he followed it toward the door, staggering as the voice hurled something yet again, something that felt like a rock with hard corners.

"Damn it! With no blender, I guess it's bye-bye Margarita Saturdays."

Nearing the doorway, it saw the usurper standing on the wooden thing it had knocked down, standing on it with her sword drawn.

"Krakeen demon, this woman will make the demon pay for daring to come here."

It roared a challenge; it hungered for her blood, her blood for its people, for its land, for the crown she had wrongfully stolen—stolen and then fled!

"You dare come to this land, my town? You dare pollute this place with the stench of your hide? This woman cannot even make clothing out of your skin, you stink so badly."

It gnashed its teeth and rushed at her, ducking under her swing and slashing at her. She wrenched herself back, and all it could do was scratch her, not gut her as it had intended.

"He shoots and he misses and, oh, ladies and gentlemen, have you ever *seen* such humiliation?"

Yes, it would kill the dread queen, and then it would hunt down that bedamned voice and kill it, too!

It followed up, swinging its long arms, each finger tipped with a razor-sharp claw an inch and a half long, and she had to backpedal out the doorway to avoid getting cut again. It ducked as she swung, but not quite fast enough, and it lost an ear.

"Oh, man! She's cutting pieces off you! And you're the best of the bunch? How embarrassing is *that*?"

"A fine point, Krakeen," the usurper said and bared her teeth at him in what the soft pink things called a "smile."

"Rae, remind this woman never to anger you."

"D'you know how long it's going to take me to fix this door?" the voice griped in response.

The Krakeen kicked, its powerful feet also tipped with sharp claws, and the dire queen backflipped out of the way, catching it on the underside of its chin as she did. It shook its head and went after her again, only to find its feet were stuck in the hard walk outside the house. It wrenched itself free easily enough and stepped onto the grass, where it caught the usurper's sword with one hand as the blade descended.

Got you now, dread queen! Your guts will feed my young! Ignoring the blood pouring from its hand, it held the blade away from ifself, readying its other paw for the killing blow, when she abruptly let go of the sword. As it staggered in surprise, it felt something hot slide into its throat.

Hot, and then very, very cold. And something was wrong with its throat. It was getting its chest wet. It was getting dizzy. It tried to swing at the dread queen and missed by too much, missed, and then the odd colored grass was rushing up to its face, and the Krakeen demon knew no more.

Seventeen

Withering stepped back, neatly avoiding the splash, and coldly watched the Krakeen fall facedown onto Charlene Hautenan's lawn. Then she looked up into the nearest oak tree.

"This woman would ask her sisters to come down."

"Why? We helped, didn't we?"

"There may be more, dear ones, and this woman would not see you hurt. It is bad enough," she added sternly, "that you disobeyed me in the manner of following me here."

"Point," Scornful replied, and they both climbed down with the speed of monkeys on crack. Then they stood over the body of the dead demon, which was bleeding black all over the grass. "Guh-ross!" she continued. "Those things come from where you used to live? This one's even nastier-looking than the other one. It's a miracle you made it out alive!"

"Mom's gonna freak," Derisive added.

"Only if you tell the good lady," Withering said, squatting to wipe her blade on the grass, retrieving her sword, then standing in time to see Thad's pizza van drive over the curb and straight up to the house, ruining more grass. He leaped out, leaving the engine running, and nearly fell onto the corpse.

"Are you okay? I got your sister's message. One of your sisters. I don't know which. Are you okay?" He took her into his arms, feeling her for injuries. "Withering, you nut, you shouldn't have tackled that thing by yourself!"

"Why?" she asked, honestly puzzled. "Who else should have 'tackled' it?"

"You dope! You could have been sliced! Chewed! Skinned! Gutted!"

"Indeed, the Krakeen would have seen to all those things if it could."

Thad actually staggered. "That statement did not make me feel better. At all."

"But it did not, and will not, ever." She gently divested herself of his frantic grip and slid her foot under the body.

"Careful," Scornful warned. "In the horror movies, this is where it leaps up for one last scare."

"Not once my knife has been in its throat." She flipped the body over and examined it carefully. Finally, straightening, she said with surprise, "It *is* a Krakeen."

"Yeah, you said that. You called it that. You also mentioned it would have gutted and stabbed and mangled and mutilated you. So?"

"So. Krakeens inhabit the other side of the planet. It once took me the better part of my sixteenth year to reach their territory. This one could have been nowhere near the thin spot where I fell through and, later, returned. That means—"

"I don't care what it means!" Thad shouted. "You're not leaving me—or Mysteria! This is your home, and nobody made you killer of demons and giver-upper of a social life."

She squinted at him. "That doesn't make any—"

"I don't care if this thing was from halfway round the planet or the house next door; *you're staying*."

"What he said," Derisive said.

"Yeah, except without that weird 'giver-upper' line," Scornful added.

"As *I* was saying," Withering continued gently, "it would appear the wishing well is now a conduit between Earth Prime and Secondary Earth."

"Sorry if you've heard this before: So?"

"That means a demon from anywhere on Earth Prime might find its way here."

"Gross," Scornful commented.

"Not to mention inconvenient," Derisive added.

"And unless I am here, in Mysteria, to protect its citizens, that could be disastrous. I cannot leave my dear mother and dear sisters to defend themselves against such creatures, nor any citizen of the land."

"So . . ." Thad held his breath and then, because the stress appeared to be too much, let it out in an explosive sigh. "So you're staying."

"Yes. I must. I do not understand why I did not see it before."

"Because you were too busy jumping Thad's bones?" Scornful suggested.

"And learning how to pick up a spare?" Derisive added.

"I suspect," she said, kindly enough, "it is because I was confused about exactly where my responsibilities lie. But I can no longer return to Earth Prime, no matter how noble my intentions, if it means leaving my town exposed to any demon with a whim to take the crown."

"Where'd Char and the baby go?" Thad asked, seeming to realize their absence all of a sudden.

"To our house, where they remain."

"You better go tell them they can come back, that Withering took care of their little infestation problem."

"*Little?*" Scornful snorted as they started down the street.

"Oh, he just wants to mack on her in private."

"Perv."

"Double perv."

"I can hear you!" Thad called after them. Then he turned to Withering. "Although they have a point."

"That you are a double perv?"

"No. That I want to do this." And he took her in his arms, no pretense of looking for injury *this* time, no indeed, and kissed her, a long, bruising, possessive kiss.

When they came up for air, Thad said, "Don't even think about leaving this town without me."

"I won't even think of leaving this town, if you find that helpful."

"My front door!" someone wailed, and they turned to see Char and her husband coming up the sidewalk. The baby, Withering presumed, had been left in Mrs. Desdaine's care. "All smashed up!"

"Wait till you see the inside!" Rae called, though it was difficult to hear her outside the house. "Also, I've taken a lover, and he'll be moving in as soon as I get an extension built."

"Fine, Rae, fine." Char and her husband were staring at the corpse on their front lawn. "That'll be—wait. *What?*"

"Oh, like you two aren't doing it every half hour of every day," Rae snapped. "Don't judge *me*, honey!"

"I wasn't. I just—" Charlene gestured vaguely: at the corpse, at the van parked in her begonias. "This is a lot to take in at once."

"Welcome," Withering said dryly, "to Mysteria."

THE
NANNY
FROM HELL

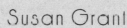

Susan Grant

For three amazing, talented women: MaryJanice, PC, and Gena. What an absolute pleasure to revist Mysteria with you all.

Prologue

*

> *Once upon a time there lived a demon*
> *with a secret wish to be human.*
> *It made Satan very, very unhappy . . .*

CIRCUS MAXIMUS, ANCIENT ROME

One hundred and fifty thousand spectators lunged to their feet, cheering as the chariots flew out of the starting gate. Everyone from the lowliest slave to the emperor himself added to the deafening applause. The attention, the excitement, the anticipation: Shay reveled in it, savoring every aspect of the races from the dust churned up by chariot wheels to the dizzying sensation of sheer speed. Most racers conserved energy in the early laps in order to give it their all in the final stretches. Bah! Rules were for mortals. Full speed ahead!

Four powerful horses tugged on the reins wrapped around Shay's fist and down her arm to her waist. If she were to crash, she doubted she'd have time to cut free with her dagger before being trampled or dragged to her death. Not that she worried about such frivolous things as dying.

Shay threw back her head and laughed. Dust billowed into the air and settled like fine powder over her toned, slender arms and her black racing colors. The fabric fluttered around her breasts, barely concealing them. She heard shouts of surprise. "A woman!" they cried.

"A she-demon, actually," she murmured smugly. Not that they'd care. Men never seemed to mind as long as they thought they were getting what they wanted from her.

In particular, she noted the emperor's hot, interested gaze, dismissing it as a mere annoyance. Warlords were sometimes diverting, yes; chieftains, too. But emperors? All pomp and little circumstance. She wouldn't bother with this one unless she was very, very bored. And she doubted she'd be bored today. There was much to be done.

A blink of her eyes, and two chariots collided. Spectacular! Ooh, and a trampling, too. Score!

Shay couldn't remember the last time she had so much fun. She was sent by Lucifer all over the world—a plague here, a fire there—but she'd rather be here. Something about racing made her feel so *alive*. So . . . real.

She cringed. *Cease that drivel!* If the Dark Lord ever got wind of her addiction to earthly life, he'd snuff out her existence like a boot crushed a flickering ash. He'd told her as much, countless centuries ago when he'd suspected she was hanging around an Ice Age settlement because she'd taken a fancy to nights spent cuddling in the furs with one of its hunters, Swift River. Master had been right, of course. With the fear of permanent extermination hanging over her head, she ended the affair with a good-bye kiss and an avalanche and went on her way.

Shay pushed the painful memory away. Her job was to break hearts and tear families apart, not to pretend she was human. Not to pretend *love*. Especially not at the risk of her own existence. Something about ceasing *to be* frightened her. She'd do everything she could to avoid that fate.

Snarling, Shay punched her fist to the side. The horses pulling the chariot next to hers went wild, yanking their rider toward the wall with a snapping of wood and the scraping of metal. The champion's scream was cut short. "Buh-bye, Scorpus." He'd won far too many races, anyway. It was time he retired.

Dust rose from the wrecks as the remaining racers plunged down the straightaway. Easily, Shay commanded the lead. Only one other racer had the stamina to keep her pace. Aquila. The shaggy-haired up-and-coming champion seemed to have it all: looks, youth, a beautiful wife and child, and all of Rome at his feet. Sensing she was pulling ahead, Aquila slid his narrowed eyes in her direction, sizing up her chariot, her horses, and her technique. Roman sunshine gleamed on his sweating skin. My, but he was nicely muscled. She could tell by his glance that he saw her as simply another competitor and not a potential lover. Probably because of his pretty little wife and baby. Aw, he was in love. How easy that would be to change. In fact, she'd keep him alive just to prove the point!

Laughing, Shay urged her horses on ahead, just like she'd urge on Aquila in bed after the race. Feeling generous, she'd even let him win. What did it matter? He'd lose later. They always did.

Neck and neck, they careened around the last turn. Who would win? Who would lose? In those final, breathless, exhilarating moments, Shay allowed him to drift into the lead. He beat her by a length. The crowd's applause was thunderous. They had a new champion!

Magnificent in his crimson racing colors, Aquila beamed as he received his palm branch and wreath from the magistrate. Shay shook out her hair as she jumped down from her chariot. As the silly Romans fawned over him, she undulated her hips as she sashayed past, brushing her finger down his arm. In his mind was planted a vivid image of her moaning and naked, submitting to his every desire. His dark eyes flashed with sudden awareness. It was done.

Away from the circus, she'd barely breezed into her tent when he came striding after her, stripping her out of her clothes before she reached the bed. He threw her on her back, impaling her with his body, pumping with sweaty, dusty, postvictory vigor. Mentally, she took control, making him believe it was the best sex he'd ever had, and that she was first in his heart. *You'll love me to the end of time, Aquila.*

"To the end of time . . ." he breathed in her ear.

Stupid mortal.

The tent flap eased open, and a woman stepped in. A babe

on her hip, she took a moment to let her eyes adjust to the shade and to the sight of Aquila's pumping bottom. Then she met Shay's amused gaze.

He loves me. Shay planted the realization in the woman's mind. One startled sob, and the wife was gone.

Shay vanished herself—at the very moment of Aquila's release. He spilled his seed on an empty bed, not knowing what had happened to her, to him—or to his little wife when he returned to an empty house later.

Love, Shay thought with disdain. It was her mission to destroy it. It was her entire reason for existence. When all was said and done, she had to say she was very, very good at her job.

One

Wanted: Loving, live-in nanny to care for working couple's only child. Must be willing to relocate to Mysteria. Private bedroom in home. Call for salary and details.

"Demon!" Lucifer bellowed loud enough to shake the depths of Hell. Molten rocks fell from the walls, sending shrieking banshees into the shadows and waking every manner of dark creature.

Head bowed, her hands clasped in submission, Shay scurried forward to answer her master's bidding.

"You're late!" Lucifer tugged on his black goatee. "What's your excuse this time?"

"This demon offers exquisite apologies, my lord. This demon had a raft full of orphans to set adrift in shark-infested waters."

"And did you?"

"Yes, Master." She chanced a peek at him. "Is something amiss, Master?"

His horns pulsed as he sank his pitchfork into solid rock and bellowed once more in rage. It was clear that something had made him very, very angry. Shay hoped it wasn't anything she'd done. How quickly he could change her back into what she was at the beginning of time: nothing. "I will never surrender to the spawn of a demon whose ass I fired for committing random acts of kindness!" He jerked a claw at the cave wall. The stones shimmered and opened up to a view of a charming town.

A tall man of dark good looks strode down a road leading to a cottage and a small church. "Damon of Mysteria . . ." Shay narrowed her eyes, scanning the scene with slitted pupils. She was starting to understand the reason for her summons. For ten centuries Damon had served as Lucifer's Demon High Lord of Self-Doubt and Second Thoughts . . . until he was caught, redhanded, committing random acts of kindness. After a couple of hundred years of torture, Lucifer made him mortal, sentencing him to live out his days in Mysteria, the very town he'd saved hundreds of years before. Such a mundane, pitiful existence was every demon's worst nightmare.

Except that Damon didn't seem to be suffering at all. He'd fallen in love, not only with his sorry life but with a human woman. A woman of God, no less: Harmony Faithfull, who presided over Mysteria's silly little house of worship.

Not that Lucifer had taken it sitting down. Rumors circulating around the lava pools reported that the Devil had been acting downright petulant about Damon's—dare she say it?—*contentment*. The Dark Lord had sent wave after wave of subdemons and other obnoxious creatures up through the gates of Hell to torment Damon and his new wife, along with the residents of Mysteria, many of whom were undead themselves. Each time, the town fought back. No one was quite sure how or even why they could, but the matter was being investigated.

Now the couple was married. Harmony was said to adore the former demon beyond all reason. Shay snorted. No man was worth that kind of dreamy, addle-brained worship. If that wasn't bad enough, they'd spawned a child.

It was all so revolting! Shay made a face. Clearly, Lucifer wanted the family broken apart. "I'll bed him as soon as I arrive there, Master. Or, perhaps, her. I can do them both."

"No, you stupid creature!" He hoisted her off her feet. "I do not want you to bed them. I want you to destroy their child!"

Shay hung, trembling, from her master's clawed hands. His crimson eyes were whirlpools of lava, threatening to suck her in, luring her deeper and deeper. If she lost herself in those eyes, she'd be trapped, unable to free herself. She would . . . end.

A slow smile revealed his glittering fangs. "You fear the end of your existence."

He knows.

Of course, he did. Did she think she could keep her deepest fears secret? "Answer me, Demon!" He shook her hard. Goblins and gargoyles somersaulted through the shadows, fleeing the chamber and Lucifer's wrath.

"Yes," she wheezed in his grip. "This humble demon fears being no more."

His fanged smile widened. His glowing eyes sparked with malice. "Then you will not fail me."

"No, Master."

"Win their trust so they let you near the child."

"Yes, Master."

"And stay away from the fountain," he growled.

"What fountain?"

"*What fountain?*" He shook her, fire erupting in his eyes. "If only you were as smart as you are evil! Mysteria's fountain, stupid demon. The wishing fountain. Do not go near it."

"Why?" Even as she asked, she knew it was a mistake to do so.

He shook her so hard that her ears rang. "My word is law! It is not to be questioned. Go earthward and win the trust of the family. Then kill the child and bring its bones back to me. Fail and . . ." He brought her face-to-face with him. "I will erase you, eradicate you, stamp you out—for all eternity!" His roar shook the entire cave. "No matter where you run, no matter where you hide, I will find you, and *end you.* You will never escape your fate."

Sputtering, he threw her to the ground. She scrabbled backward to her feet, stumbling away from his threat: "*I will find you, and end you.*" Humans had their Heaven (or Hell). Angels, also, could look forward to Heaven. As well, all matter of undead creatures had a future ahead of them, whether they were vampires, shape-shifters, or even ghosts. But for a ruined demon, eternity meant nothing, zero, zilch. She simply would no longer *be*.

The prospect frightened Shay more than anything else. She would find the child and kill it. There was no other choice. Failure was simply not an option.

Damon, new father and ex-demon, climbed the porch stairs to the home he shared with his wife, Harmony, Mysteria's minister. Their black Lab Bubba bounced around his heels, barking happily. Before Damon reached the top of the stairs, Dr. Fogg burst out, juggling his black medical bag and his ever-present BlackBerry as he pushed his glasses up his nose.

Damon's heart rolled over. His wife, his babe—he couldn't bear the thought of any harm coming to them. "Is everything all right, Doctor?"

"In your house, yes. My visit with your wife was interrupted. They need me at the high school. Fighting Fairies practice was a little rougher than usual today."

"I do like American football," Damon admitted.

"Football? It was the cheerleaders." Fogg ran a finger around the inside of his collar as he trotted the rest of the way down the stairs.

Despite his intellectual outward appearance, Fogg had taken a wild-elf princess as a wife. Wild-elves lived outside Mysteria and outside the law. When they mated with humans it was usually by force. A month into the surprise marriage, the elf left him. The mild-mannered doctor had referred himself to Harmony for spiritual counseling. Today had been the first session.

Harmony stood in the doorway. "Well," she said with a sigh, "that was interesting."

Damon lifted a brow at his worried-looking wife. "He doesn't look well, lass."

"He's not, the poor man. He's been through a hard time. I think today helped—a lot. He'll be back. As for you, come here, honey. I need a kiss."

The lass knew how to do things with her mouth no woman of God should know how to do, but he was glad of it. He took a moment to hold her close, cupping her sweet face in his hand, savoring the feel of her skin and the love shining in her eyes as she smiled up at him. He'd existed ten thousand years before Harmony. In his mind, life had only just begun.

He brushed one more kiss across her lips and took her hand. "Damon Junior misses his daddy," she said, leading him inside.

In the kitchen, little Damon sat in his highchair. He squealed in delight, seeing his father. "Papa!" The vase of flowers on the kitchen table jumped, took two hops, and stopped.

"Omigosh," Harmony cried, running for a dish towel to mop up the spill as Damon said sternly, "Son, I told you no moving furniture—or any other items—without my or your mother's permission."

Harmony paled, the damp cloth dangling from her hand. "Are you saying little Damon moved that vase?"

"Aye. I saw him do it for the first time the other day. When you came home from the store and the lamp fell."

"That was the wind."

"Nay," he said quietly.

"You mean our baby has . . . *powers*?" she practically squeaked.

He tried to reach for her hand, but she'd shoved it through her hair. "We talked about that possibility when you were pregnant, love."

"I know, but . . ." She sighed. "We thought the chance of your demon powers being passed on in your DNA was remote if not impossible."

"Impossible is a woman of God falling in love with an ex-demon," he said tenderly. "Impossible is a former minion of Lucifer finding out he has a soul. And yet, both happened. Aye, love, who are we to say what is possible and what is not? Besides, I'm not the only one with powers in this relationship." Harmony was a powerful seer, a talent she'd inherited from her great-grandmother. She hadn't yet fully come to terms with what she was. He wasn't surprised she'd "forgotten" that he wasn't the only one supplying their offspring's supernatural genes.

The vase jumped again. Harmony turned to their son, shaking her finger at him. "Damon Junior! You heard your father, no . . . no *telekinesis*!" She made a face. "I can't believe I just said that."

The babe flashed a blinding grin, and Harmony melted. "The little charmer. He has your smile, honey. I'm going to have to become immune to it if I'm ever going to effectively discipline this kid. Oh, Damon, what are we going to do?"

"He's only a year old, lass. In time he'll learn to control his powers." Powers that Damon predicted would grow even stronger as he aged. "It's of utmost importance that we keep his abilities secret from Lucifer."

"I don't think that'll be a problem, seeing that I haven't talked to your former boss in"—Harmony pretended to concentrate—"ages. Our paths just never seem to cross," she quipped sarcastically. Then she noticed how serious he was, and her eyes opened wide. "Will Satan be able to sense him? Will he know what our baby can do? Oh, Lord, Damon, will he try to hurt our child?"

Fear gripped Damon. Anger, too. "We'll do everything in our power to ensure that never happens, lass. But one day the boy will rise as a powerful rival to the Devil."

Little Damon giggled, and the ice cubes in the pitcher of ice tea rattled. "Damon Junior!" Harmony scolded in unison with Damon. Then she whirled on him, eyes ablaze. "As for your last comment, Damon of Mysteria, don't think I didn't notice you sneaked that in. There will be no ultimate showdowns between our baby and the Devil. Do you hear me? I forbid it."

Outside, thunder rumbled as Harmony took a seat at the table. She mumbled grace before serving lunch, which they ate awed into silence by the prospect of epic battles of good and evil. A few moments later, the first raindrops began to fall.

The doors to Hell opened with a belch of heat, expelling a single demon before slamming closed again. The forest sang with the squeaks and scrabbling of the few winged subdemons and goblins released when the hellhole opened. The lesser beasts scattered into the mist, off to their wanton mischief, but the demon, experienced and centuries-old, scurried with purpose through the rain. There were miles yet to cover before reaching the hamlet of Mysteria.

Mindful was the demon of keeping out of the sight of humans. It could not be interrupted, stymied, or sidetracked. It had a job to do. Find the child. Kill it before it grew to adult hood and challenged Lucifer himself.

"Fail, and I will erase you, eradicate you, stamp you out— for all eternity! No matter where you run, no matter where you hide, I will find you, and end you."

The she-demon cowered and hissed, crouching out of sight as she took on her traditional human form. Her coarse red hide fell away, replaced by smooth, creamy flesh. Cloven hooves elongated into two feet, complete with ten perfect shell-pink toenails. Gone were the horns sprouting from her skull; in their place were jaw-length waves in rich, reddish brown. Slits no longer dominated her copper-colored eyes. They were rimmed with dark lashes, appearing completely human. No one would be able to tell what she was and what she'd come here to do.

Kill. The wind howled and shook the canopy of rain-drenched trees. Under the cloak of low-hanging clouds, Shay lurched forward and down the hillside, knowing *exactly* where to go.

Two

"Can you really smell a demon a mile away?"

Quel Laredo stood in front of Mysteria's wishing fountain, surveying the town square. A breeze whipped his duster around his long, denim-clad legs. Water from the fountain sent mist into the dry, Rocky Mountain air. Sniffing, his eyes in a perpetual squint, he sampled that air, tasting it. The storm had passed, allowing the sunset to break through, but something wasn't quite right about this twilight. He couldn't figure out what.

"Can you, Mr. Laredo?"

"Yeah." The wide-eyed boy was one of the O'Cleary grandchildren, he guessed. He'd lost count of them all. They weren't a family; they were a herd. "Two miles if the wind is right."

"Like now?" the boy breathed in fearful wonder.

Nodding, Quel peered into the deepening shadows in the woods at the edge of town. The scent of evil was growing stronger. There was definitely something out there.

"Hey, Laredo, do you want to buy me a drink? Come on, you know you do." A comely enchantress brushed her hand along his arm as she passed by with her female friends. "We'll be at Knight Caps. Afterward, I'm free."

"I'm working."

"Late?"

"Late."

"Shame." Her voice turned husky. "All work and no play makes Quel a dull boy." In the face of his silence, she tried to recant. "I mean, not that I find you dull. Not at all. It's just a saying."

He tipped his hat. "That's all right."

Smiling, she backed up, almost stumbling on her high heels before hurrying away to join her friends.

Her lush little ass swayed as she shimmied away. A nice piece, but Quel didn't feel much like company. There was something about the air tonight. It was different from anything he'd detected before. Something very old and very dark had been unleashed, and he wouldn't let down his guard until he figured out what it was.

Making snuffling sounds, the boy screwed up his face. "You smell anything yet, Mr. Laredo? I don't."

"Hurry on home, boy. Your mama's going to be worried."

Half in awe, half-terrified, the boy ran off. Not all that different of a reaction from the women in town, Quel thought. Not that he blamed others for the way they acted around him. He'd grown up tough, eight foster families in ten years, but that wasn't it, entirely. It was what people saw in his eyes that scared them away. His eyes reflected what he'd seen—and continued to see: demons.

Growing up, he thought demons were make-believe. Now he knew more about them than he wanted to know. The first time he'd laid eyes on a demon was on a battlefield in Iraq. He'd woken up bleeding from his head and chest after a roadside bomb had taken out the convoy he was escorting. He'd been working private security for Blackstone, he was experienced and sought out for it, but this time the terrorists had been kids—nothing but damn kids, no more than fourteen, fifteen years old. They did what few others had ever been able to pull off: they caught Quel Laredo by surprise. The attack was quick and on target. He'd woken to see a gangly, leather-skinned monster crouched next to one of the wounded soldiers. At the time, Quel was sure he was hallucinating. "You see that?" he croaked to his buddy, Hauser, who'd dragged him out of the hot sun.

"We're gonna get you patched up, Laredo. Hang in there."

Hang in there? As clear as day, Quel saw a medic fighting to save the soldier, pumping his heart even as the demon drained his soul. "I'm losing him," the frustrated rescuer shouted, oblivious of the demon.

Quel fought off Hauser. "Get it the fuck away from him!" The soldier would die if they didn't. Quel got to his hands and knees and dragged himself to the dying man, shoving the demon off his chest. The monster came back—this time for him. *Don't look at its eyes.* Quel remembered thinking that. The whirling red balls sucked his strength, his very life, leaving despair and terror in its place. *No!*

They rolled over the sand, grabbing for each other's throats. Then, remembering every last horror movie he'd ever seen, Quel stabbed him with the cross his mother had given him before she died.

Quel wasn't religious—he didn't follow much of anything—but the necklace was the only link he allowed to his past. The silver sank between the demon's ribs, sizzling as the creature convulsed, shrieking. By the time the surviving guys on his team got him wrestled to the ground, the damn thing was dead.

Everyone assumed he'd suffered a hallucination. So did Quel, until he started seeing demons all across Iraq. No wonder there was a damned war going on. Evil fueled it.

He put in his papers and left the Gulf. After a few months kicking around a friend's ranch in Montana, dogged by restlessness and too many memories, he ran into more demons. This time he knew what to do. People were more grateful than they were skeptical, and now even more afraid of him, but he was used to that. Might as well use his ability to see demons to make a living. Now he was Quel Laredo, demon hunter. It kept him on the move. Moving was good. It gave him less time to think. As a demon hunter, he could do some good, and he didn't have to face his past. A win-win situation, in his mind.

He had a lot to learn at first, and there was no shortage of people wanting to help him. Over the years, he'd studied with everyone from ninjas to witches. He learned that some demons were obvious to the human eye and that others preferred to be invisible, either by disguising themselves as humans or by using dark magic to remain unseen. Quel grabbed freelance demon-hunting jobs where he could find them, never staying long in one place or with any one person. He was like a swift river, sure and cold, always moving on. When Mysteria was hiring, he took the job—just for the winter, he'd thought—but he ended up staying. It had been a year now. He liked it. Maybe he just felt at home with the collection of other lost souls there.

The lost souls he'd sworn to protect.

Quel checked for his rifle, pistols, ammo, silver BBs for the smaller creatures, garlic, and the cross hanging from his neck as he paced in front of the fountain that was the center-piece of Mysteria's town square. The water bubbled, sending up spray. The townspeople insisted the fountain was magic, that wishes made there would come true. Hell, he wouldn't mind the help. He'd find his demon that much sooner.

Frowning, he tasted the air again. Yeah, definitely demon. It was getting stronger, too—the scent of demon mixed with something sweeter, almost distracting. He didn't like that. No one distracted Quel Laredo.

He pulled on the brim of his hat and kept walking. There was a demon about, and he'd find it before sunrise . . . like he always did.

The night had cleared. Stars had come out. In the moonlight, Shay followed the road leading into Mysteria. She attracted less attention now that she was no longer naked—thanks to the generosity of some campers. Oh, they were startled to see her waltzing into their campsite wearing nothing but her bare curves. A well-placed thought, a blink of her eyes, and they let her take what she needed, convinced they'd done a good deed. Shay liked to leave mortals believing they'd done good, even when they helped her do things that were very, very bad. Yes, she was like the Good Samaritan except with ulterior motives.

The jeans were a little tight in the butt, but the T-shirt was just perfect, snug and smooth. ANGEL, it said, BY VICTORIA'S SECRET. Well, Shay had a secret, too: she was no angel. Her laughter floated in the damp, chill air of the mountains as she smoothed her hands over the outfit. She enjoyed showing off her assets. This body was her favorite. It had served her well for most of the last few thousand of years. Why not showcase it—to Damon's downfall? *You're not to bed him. You're to kill the child.* Yes, she must remember, no sleeping with Damon. She must keep focused on her mission, even at the temporary expense of fashion. Lucifer wanted no delays.

Eventually she came upon what looked to be an inn. Inside, several couples shared a table as they ate dinner. She sashayed past the line of parked cars, brushing her fingers over the hoods, and paused next to a little red sports car. Her driving had never been as good as her chariot skills, but then she'd not had as many centuries to practice. Still, how could she walk away from this sweet little Porsche, irresistible in devil red? She had a job to do, yes. No one said she couldn't have some fun while doing it.

A blink of her eyes, and the locks popped open. The diners behind the restaurant window glanced her way, alarmed. Shay blinked, placed the thought: *You see my taking the car as a favor. You want me to have it. Think of it as a little gift. Your generosity makes you feel good.*

They went back to their meal. Smug, Shay slid in behind the wheel and started up the car. A blink of her eyes, and the license plates and registration reflected her human alter ego: Shay d'Mon. She giggled. Oh, how she enjoyed a good play on words. Yes, Miss d'Mon, single, white, twenty-five years old, complete with no living family and a teaching degree. With the engine purring, she smiled and pulled onto the highway and shoved the gas pedal to the floor. "Full speed ahead."

A pair of headlights appeared on the road that wound down through the hills into town. Someone was driving way too fast. Outsider, Quel thought, testing the air. Demon. He smelled demon. Yeah, demon and that sweet hint of something delicious underneath that somehow didn't belong.

Maybe the car had come in contact with the demon and didn't contain the creature itself. He'd never known demons to drive, but they were crafty; they adapted. He wouldn't know until it got closer. Quel cradled his rifle in his arms and waited.

The car sped toward town, barely staying on the rain-slick

road as it made the switchback turns. It was either a demon without a driver's license or a dumb-ass city boy playing NASCAR.

A pack of werewolves scampered across the square, headed toward the woods. They'd have to cross the road to do that. Quel glanced at the rising full moon and swore. They'd be too crazed by their hormones to see the danger careening toward them.

"Watch out," Quel shouted as the car sped toward them. The sound of brakes being applied shrieked in the night. Werewolves scattered. The car fishtailed and spun. A rear wheel clipped the shoulder of the road, flipping the vehicle over. It rolled all the way down the embankment and landed right side up in the center of the fountain with one helluva splash.

Now he'd seen everything. Quel cocked his rifle and headed that way. Whoever—or whatever—was driving that car sure knew how to make an entrance.

Three

✳

Satan's stones! One minute Shay was swerving to avoid hitting what looked like a dog pack, and the next she was submerged up to her neck in cold water that smelled like a stale pond. Her legs were pinned by the crushed front end of the car, while the rest of her was being crushed by something that felt like a giant balloon.

Cursed air bags. Safety devices were for cowards and mortals with finite life spans.

It took a few seconds to register, but the water was rising—and rising fast. It bubbled over her chest to her shoulders, creeping toward her neck. She couldn't kick free; her feet were wedged in too tightly. Her hands hunted for something to hold onto, flailing and splashing. Hell's bells, she felt like a landed trout!

More like a landed piranha. She was that angry—at herself. She liked attention—adored it, actually—but not this much attention. The crash would wake everyone in town and maybe put them on guard against her. She was a stranger on a secret mission. *Win their trust,* Lucifer had advised her. Escapades like this were not going to get her closer to the child.

The rising water now sloshed at chin level. She sputtered, swearing. Instead of succumbing to panic, she followed the pull of a new and all-encompassing urge—the will to *survive*—and tried to claw her way out of the air bag.

Something banged on the outside of the car. A shadowy form moved outside the shattered windshield. "Here," she called. Fires of hell, *here*. Never had she been so happy to see a mortal, a silly, selfless human who'd come to save her. She couldn't afford to drown.

If she destroyed this body, she'd have to return to Hell and get a new one, starting all over again. What would the Dark Master think of that? Not much. She could picture him now, pacing and spitting in fury. Not a day into this mission, and she'd already faltered. *"I will erase you, eradicate you, stamp you out—for all eternity!"*

The human was pounding on the door now, mere inches away. *Please,* she thought. *Please?* Since when did Shay beg for anything—or anyone?

"Snap out of it, Shay," she muttered through gritted teeth. She used to be resourceful. She tried to reach the door handle herself, but her legs were pinned, wouldn't let her stretch far enough.

The urge to survive expanded, filling her chest, growing more powerful with each beat of her heart, as if she were indeed truly alive and not pretending. She'd long wanted to know what that felt like. Now she never would.

Oh, how she wished otherwise. Over the centuries she'd barely touched what it meant to live, to feel, always wanting more depth of emotion, craving it, but unable to cross the line separating her from what she was and what she'd secretly yearned to be. Always, Lucifer would figure out what she loved most and take it away: Circus Maximus and chariot racing, cuddling in the furs with Swift River on glacial, star-filled nights. He took them all. The poignancy of loss sliced deep— that which was dealt her and that which she'd caused.

She'd inflicted much pain. She'd never cared before. Now the knowledge of her deeds hurt in a way she'd never thought imaginable. She regretted not only her recent misdeeds but every evil act she'd ever accomplished.

You shouldn't have sent those orphans on a one-way voy-

age into the sea. Or bedded Aquila the day after his wife told him they were going to have another child.

She even regretted stealing the red sports car and wrecking it. Remorse and shame flooded her, choking her. *I'm sorry . . . Truly sorry.*

She was evil. She deserved to die.

No, only living creatures died. *Monsters like you cease to be.*

Shay tipped her chin up and stole a few last breaths before the water caught up, rising over her eyes, her forehead, and submerging her fully. In no time she'd be waking up back in Hell with Lucifer kicking her ass.

Instead, a soft, white cushion enveloped her, something she'd never remembered experiencing after her previous accidents. She went from acute remorse to utter serenity and did not question it. The roll bar slipped from her hands, but somehow she knew everything was going to be okay. The feeling of trust was instinctive, all-encompassing.

For the first time in her life she felt at peace.

It was no longer dark. Shay looked around in wonder. A field of endless soft snow surrounded her . . . so white, so beautiful. And there, across the way, Swift River waited, dressed in furs, his hair flowing in a wind she couldn't feel. He opened his arms. Smiling, she took the first step toward him.

"Goddamn it, *breathe*."

Reality returned in jagged slices. Someone pushing on her chest. A warm mouth sealed over hers. Air swelling her lungs. The scents of sweat and leather, dust and man filling her nostrils. Then she was coughing, her lungs on fire.

Another flash: her eyes opening, a face looming inches from hers. "About damn time," the male voice muttered. He cushioned her skull from the ground with a hand buried in her soaked hair. Water fell nearby, misting, gurgling, soothing in contrast to the agony hammering inside her skull. "Thought I was going to have to call the coroner," he growled. "You saved me the trouble, but don't get me wrong, lady, you're still a pain in the ass."

Her vision cleared, and the face came into focus: handsome, raw-featured, and eyes so blue it hurt to look at them. *The color of cold, deep water that all but begged a probing of their bottomless depths.* She knew that face and those eyes. "Swift River . . ."

"River?" His laugh was quick, derisive. "You landed in the damn fountain."

She tried to make sense of his modern speech. And his apparent anger. "What happened to the snow?" Her speech sounded a bit slurred to her ears. "All the pretty white snow . . ."

He muttered what sounded like an exasperated curse. "You damn well better not go into hypothermic shock. That'll really piss me off. Here, put this on." She was as limp as a rag as he jostled her, lifting her gently to wrap her in a coat—his coat. That's when she realized she was shivering, her teeth clattering together.

"It's b-been so long." She soaked in the sight of the man she never thought she'd see again. Centuries hadn't erased the memory of his eyes that could alternately turn dark with passion or shine with intelligence, cruelty, or mischief. *Lucifer took you from me. He made me hurt you.*

How could she have done what she did? Her throat ached. Tears welled up in her eyes. Real tears, not the ones she was so good at simulating. "I made the avalanche," she confessed in a whisper. "I buried you. I destroyed the settlement."

Swift River bent forward, coming closer. To kiss her, she thought. She hungered for the touch of his lips. Her entire aching body strained upward to meet him halfway.

He didn't kiss her. He didn't even touch her. He sniffed the air as if trying to detect an odor.

"I like your smell, woman," Swift River used to tell her. He told her so many things; *"I love you,"* even, although she'd implanted that thought in his mind. Still, a part of her sensed, *hoped*, he may have meant it.

She brushed her fingers across his warm jaw. "I'm so sorry . . ."

Sighing, he took hold of her hand, removing it from his face. For a second, she thought there might have been a softening of his hard expression; then he spoke, spoiling the illusion. "I'd be sorry, too, lady. Someone's going to be mighty pissed you wrecked their pretty red Porsche."

A siren wailed in the background, piercing her head with pain and bringing her back to her senses. The snow was gone. People had gathered around, murmuring in hushed, concerned voices. The man crouched next to her wasn't Swift River, though the resemblance was strong. This wasn't the Ice Age; this was Mysteria, and this angry, modern-day man wasn't her lover. Not even close. By now Swift River would have had her out of her clothes and under the furs with him, hot skin, cold nights. Bliss.

The blue-eyed stranger observed her with a curious expression on his face. He shifted his weight, his boots creaking, his narrowed eyes darker. Had he guessed the direction of her thoughts?

"I thought you were someone else," she explained.

He gave the air another sniff. "That makes two of us, sweetheart."

Sweetheart. An endearment, but spoken without any obvious tenderness.

You love me. You adore me. She planted the thought in his mind. She'd rather face a simpering love slave than this man's indifference. His expression, however, remained unchanged.

What, was he immune to her powers of persuasion? She didn't sense dark powers in him. Bat bugger, she didn't sense anything at all. Something wasn't right. An uneasy glance around made her aware of the gathering crowd. Why was she still here in the human's world, anyway? It made no sense. She'd died—or at least she'd experienced a demon's version of dying. *Except for the haunting vision of the snow, and all the white light.*

It was so beautiful . . .

Shay gave her head a small shake. Mistake—the sharp pain nearly blinded her. She moaned. Maybe she *was* back in Hell, and Lucifer was playing with her, teasing her with images of her Ice Age lover. More than any other demon, Lucifer liked to torment her. She'd eventually learned never to reveal partiality to anything—or anyone—because he'd force her to give them up.

The blue-eyed man stood as the ambulance pulled up and stopped. Doors slammed. A man with tousled brown hair and glasses, a wrinkled shirt, and loosened tie elbowed his way to where she lay on the pavement.

"I'm Dr. Fogg," he greeted. He immediately took out a flashlight and shined it in her eyes. Grumbling, she tried to turn away, but he wouldn't let her. If she hadn't been hurting as much as she was, she would have gotten up and left the scene, leaving them to practice their mortal medicine on someone else.

The blue-eyed man watched the doctor's every action—and hers. His glare was intent, unwavering. A rifle hung from one hand. "You'd better take a good look at her, Doc. She's been babbling. She thinks it's snowing."

Babbling? Suck a frog, mortal. She shot him a glare, but it made her head spin. He seemed to notice, his mouth twitching ever so slightly in amusement, almost as if he'd provoked her on purpose. Then he sobered, sniffing the air again and frowning. She was tempted to conjure up some exotic perfume—the Egyptians were quite good at crafting it—but she didn't want to call notice to her identity. She was here undercover.

A dark-haired woman wearing a khaki uniform and a star pinned to her chest showed up, jotting notes on a pad. She had a pretty face and a boyish way about her. "Sheriff," the blue-eyed man said, nodding.

"Laredo," she greeted back. Surveying the Porsche with its front end submerged in the fountain, she sent Shay a withering look. "A dead-on dunk by a drop-down drunk. Now, this is a new one on me."

"I'm not drunk," Shay said.

"High, then."

"No."

The sheriff made a quiet snort. "Miss, how fast were you going? Was there a reason you were in such a hurry?"

The doctor removed his glasses to frown at the sheriff. "She's in shock and probably has a concussion. Save your strong-arm tactics. I'll give her a blood test at the hospital. In the meantime, no more questioning until she's stabilized."

That suited Shay just fine. With her powers of persuasion apparently on the fritz, she'd be forced to make up a story. Mortals were basically smart; they wouldn't believe just anything. Whatever she fabricated had to be convincing.

"Can you touch your right finger to your nose?" the doctor requested.

"Of course." Shay's finger landed on her upper lip.

"Must be that alcohol she's not drinking, or the drugs she's not taking," the sheriff muttered.

Blue eyes—Laredo—chuckled. Shay's temper burned. No one laughed at her. She'd show him the consequences of his error. *You fall to your knees, sobbing as you beg forgiveness.* She blinked, implanting the thought. Nothing. It bounced right off his mind. Fuming, she turned to the sheriff. *You itch terribly between your legs.*

The woman continued to scribble notes on her notepad. Shay felt the first tingles of fear. What had happened to her powers? She felt as disoriented and defenseless as a gladiator standing in the middle of the arena who just realized he'd left his weapons behind.

"Hey, Laredo," the sheriff said. "Doc Fogg says you pulled her out of the wreck and resuscitated her. That's hero stuff."

Laredo shrugged off the sheriff's compliment.

"Just doing your job, I know. Consider me impressed. When I hired a demon hunter, I thought I was getting a killer not a lifesaver."

Shay's gaze whipped back to Laredo. Satan's stones! He was a demon hunter? How could she have let him get this close without sensing what he was? Then it hit her that he didn't recognize what she was, either. If he had, he would have killed her, not revived her.

He wasn't completely fooled, though. He acted suspicious but not certain—but to a demon hunter, a demon of her caliber should have been obvious. It was clear something had neutralized her dark powers.

"You landed in the damn fountain."

She remembered Laredo's words with sudden unease. Lucifer had warned her to stay away from Mysteria's wishing fountain. *This* was why. The "damn fountain" had stolen her powers and rendered her helpless. Well, if not quite helpless then very much human.

Human . . . Something inside her leaped at the thought. All her long existence had she not fantasized about being human? *Mortal.* Craved the thrill of feeling real emotion, of knowing she walked along a finite road of destiny under the constant threat of death? How exhilarating it was to pretend; doing it for real was another thing entirely. The vulnerability was breathtaking.

Terrifying.

And most certainly terminal.

"I will find you, and end you." Lucifer's threat strangled her silly daydreams and dragged her back to her senses. *"You cannot hide."* Panic gnawed away at her composure, worsening her all-too-human headache. This condition had better be transitory, or she was history. Literally. How could she complete her mission if she was weak and had—she cringed—emotions? Hell's bells, she'd been bawling only moments ago, thinking Laredo was Swift River. Ugh—how weak! How human. Even now her heart—or what passed for a heart—leaped every time their eyes met. Which was every damn time she glanced his way.

Even as she formed the thought, Laredo was watching her, hard—and not because his heart was leaping (or any other part of him) with the sight of her, she'd bet. He wanted to kill her, not kiss her, and wouldn't hesitate if she gave any hint of being a demon. In her weakened state, he might very well finish the job.

A woman squeezed past the people surrounding the scene. "Hello, honey." The woman dropped to a crouch next to Shay and took her hand in hers. She had creamy brown skin, black curly hair shot through with copper highlights, and a smile that could melt glaciers. "I'm Reverend Harmony Faithfull. How can I help?"

Shay's gloom vanished in a *poof*. Harmony Faithfull. The mother of the child Lucifer wanted destroyed had walked right into her clutches. What a stroke of devil's fortune, she thought with a slow smile. Suddenly, things were not as bleak as they seemed. "You already have helped, Reverend. More than you know." Yet, the thought of hurting Harmony or anyone else gathered around left her feeling sick to her stomach.

Once she got away from the damn fountain, she'd be fine. By morning she'd be able to commence her mission.

As the doctor checked Shay's blood pressure and other vital

signs, Harmony took out a cell phone. "Is there someone I can call for you? Your family? A husband?"

At the mention of a husband, Shay felt Laredo's stare sharpen. Jealous, was he? She ignored him, trying to project instead a quiet sadness as she shook her head. She needed to throw her whole being and many millennia of lying into convincing Harmony to trust her around the babe. The thought made her stomach clench and her mouth go dry.

Before she had a chance to answer, the sheriff returned. "I ran your plates, Miss Shay d'Mon." Shay cringed at the surname she'd chosen. It had seemed a good idea at the time. Now she regretted it. Laredo's suspicious stare was fierce. She didn't want that man making any connections between her and the underworld, especially not while her demon powers were down. "Your record's clean. Nothing on you at all. Yet, here's your car, swimming in our fountain. What did you do? Fall asleep at the wheel?"

Shay's gaze shot to Harmony's. She couldn't have the woman thinking she was irresponsible. *I'm hardworking, honest. I'm the perfect woman to trust around your son.* She blinked, planting the thought in Harmony's head.

The minister's expression remained exactly the same. Serpent's breath! Without her legendary powers of mental persuasion, she'd have to rely on her wits. She was sure she had some; she'd just never had to rely on them before.

"Aw, honey. It'll be all right." Harmony took her hand, squeezing it. Her gaze intensified as she held fast to Shay's fingers, conjuring the unsettling feeling that the minister saw much more than she let on. Shay's instinct was to pull her hand away, yet there was something so compelling about the reverend's regard that it kept Shay in place. In Harmony's gaze, she felt accepted, forgiven . . . *good.* Yes, good. In that breathless moment that seemed to hang still in time, Shay was no longer evil.

No longer a monster.

Then Harmony patted her hand, breaking the spell. Her eyes were moist; a sheen of perspiration shone on her forehead. She appeared almost as unsettled as Shay. "You have a soul," she murmured. "A good and sweet soul."

Shay covered her appalled snort with a fake coughing attack.

"Leave her be, Reverend Faithfull," Dr. Fogg scolded. "This young woman needs to rest. She's in shock."

If she wasn't in shock before, she sure was now. Shay hoped Lucifer wasn't eavesdropping on any of this. Withering warts, a soul! And not just any soul, a "good and sweet" soul. Bat bugger. She hoped to hell the condition wasn't permanent, merely a trick of the fountain.

Some trick. If it could implant souls in demons, the fountain was more dangerous than she'd thought. Lucifer should have been more specific. *Unless he didn't know.* If he didn't, and these mortals did, it could prove the undoing of the entire dark empire.

Well, no matter. If a soul got in, she could get it out. She'd worry about that tomorrow. As long as her master didn't know anything was wrong, she was fine.

Harmony stood. "I'll be out of the good doctor's hair now, but if you need anything, call." She smiled once more before disappearing in the crowd.

At the doctor's direction, the ambulance crew transferred Shay to a stretcher. Going to a hospital was a delay she couldn't afford. What choice did she have? She didn't know how severe her injuries were. Without her demon powers, she'd have to rely on the mortals to repair her. Then again, Harmony Faithfull was coming to her hospital room in the morning to see how she was doing. Shay didn't have to lift a finger to lure her there.

A soul, a good and sweet soul. The woman's pronouncement haunted her. On the bright side, a soul would throw Laredo off her scent. She stole another glance at the man working so hard to figure her out. Her heart gave another little leap.

He walked alongside the stretcher as they wheeled her to the ambulance. His gait was deceptively casual. There was banked power in that walk. Killing power. He was impressively built, though his frame tended toward leanness rather than bulk. She imagined he hadn't an ounce of fat on that body. He didn't seem to be a man who tolerated overindulgence in himself or in anyone else. Shay, on the other hand, loved to indulge, which, of course, underscored the fact that they'd never get along.

Much to her annoyance, Laredo stayed close as she was loaded into the rear of the ambulance. Was he that worried she'd escape? She could hardly lift her aching head much less sit up or walk.

With his rifle cradled in his arms, the demon hunter waited in silence until the doctor and medics had settled her in. "Your coat, Mr. Laredo." A medic handed Laredo the coat he'd draped over her. It left her top half uncovered. Her soaking-wet pink T-shirt was molded to every curve and contour of her breasts.

Laredo read the slogan scrawled across her chest. "Angel?" His smile was slow, feral. "We'll see about that, Miss d'Mon." To her disgust, her heart leaped with the heat and the challenge of his dark stare. Slamming the door closed, he walked away, shoving his rifle back in his holster.

Shay glowered after him. Let him see if he was as arrogant once her powers of persuasion returned!

Four

✳

The morning Shay d'Mon was released from Mysteria General, Quel blended in with the crowd gathered in the town square for the weekly farmers' market. He bought an apple from a vendor and leaned back against a light post, biting into the fruit while keeping an eye on the Faithfull family: Harmony, Damon, and their boy. The couple had picked up Shay the moment she was discharged. Now, after taking her to lunch, they were giving her the grand tour, including introducing her to what townspeople hadn't witnessed her infamous crash into the fountain.

They exited an ice cream shop. Shay ran a pointed tongue around the base of the ice cream. It was just a damn ice cream cone, but the woman put her whole focus into indulging in it . . . licking . . . savoring. It was probably the thousandth time she'd eaten ice cream, but she made it look like it was the first time and the best damn thing she'd ever tasted. Swearing, he forced his eyes away from that mouth. He'd been all about resuscitating her the night of the crash, but he hadn't forgotten the way those lips felt. She was dressed in the same clothes. Laundered, they fit just right on her tight, toned little body.

"Angel," he muttered, shaking his head as he read that damn pink shirt of hers. "We'll see . . ."

As if she'd sensed his attention, Shay turned his way. Quel touched the brim of his hat and nodded. *Yeah, darlin', I'm keeping an eye on you.* There it was again, always that look of surprise chased by sadness and unmistakable heat. Just like the other night, it got to him, and he didn't like it, not one frickin' bit. If he didn't know better, he'd say she missed him. But, hell, she didn't know him—and probably didn't want to, based on his record with women. He probably reminded her of someone who'd done her wrong. Or maybe his little "angel" had done the man wrong.

Then she was whisked away by the Faithfulls without another glance in his direction. Quel narrowed his eyes and took a sniff. One taste of the air brought the unmistakable scent of *her*.

Not, he acceded stubbornly, a demon.

Bullshit. He took a brutal bite of the apple, frowning as he chewed. He'd smelled that she-demon the moment it came down the hill. If it wasn't Shay, then somewhere, somehow, a demon had done a bait and switch. All he could do was lay in wait for it to make a mistake.

"Take him," Harmony said, grinning as she dropped a wriggling little boy in Shay's arms, drawing Shay's attention away from the enigmatic demon hunter who'd been shadowing their tour of the town. If only Quel Laredo would go away and stop reminding her of what she was—and what she could never be.

Awkwardly, Shay juggled the squirming weight in her arms. Satan's stones—here she was, pretending to be a childcare provider, and she'd never once held a child. She'd never wanted to. Harmony, thank the Dark Lord, didn't seem to notice. "He's a handful, isn't he?"

Shay swallowed hard. It wasn't her intent or desire to get to know the boy. Especially since she was going to have to—

"Park!" The boy strained in the direction of the lawn and play area across the street. Other children played, their mothers watching, smiling as if their offspring were the cutest things on earth.

To Shay's shock, disgust didn't fill her as she'd expected. Nor, however, did she want to join the group. It was too far outside her experience—and interests. *It's a chance to get the babe alone.* Yes, but she couldn't kill it here, not in front of everyone. The thought of killing it at all was growing increasingly repulsive. As soon as she recovered, her reservations—*her conscience*—would pass, she was certain. Meanwhile, she'd better role-play and strengthen the family's trust in her.

"Take him to the swings, if you like," Harmony coaxed. "Damon and I will stay here. It'll give you two a little time to become acquainted."

Forcing a smile, Shay hoisted little Damon higher on her hip. "Let's play while your mama and papa finish their ice cream." She remembered to look both ways before crossing the street—pretending to be mortal required so many little details—and headed toward the park.

The babe brought a warm sticky hand to her cheek, holding her gaze in a direct, quite disconcerting way, much like his mother. "Shay good."

A low laugh escaped her. "I wouldn't jump to conclusions."

"Good Shay," he insisted.

Wincing, Shay took the babe's hand, holding it in hers as she lowered it. She wasn't good. Not at all. She was a monster of the worst kind. Soon, very soon, the babe would learn the truth about her.

"Hey, Laredo, what do you think of the Faithfull's new nanny and Mysteria's newest citizen, Shay d'Mon?"

Quel almost choked on the cup of coffee he was about to gulp. "What?"

Jeanie, the sheriff, slid onto a stool next to him in the coffee shop. "Yup, our little fountain splasher. Hired. Yesterday. I'll take the special, Elvira," she called to the waitress.

Quel drained his coffee cup and rammed it down to the counter. He grabbed his hat and coat, grumbling, "See you, Sheriff."

"Where you going?"

"To talk some sense into those folks."

"Harmony and Damon? They know what they're doing."

He snorted. "Doesn't much sound like it. Look, you hired me to look after the people here, and that's what I'm going to do."

"I appreciate that, Laredo. You know I do. But her background check came back clean."

"As clean as an unemployed, midwestern schoolteacher who crashes sports cars willed to them by their deceased parents can be, I guess." If Shay had relayed that information with her own lips, Quel would have laughed it off as lies. But the woman didn't have to say a thing. Jeanie had found it all using the info from Shay's license and registration. "A sweet smile or two, a pure-as-driven-snow background as a kindergarten teacher, and she goes and gets herself hired as their nanny? Do they have any idea who—or what—she might be?"

"Like you just said, a small-town teacher with a spotless record. Not even a traffic ticket. Well, before last Tuesday."

"You gave her a ticket? Well. There's justice in this town, after all."

"Shay owes me community service in lieu of a fine."

"Let me guess—at the car wash." Quel threw the tip on the counter and headed for the exit. "Now, if you'll excuse me, I'm paying the Faithfulls a visit."

"Or maybe it's just an excuse to say hello to Miss d'Mon. There's more than a little electricity going back and forth between you two. I'm not the only one who's noticed."

Quel stopped short, his back aimed at the sheriff. *Electricity?* He removed a toothpick from his pocket and slipped it between his lips. "The only thing going back and forth is my investigation and Miss d'Mon not liking it."

Then he pushed out the swinging door into the sunshine, scowling as he did so. Since when had he become such a rotten liar?

In the cottage that Reverend Faithfull shared with her husband Damon, Quel stalked past a kitchen table topped with brownies and milk. His boots scuffed over the hardwood floor. His silver-bullet-loaded revolver rubbed against his hip. "Reverend Faithfull—"

"Harmony," she corrected with her usual bright smile.

"Harmony. Jeanie tells me you're thinking of hiring Miss d'Mon as your new nanny."

"We already did."

"Because you think she has a good soul," he said, skeptical about the minister's purported talent as a seer that the entire town took for granted—except him. "How do you know for sure?"

"It's my job to know." The reverend wore her pastor's face that tried to get him to feel guilty about never setting foot in her church. Thing was, he had more things to blame God for than to thank him for. Since church was for praying and thanking, and not blaming, he never showed. The way he saw it, he killed demons for the Big Man. That should be enough. "And," she said, blushing, "I can see things other people can't, Mr. Laredo, just like you can sense demons. Shay has a good soul. I saw it. I *felt* it."

"It's a demon trick. That's what they do. Your guard goes down, and they get you. Or, in this case, your kid."

Her husband spoke up. "Demons can do many things, aye, but they can't replicate a mortal soul." Damon was a former demon high lord. If anyone knew about demons, it was this man.

"All I know is that I never sensed anything that powerful. Whatever came down that mountain was old as shit. I had one thing on my mind: get it out of the car and kill it before it killed any of us."

Harmony lifted a brow. "Glad you took a moment to access the situation."

"That's the thing. I didn't. By the time I got to the wreck, it didn't smell like demon anymore. It didn't smell like anything I've ever come across, either." Not exactly demon, not exactly human.

But 100 percent woman. A damned sexy woman, too, with all the right curves and attitude to spare. He couldn't stop thinking about how the hell stench had morphed into a hot little thing with an innocence about her that didn't fit the heat in her eyes. His senses blasted on high alert whenever their eyes met. No one had ever looked at him with that much hunger, that much longing. Even if she did admit she'd mixed him up with someone else, it was damn unnerving. Damn arousing.

Laredo, focus. You gotta think with your head not your cock. Hell and damn. Since when did he ever have trouble keeping the two apart? It was all jumbled up. He was all jumbled up.

"Shay has no defenses, Quel, none," Harmony assured him, clearly trying to sway his opinion. "I can see right through her. There's goodness there. She's also conflicted, lonely. Afraid."

He remembered Shay's tears. Yeah, they'd looked pretty frickin' genuine. Damn lucky he came to his senses before he wiped them off her cheek with his knuckle like he wanted to. He frowned. Quel Laredo didn't wipe away tears. He didn't know how. Yet she had him wanting to learn. She'd gotten under his skin, skin so thick he'd long since assumed it was impenetrable. Maybe Shay *was* an angel, and he was all wrong. Maybe he'd been around the wrong kind of woman for so long he didn't know how to recognize the right kind.

Quel glanced out the kitchen window and into the backyard where the couple had told him Shay was spending time with the boy. Standing by the pond near the barn, she held the child in her arms, handing him bread crusts to throw to the ducks. The breeze lifted and tossed her curls around her neck and jaw. Suddenly, she looked sweet and vulnerable, like a young mother. Was this the monster he thought he'd find in the sports car? A woman with the face of an angel, the shirt of an angel, and the devil in her eyes. Damon and Harmony trusted her. Was he wrong not to?

Exhaling, Quel tiredly rubbed his face. He hadn't shaved. He'd hardly slept. "I know what I sensed that night, Damon. As clear as day I know. My gut's telling me whatever came down that hill didn't up and disappear. Yeah, maybe it's not Shay, maybe it's not in Mysteria at all, but I won't ignore my instincts. I did, once, and half my convoy got taken out in Iraq. Now I pay attention. I'm not letting down my guard. I advise you don't, either."

"I trust my wife's instincts. I'll take yours into account, as well."

Quel nodded. His attention drifted outside again, where Shay hugged the boy close as if he were her own. Quel had a fleeting memory of being hugged by his mother in the early years before she left. After that he adopted such a fierce outside shell that few risked reaching out. He never made it worth their while. Though if they'd tried a little harder, tried more than once, he might have let them in. No one ever did. He didn't need cowards in his life then or now. He'd raised himself and was proud of it. Yet he had to wonder what he'd missed with the absence of any softness in his life.

With the child in her arms, Shay disappeared behind the barn. A chill washed over him. It was as if the sun had gone behind a cloud. He made fists, trying to resist the urge to follow—to chase down the sun. Impossible, he realized, and grabbed for an excuse to see her again. To see the pining in her eyes again. Hey, so he was being soft. So what? Sue him. If he liked the way a woman looked at him, no one needed to know. "Now that she's going to be staying here, I'd better go and reintroduce myself."

Harmony frowned at him. "It took us weeks to find a nanny. If you scare her away, Laredo . . ."

"I'll be good. I promise."

The couple sitting at the table didn't look convinced. Damn, his reputation was worse than he'd thought. No one, not even the town pastor, wanted him near the woman. "I'll play nice. I do know how." So he was a little out of practice. No one needed to know that. In the meantime, it wouldn't hurt to get to know Miss d'Mon a little better, angel . . . or not.

Five

If ever the moment to strike was right, it was this one. Here she was, alone with the babe, unwatched. Now was her chance.

Pink-cheeked, little Damon sat perched on Shay's hip, giggling at the ducks. The idea of murdering the child and taking its bones to Lucifer threatened to make her violently ill. She'd killed men with a blink of her eyes. Now she was paralyzed by guilt and disgust at the thought of betraying the mortals who trusted her. The sensation had gotten worse over the past few days, not better.

Bat bugger. It was the blasted soul. *Out, out,* she chanted in her mind. Ever since she rode the ambulance to the hospital, she'd been willing the soul to leave her body, begging it to go away throughout her treatment by humans who seemed to care for her despite her sloppy entrance into town, despite her being a stranger. No matter how hard she tried, she couldn't get rid of it. Worse, kindness was feeling pretty good when it used to make her sick. How much longer could she fool Lucifer into thinking she was doing her job? If he found out what had happened, she was toast. And if the Faithfull family learned of her true mission . . . well, she was still toast.

Think of something, Shay. Think!

No plan beyond hiding out came to her. No ideas. No strategy. Where were those wits she was so sure she possessed? *"You stupid creature."* She squeezed her eyes shut, remembering Lucifer's tirade before he sent her from Hell. He made no secret that he thought her stupid. Vile, yes, but lacking in the wits department. Anger lanced through her, and she opened her eyes, glaring at the pond. She was smarter than her master thought, and she'd prove it. How, she didn't yet know, but it would come to her, surely it would.

By now, Lucifer would be wondering why she hadn't reported in with her status. Soon she had to send word of her progress, or he'd grow suspicious. Her master knew her weaknesses. Even now he might be watching her holding little Damon, the scene projected on the molten walls of his lair.

"More!"

She pressed more bread into Damon's outstretched hand. His baby fragrance drifted to her. Babies mystified her; she knew little about them and wasn't interested in learning more, yet there was an innocence about them, a goodness, that she'd never really noticed before. *Perhaps you were not capable of noticing.* Glancing around to make sure no one was watching, least of all Lucifer, she touched her lips to the top of little Damon's head, her favorite spot. Soft, warm skin, silken curls. Her hand drifted lower, down to the babe's fragile neck, so easily snapped . . .

No.

Gasping, she snatched back her hand. Assassinating the babe ensured her master's future. Letting it live assured her master's end. Kill or spare the child: each of her potential actions contradicted the other. She'd seen people tortured on the rack during the Middle Ages, pulled apart by opposing forces. Torn between good and evil, between conscience and duty, she decided the rack could not have been any worse than this.

Tiny fingers landed on her cheek, turning her head to bring her eye to eye with the child she was supposed to kill. Those gray blue eyes searched hers, deeply and with disarming intensity. Swallowing, Shay turned her eyes away, lest the little one see her purpose and her true nature.

The boy's sticky hand pressed on her chin, forcing her gaze back to his. A year-old babe imposing his will on an ancient demon! No wonder her lord wanted the child dead.

"Shay . . . good," the child said. "Good Shay."

Choked with guilt, she hugged him close, burying her nose in that pile of curls. "You know I'm not good," she whispered. "I'm a monster. But I can't do it." *Yet.* "You're safe." *For now.*

The only certainty was her demise. No matter what her decision, it would bring about the end of her existence.

"Birdie!" Shay lifted her head at little Damon's cry. With the child cradled close, she turned around. A raven had landed in one of the surrounding trees. Even without her demon powers, she sensed something amiss in its presence. Was it Lucifer's minion, here to check on her? Or was she just being paranoid, hindered by her new, humanlike weakness?

"More birdies!"

Several other ravens flew into the trees, ruffling their shiny black feathers as they settled in to watch her. Their small, obsidian eyes followed her every step.

The sound of more approaching ravens came from behind her. A pinpoint of red glowed in their eyes now. Subdemons. Her pulse quickened. *Don't act afraid.* Lucifer will sense it. Shadows flew all around them, swooping uncomfortably close. She glanced wildly in the direction of the house. The more mortals to stand against subdemons, the better the chances of success. Even Lucifer accepted that. It was why he sent the inferior creatures in large numbers. She opened her mouth to call for help.

And stopped before she uttered a cry. To call attention to the sudden interest of the subdemons in her and the babe was to risk raising suspicion as to what she was and why she was here. She could—and would—handle this on her own.

She kept her voice calm. "Shall we go inside, little Damon? I will feed you one of your mother's brownies." A confection Shay had quickly become addicted to, she was happy to say. She deposited the babe in the stroller and gave the contraption a shove. It might not be a chariot, but she could steer it like one if she had to.

The ravens cawed, as if calling her back. *Speak with us.* The command rang in her head. She ignored them. *The Dark Lord wants an answer.*

"Shove it up your arses," she muttered.

"Arses!" the babe repeated.

"I will complete this mission in my own time," she sneered at the demons. "I will not be rushed. Do you hear? Tell your master to leave me be, or the trust I have gained with the family will be for naught." She jogged away from the pond, pushing the stroller along a dirt path. "Don't say *arses*," she told the babe. "It's not a nice word."

The cottage came into sight. Seeing it, she almost sobbed with relief. Then a deep, threatening growl brought her to a halt.

Damon and Harmony kept several goats. One of them stood in the middle of the path ahead. Its eyes were unnaturally bright—bright red. It should have been calling "Maaah." Instead it was growling like a wolf, its lips drawn back over yellowed fangs.

Little Damon pouted. "Bad doggie."

Shay grabbed a fallen stick and turned to face the new subdemon. "Go! I gave you my answer—go *now*."

With a breathtaking purpose, it clawed at the dirt with a cloven hoof and advanced on them. Shay stood between the stroller and the creature. It would have to kill her, or at least hurt her badly, to get past. She didn't want to think about that right now. *Keep positive*, she told herself in disgustingly optimistic mortal fashion as she held the stick out in front of her. Without powers, it was all about appearances, she realized. She put all the menace she could muster in her face and body and assumed the stance of a warrior.

The goat leaped. Shay raised the stick, gladiator-style. A loud pop tore through the silence. A second later, the goat was lying still on the path many feet from the reach of her stick. How?

Several smaller pops followed. Dark feathers and silver pellets rained down. One by one, the ravens disappeared from the trees. Then, like a vision of vengeance, Quel Laredo strode out of the woods, a weapon in each hand.

"Hello, angel," he said. "We're gonna have to talk about the company you keep."

Six

"My, aren't we the center of attention," Quel said as he saun-
tered toward Shay.

She stared at him, her lips parted in surprise, the stick still
gripped in her fists. This time there was more tenderness in
her gaze than heat, more apology than anger. For a second he
thought she'd run headlong into his arms. A kiss of gratitude
with the promise of more to come would hit the spot. No such
luck. He knew what he looked like: his narrowed, mistrustful
eyes and guarded expression kept her rooted to the path. "Any
reason I should know about for why there are suddenly so
many subdemons, Miss d'Mon? The town's been clear of
them for months."

"I don't know. You're the demon hunter, not me."

"Any prior experience with demons?"

"That's irrelevant."

"I don't think so."

"If you feel the need to interrogate me, call the sheriff and
make it official." She looked him square in the eye when they
spoke, and she spoke what was on her mind, holding nothing
back. She seemed afraid at times, just like Harmony said she

was, but not afraid *of him*. Not one frickin' bit. She held her ground, didn't let him intimidate her. It had him aching to get her into bed. To see how she looked at him then. To see if she maintained eye contact when he made her come. When he made her beg for more. Yeah, that'd be something.

She reached for the child, lifting him out of the stroller. Her voice lost its edge. "Thank you for saving us."

"That's what they pay me for, ma'am." His hunter senses were turned on so damn high that he could feel the surge of heat in her body as he took another step closer. Longing and hunger flashed in her eyes. Her scent washed all around him. It was a frickin' aphrodisiac.

"Stop it," she whispered.

"Ma'am?"

"The way you look at me, it drives me crazy."

"Nice to hear it's mutual."

"Shay! Damon Junior!"

The boy squealed at the sight of Damon and Harmony jogging toward them. "Mama! Papa!"

The reverend reacted in obvious terror, seeing the dead goat, the fallen ravens, and scattered feathers. "Subdemons."

"Aye," Damon said, grim. His wife gently took the boy from Shay.

"You okay, honey?" Harmony murmured to Shay.

"Fine!" Her voice was overly perky. A sign of guilt, but she'd done nothing to warrant it. It added to the mystery Quel was determined to figure out.

"Miss d'Mon was no mere observer," Quel told them. "She was fighting them back with a stick when I got here. Defending your little boy."

His compliment drew praise from Harmony and Damon yet seemed to make Shay uneasy. In fact, her obvious embarrassment told him she'd prefer the topic to go away completely. Why?

Damon's hand fell on Quel's shoulder. "You protected my son—both of you," the former demon said, his voice deep with emotion, with accent thicker. "You have my loyalty and my gratitude." He gave Quel's shoulder a hearty squeeze before turning back toward the cottage with his wife.

"Would you like a second chance at those brownies, Mr. Laredo?" Harmony called over her shoulder.

"No thanks, Reverend." He wanted a second chance at Shay d'Mon.

She started to follow the couple. Quel cleared his throat. She stopped, glancing over her shoulder. "Woman, you ought to take credit where credit is due. You did a damn fine job with those subdemons."

"The credit's yours. You killed them."

"You're no coward. That's something to be proud of, not ashamed of."

She sighed in exasperation. "I don't want to talk about it." She started walking away.

"You want to get a drink?"

She halted. "What?"

"A drink. On me. At Knight Caps, the bar on Main."

The breeze tossed her curls and the hem of her soft shirt. Her silence made him feel like an idiot for asking her out.

Since when had he ever cared whether a woman took him up on an invitation or not? When they said no, he'd call it their loss. Hell, usually he wasn't ever doing the asking; he didn't need to. Women were buying him the drinks, not the other way around. That's not how he wanted it with Shay. Suddenly it became pretty damn important that she said yes. "When's your night off?" he persisted.

"Tomorrow. I'm off at six. Six until . . . until dawn."

He lifted a brow, waiting. As much expectancy as reluctance filled the new silence. Maybe she was in as much doubt about him as she was her. He didn't blame her.

"Knight Caps," she said finally. "Tomorrow, six o'clock."

He touched a hand to the brim of his hat. "Yes, ma'am. Six works." The "until dawn," he figured, was still negotiable.

Laredo walked her all the way back to the house. Thunder rumbled distantly. The scent of rain was acrid in the air. Then the first drops fell, wetting her skin. An image of stripping Laredo out of his clothes and making love on the wet lawn filled her mind with vividly erotic images. She sucked in a quiet breath, trying to control this new body that seemed to have a will of its own. Her arousal added to the many sensations, internal and external, colliding in a vivid, exhilarating storm. All these long centuries, she thought she knew what it was like to be alive. She hadn't known squat.

The demon hunter stopped at the base of the porch steps, turning up his collar against the rain. His right cheekbone had a small scar. A bump on the bridge of his nose hinted at a long-ago break. He hadn't lived an easy life or even a happy life; even without her demon mental powers, she could tell.

It made her want to make it all better.

Stop! It was bad enough he hunted demons. Why did he have to look like the only mortal she ever cared about and would have lost her heart to, had she a heart to lose? Acquiring a temporary soul may have heightened her ability to feel emotion, but she sure as snake's scales wasn't going to let it turn her into a simpering, lovesick fool. Her weakened state was humiliating as it was. No need to make it any worse.

"Before I go, since you have such a nasty habit of attracting subdemons"—he lifted his silver cross off his neck—"use my talisman to ward them off." He dropped the chain over her head.

Cool and smooth, the cross dangled between her breasts. She gasped, half expecting some sort of sizzling to begin, the silver burning her demon flesh, the cross shredding her, but her skin didn't react. In wonder, she fingered the cross. This body of hers was unlike any other she'd inhabited. "It protects you?" she asked, trying to hide her shock.

"I'm still here, aren't I?"

That had more to do with the fact she'd been avoiding him, fearing Lucifer would sense her attraction to the mortal. Now she'd gone and agreed to meet him—at a bar, no less—like a common human.

"Well, I'd better get going, Miss d'Mon."

"I guess so," she said.

Hesitating, he acted as if he wanted to say more. She knew *she* did. The intensity between them made no sense, considering they hardly knew each other. Their inexplicable connection seemed to prove what she already sensed herself. They went back, *way* back. Fifteen thousand years and counting. Call it reincarnation, whatever, but they'd been down this road before: Laredo as a doomed Ice Age hunter and she as an inexperienced demon who thought she could live as a human. With deadly consequences.

Then why was she heading down this same road again, knowing where it ended? *This time, you won't let it get that far.*

Laredo tipped his hat. "Good day, ma'am." Swinging his rifle from his hand, he walked away, his long legs carrying him swiftly out of sight.

Sipping a scotch, Quel waited for Shay the next day in Knight Caps. The bar was filling up. The music was loud. The fairy-goths were stirring up the usual trouble, and a trio of witches near the back were having themselves quite the party with a sullen-looking vampire. Quel had saved the stool next to him. It had taken some work keeping it empty of the shapely asses of the women he didn't want sitting there, which was every other female in this bar.

He glanced at his watch. It was almost seven, an hour past the time Shay said she'd meet him. What had he been thinking, giving her the cross? It was his mother's cross. Shay was a stranger. *No, she's more than that.* He damn well couldn't figure out what, though.

Frowning into his drink, he pushed his thumbs impatiently around the rim of his glass. Then he downed the drink he'd been nursing for an hour. He'd wanted to be sober when she got here. Guess it didn't matter anymore. He flicked a finger at the empty glass. The bartender, Falon, poured another scotch—straight up, no ice, no water.

Then a woman's voice: "Nothing gets in the way of you and your scotch, I see."

She came. He slid around on the stool to face her. Shay wore a black tank top cut low enough to show off the rounded tops of those amazing tits, a pair of faded jeans, and stilettos with heels high enough to give someone a nosebleed. Her tanned skin sparkled like the cross she wore around her neck. She'd glazed her skin with some kind of lotion. *Everywhere?* He couldn't help wondering. This wasn't the timid schoolteacher-nanny; this was the crazy girl who'd driven that Porsche. "I like my scotch the way I like a woman," he drawled. "Real, undiluted, nothing in between me and her."

There it was: that flash of heat again. He wanted to press his lips to her neck where those hoop earrings glittered in her soft halo of curls. He wanted to grab her thighs and haul her legs over his hips, right here in the bar. No, he wanted her in private, hard and up against the wall in his small room. Then, when he'd slaked the fire burning in him all damn week, he'd take her nice and slow.

Shit. He hadn't moved, and he'd already worked up a sweat, not to mention one helluva hard-on. He motioned to the bartender. "Give me a couple of cubes." Ice splashed into his drink.

"What happened to undiluted?"

"You showed up, Miss d'Mon." He turned the stool to face her. They sat, jeans to jeans, knees almost touching. "Woman, you got a way of looking at me that . . ." He let his words trail off, shifting his focus to the drink. He wasn't used to this kind of frank talk. Revealing talk. Telling people his feelings.

"That . . . *what?*"

He shook his head. "Who do you think of when you look at me?"

This time she glanced away. "Wine," she told the bartender.

"Red or white?"

"Roman."

The bartender glanced at Quel for enlightenment.

"Italian," Shay corrected.

"We've got Californian." The wall behind the bar was filled with wine bottles.

Shay pursed her lips and pointed to one, seemingly at random. "I'll have the red."

Her first sip was a hearty one. Shay d'Mon definitely attacked life with gusto. He liked that. Careful women bored him. "You never answered my question," he said, low in her ear. "Who are you thinking of when you—?"

She sealed her mouth over his. He almost fell off the stool. Two heartbeats: that's all his surprise lasted. Then he took hold of her soft hair and kissed her back. The soft little sound of pleasure she made drove him crazy. His hand fell to the side of her throat, resting on her throbbing pulse. The scent of her skin and her perfume filled his nostrils along with another scent that threatened to make him drunker than the scotch: he couldn't make sense of it; he only reacted to it, as he had the night she'd driven down the mountain. It seemed like a scent that he already knew—deep down, a memory he'd always carried without realizing it, just like he felt he'd kissed her before. It was impossible. No way would Shay have entered his life and sneaked out of it without him noticing. And she definitely wasn't sneaking out now. No damn way. He suckled her tongue, devouring her lips like she was the best damn bite of candy he'd ever tasted in a life of savoring every last piece thrown his way.

He became aware of a roar. Not the one in his head. The crowd in the bar was cheering.

Shay pulled back. "You," she said. "I think of you."

"Liar."

She blushed. "You can tell?"

"Yeah, I can tell." He reached for her, needing to touch her again. His fingers trailed up and down her back, following the bumps of her spine. He liked the goose bumps his caress raised on her bare arms. "That will come in very useful, too, angel, knowing how bad of a liar you are."

She shot him a panicked glance. "Because," he brought his lips to her ear, "when I kiss you again, I'm going to ask that same question. You're going to tell the truth this time, and the answer had better be me."

He saw her throat move before she glanced away. The song that had been playing ended, and a slower tune came on. "I'm thinking you dance as good as you kiss," he said.

"Maybe . . ."

"Let's get out there, and you can show me." What was with him? He never wanted to dance.

She sent a look of longing to the dance floor. "I used to like dancing."

"With so-and-so?"

Lifting one reddish brow, she shot him a confused look.

"The guy you think of when you look at me."

She shook her head. "We never danced."

It had Quel wondering what they did do that had been so memorable. He took her hand. "It's been a while," she warned.

"We can fix that."

He sensed only a moment's resistance before she let him lead her to the dance floor. He found a place in the middle of the swaying couples before sliding his hands over the body he'd been aching to touch all damn week. She melted against him, threading her fingers in his hair. It was like coming home. She fit him; he fit her. Déjà vu. He could almost believe he'd done this before and knew just how to hold her. Call it schmaltzy, but there it was.

Shay's body was toned and firm in all the right places, and soft where it counted. He, on the other hand, was hard where it counted, almost to the point of pain. Even harder was his ability to remain a gentleman, but he did, keeping his hips from pressing too hard against hers and giving away just how eager he was to have her.

The music stopped. They stayed there, holding each other, his lips resting on her hair. Her shirt was so thin he could feel the heat of her skin burning his palms. He didn't know what possessed him, and he kept thinking she'd chicken out, but he took her hand, steering her out of the bar. He led her around to the back alley and up the dark, narrow staircase to his room, shoving the door closed with his boot.

Seven

Shay still hadn't come to terms with the fact that she'd showed up at the bar at all, and here she was, in his room. They were kissing before the door slammed shut, the kind of deep, thorough, wet kisses she'd always loved and that too few men knew how to do right—and as skillfully as Quel Laredo. *You desire me. You can't get enough of me.* Shay instinctively sent the thoughts. Then she remembered there were no powers of persuasion to back them up. She was on her own. Nothing but chemistry fueled this seduction. She knew little of making love as a powerless being. There was no dark magic holding Quel here. There was no reason other than chemistry to make him want her. To desire her. How did humans manage it? How did they overcome the fear and doubt?

The kiss turned even hotter. Then he was pulling off her shirt and smoothing his hands over her breasts. She unhooked the bra. He threw it out of the way. His pants dropped, then hers. And he reached for a bedside box. *Protection*, she thought, dazed.

They were frantic now as he backed her up against the wall. It was a blur of sensation, uncontrollable need. Kissing wasn't the only thing that was going to be good with Quel Laredo. Of that she was absolutely sure.

He lifted one thigh over his hip. "Quel . . ." she moaned. She thought she saw a shadow of a smile as he hoisted her other leg off the floor. Then he plunged deep.

A flash of pain, a swift intake of breath. In the next breath the stinging dissolved into sheer pleasure.

"Who are you thinking of now?" he demanded. "Me or him?" He was thrusting slow, swaying just right. His eyes were dark, burning into hers.

"You," she whispered. Dark satisfaction, even triumph glimmered in Quel's gaze as he crushed his mouth to hers. Perhaps he read the earnestness there that she hadn't revealed before, perhaps, too, a glimpse of her surrender, yet she felt nothing that smacked of defeat. She'd simply told the truth, a new habit for her, but one that felt exquisitely freeing.

She clung to him as he rocked inside her, her fingers grasping for purchase on his hard, slick body. No words now, only her sighs and his groans, his scent mingling with hers. Her human body was a gift. The pleasure it brought her was intense. Sex had always been good but never like this. Never like—

"Oh!" She came apart, crying out as she writhed against him.

"Angel," he hissed, pressing his teeth to her shoulder as he thrust into her body. His peak came soon after, crashing over them both like an earthquake before subsiding into trembling aftershocks.

He swept her away from the wall and tossed her onto the bed, kissing his way down her body to where she still throbbed for him. When his lips touched her between her thighs, her body made no secret of how he affected her. She moaned, arching her back. He chuckled smugly. "Angel, we're gonna have a good night tonight."

They kissed and stroked each other until Quel pushed up, frowning down at the tangled sheets. "You're bleeding."

"I am?" She squinted in the dim light but couldn't make out much.

"Did I hurt you?"

"No." Then she remembered the pain. "Just for a minute."

He stretched out next to her, his head propped on one hand, his other flattened on her stomach. The heat of his palm, the male possessiveness in his touch, made her shiver. "It's not your period?"

"I . . . don't think so." Could this body menstruate? The other bodies hadn't.

"Shay?"

"Yes?"

One, two moments of silence ticked by before he asked, "Were you a virgin?"

Hades. That was it. She hadn't even thought about the issue of virginity. She'd been so hot for Quel that she'd forgotten all about her cover. Her demon self was no virgin, but her physical body was—as innocent and untouched as . . . that damn soul she was stuck with. "I should have thought to say something."

"Hell yeah, you should have." His gaze had changed. It was oddly soft, as was his voice. "Jesus, Shay. Why didn't you?"

"Would it have mattered?" She honestly wanted to know.

"Damn right, it would have. I would have done things differently."

Curiosity burned. She'd never experienced lovemaking where the act had been entirely voluntary—a fact best kept secret, though. "How so?"

His mouth, tipped in that half smile of his, filled her vision as he moved closer. "Give me a second to recover," he said low in her ear, "and then I'll show you."

Toward dawn, Quel gently roused her from a doze of pure exhaustion. Her human body tired as quickly as it surrendered to pleasure. The trade-off was worth it. "I knew your ass looked great in jeans." Quel nibbled and kissed his way down from her neck to the ticklish spot between her shoulder blades and lower. His heavy erection brushed against her thigh. The man was insatiable. She quite liked that. "Though I've got to say it looks a hell of a lot better without them." On all fours, he playfully bit her left cheek

She laughed then winced as she rolled over. Her body continued to remind her that tonight was its first time making love.

As did Quel. "Sore?" He sounded slightly more smug than sorry.

"Yes. A bath sounds lovely right now."

"Sorry, angel. I've got a shower, no tub. There's a new motel in town. Nice place. Maybe on your next night off we'll check in and have ourselves a party in one of those in-room Jacuzzis."

His words shattered the lovely spell she'd been under all evening. There wouldn't be a next time.

Bat bugger. What had she been thinking, coming here tonight? She should have said no to the drink, she should have stayed close to the Faithfulls' home. She'd put Quel at risk by spending the night with him. It was a selfish risk, even if she hadn't planned on it going this far. Lucifer was all too good at discovering her affinity for anyone and anything—and taking it away.

She wriggled out from under Quel's weight. "It's nearly dawn. I've got to go." She hurried around the room, snatching her clothes off the floor, blaming her mistake on her addiction to feeling alive—and her curiosity and attraction to Quel. *In coming here, you may have just signed his death warrant.* Her tenderness with the babe could be explained away as winning the family's trust, but what of the others she'd met here? She couldn't afford to get close to any of them. She had to keep her distance or risk the unthinkable. She mustn't become attached to Quel, to the babe, or to anyone. Mortals were off-limits. Starting now.

She was going to miss him. She was going to miss this life. More so than the others, this one had felt . . . real. Her body did, too, she thought with another wince. Her other bodies had all been virginal. Why hadn't they stung like this one did? Maybe it, too, like this life, was real.

The realization froze her in place. Did the soul mean she was no longer a demon? No, that was impossible.

Jeans, bra, blouse . . . one shoe, then two. Frantically she tore through the fallen garments. "Did you see my—?"

"Panties?" Propped up on one elbow in bed, glorious in his unselfconscious nakedness, he twirled her tiny undergarment on his finger. "Come and get 'em, angel." His blue eyes danced with devilish mischief of the sexual sort, reminding her all too much of Swift River the last time she saw him. The night he died. *At your hand, Shay.*

Lucifer would make her kill Quel, too. She thrust out her hand. "I have to go, Laredo."

In a move so swift she hadn't time to react, he caught her hand, yanking her across his body. She batted at him, pushing him away as he kissed her . . . kissing her until she'd melted into the embrace. It didn't take long at all to thaw her. She could almost taste the smile she was certain curved that self-satisfied mouth, a smile she sensed faded as he rolled her under his body to give her a kiss as tender as any she'd ever experienced.

When he finally lifted his head, cradling her face in his hands, she was reluctant for their lips to part. No one, not even the men she'd persuaded to love her, had ever kissed her quite like that. "That's my parting gift to you, angel," he said quietly. "A little something to remember me by."

"I will remember you." With that vow, a shiver ran through her. "Always."

Suddenly gruff, he pushed her waded-up panties into her hand. "Shower. Get dressed. Whatever you need to do, Cinderella. I'll walk you home."

"Cinderella?"

"Yeah. I gotta get you home before your coach turns into a pumpkin. As long as you leave a glass slipper behind, we're cool."

"And you accused me of babbling?"

"Hey, you're the teacher. You know your fairy tales better than I do."

Actually, she didn't. "Of course. Cinderella. The glass coach."

He gave her a strange look. "Slipper."

"Right." She bit her lip before she revealed more of her ignorance. There were many details of being a modern human that she didn't know. She'd never thought she'd be staying here as long as she had. She hadn't banked on meeting Quel Laredo.

He shook his head at her. "If it takes me the rest of my days, I'm going to figure you out."

She was going to use the rest of her days to make sure he didn't. Not that she had many days left.

The fountain was the centerpiece of the town square. This time of night the area was deserted. The sky was growing light already. If she'd been human, she'd be greeting the sunrise with all the excitement of having spent the first night with a lover she wanted to see again and again. Instead, the coming dawn brought a feeling of dread.

Oblivious, Quel wrapped his arm over her shoulders, holding her close as they walked. "That was one hell of a night. I'd like to see you again. Though if the good reverend figures out you're no longer a virgin after one date with me, she might not let you."

"That might not be such a bad thing, Quel."

His steps slowed as her heart banged hard in her throat. "What the hell is that supposed to mean?"

"I don't know if seeing each other is a good idea."

Now he stopped, holding on to her hand as he searched her face in disbelief. "Are you giving me the brush-off?"

"I can't see you anymore," she blurted out. She had to sever ties with Quel before Lucifer discovered her attachment. It was what she'd failed to do all those thousands of years ago with Swift River. Then, she'd made the one, unforgivable mistake: she'd underestimated Satan. She might not be the smartest demon, but she did have a learning curve, and she was going to prove it tonight. She'd put Quel's welfare over her own desires. "It's over. I'm sorry."

Quel swore under his breath. "I don't frickin' believe this. Shay—"

He'd stopped speaking midsentence. Reaching for his pistol, he peered into the shadows, his nostrils flaring. "Hell stench."

The thunder of small hooves drew their attention to the far side of the square. A herd of billy goats trotted toward them.

Fluffy and white, they looked like the ones in Harmony and Damon's pen. Glowing red eyes gave away their origins.

"Subdemons," Quel growled. He sprayed silver BBs into the herd, decimating it. The goats sizzled and popped, dissolving before their eyes.

A shriek sounded overhead. Something whooshed past, blowing Shay's hair. Quel took a shot. An owl fell to earth, its red eyes fading as it flapped at their feet. Even as it vaporized, the sky filled with other creatures, hundreds of them. Their flapping wings rustled like dry leaves. "Bats this time," she said. The subdemons swooped and squeaked.

Quel hauled her close, letting her bury her head against his chest as he blasted away at the beasties. More varieties appeared to replace what he destroyed. Evil soaked the very air. Malevolence, she could feel it.

And so it begins . . . Lucifer's patience had run out. Her time of freedom was up. The time to act was upon her. She twisted around. "Quel, protect yourself before me. When the time comes, you cannot hesitate. You must save yourself."

He jerked back. "Woman, you're definitely babbling now."

"Promise me you'll do it." She gripped his arms. His eyes were wide with denial. He'd rather die himself than hurt her, she knew. There was only one way to get him to do as she said, and that was to tell him what she was. "I'm a monster, Quel. A demon. Your instincts were right about me."

"Bullshit," he growled. His blue eyes were blacker now. He was angry.

"I came to kill the Faithfulls' baby. Lucifer ordered me here. He thinks the child will grow up to rival him, even defeat him. He sent me to make sure that doesn't happen."

"And you couldn't do it."

Her throat constricted. "No," she whispered. "I can't."

"You're human, that's why." Quel grabbed the cross hanging from her neck, pulling the chain taut. "A demon couldn't wear this. You can. You're mortal, Shay. You're one of us, not them. You're human."

Human . . . could it be? Yes. She was already halfway to believing it. Quel's conviction pushed her the rest of the way. Her soul, her immunity to silver, her virginity, it was obvious. "I crashed into that wishing fountain and came out mortal."

"You wished to be mortal, to have a soul, and it gave you want you wanted."

A soul. The chance to really live. For a finite period, she realized. "I'm no longer immortal."

"Quality over quantity, we humans always say."

She laughed at that until reality returned. Her new status meant she was even weaker than she'd thought. She had no powers at all to fight anything Lucifer threw at her. And these subdemons were only the tip of the iceberg.

"Go, Quel." She shoved at him. It was like trying to move a brick wall. "Get out of here. It doesn't matter what I am now; Lucifer will kill you if he finds out I love you."

For all his hardness, he gave her the classic double take.

"Yes, I love you. We go back, Quel, *way* back. It was during the Ice Age. You were a hunter, even then. I was a demon, but I fell for you. Lucifer didn't like it. He had me kill you. He'll do it again—"

"Hold on. I smell a demon." His voice sounded a little too calm, a little too steady. A glance at his face revealed alarm. Damnation, the demon hunter was nervous. Not a good sign. Whatever was on the way frightened him. "It's powerful, Shay. Ancient."

Who was it? She glared into the shadows. The oldest demons were few; she knew them all. "See? You've got to get out of here." Why couldn't he understand? She knew! She'd lived this all before. "Forget all that crap about protecting me. Go. You're in over your head."

"You got the wrong man if you think I'm going to cut and run, angel."

"I'm not an angel," she screamed in frustration.

"You are to me." Quel made a stifled groan and hauled her closer, crushing her against him. Sliding her hands under his coat, she soaked in his body heat. It didn't help her shivering. It was like the night of the crash all over again. "It doesn't matter what you were," he said in her hair. "I don't frickin' care."

A quiet laugh interrupted. "I'm jealous, Shay. I've missed you down in Hell, and here you are, once again keeping

company with mortal men. What do they have that I don't?
Feelings?"

The familiar deep, lilting voice chilled her to the core.
Nevin, she thought. Lucifer hadn't sent just any demon after
her. He'd sent the most feared high demon lord of them all.

Eight

With a tornado of bats spinning overhead, Nevin advanced on them, his eyes glowing red. "Down!" Quel shoved her to the ground and took aim.

Nevin flicked his wrist. A burst of black energy sent Quel flying backward. He hit the ground hard, his boots scraping over the dirt.

"Quel!" She bit her lip. Too late. She'd revealed her feelings.

Nevin appeared absolutely delighted by her outburst. "Master wanted me to see what was taking you so long. How quickly I found my answer. Our little mortal wannabe has found herself another man. Is she *in love*?"

"He's nothing but a bit of sport, Nevin. You know how much I enjoy sex."

"That I do." Nevin was heartbreakingly handsome. When he smiled, broad and perfect, he could bring a woman to tears. And he had, many times; she'd been witness. "You always did prefer me to the humans, dear Shay, didn't you? A real lover. A dark lover." *You want me, Shay. You desire me above all others.* His commands rang in her mind. *Take off your pants and beg me to fuck you in front of him.*

Gasping in shame, she shook her head even as her fingers tangled with the top button on her jeans. *Fight it,* she told herself.

You desire me above all others. You can't help it.

No! The compulsion to please Nevin warred with her drive not to give in. Crying out, she rolled her fingers into fists.

Nevin howled with irritation. "How do you defy my commands? You are human, weak." He blinked, sending another wave of persuasion. *Undress.*

"No." Her voice sounded guttural and surprisingly strong. How? Residual power? Sheer will?

This crazy town?

Nevin grabbed her wrist, spinning her around. He lifted his hand as if to rip off her blouse but recoiled at the sight of the cross. A shot rang out. The demon staggered backward, roaring in fury as he centered the forgotten Quel in his sights, his eyes glowing fiercely. Although obviously hurting, Quel had staggered to his feet, a pistol in each hand. The weapons and his eyes appeared preternaturally bright against the backdrop of the fountain. Did the demon hunter have powers of his own?

If so, they were not enough to go up against Nevin. The demon hurled another pulse of energy, and Quel staggered backward. Quel uttered a harsh sob and pressed a fist to his forehead. His struggle to fight off the nightmares the demon had implanted in his head tore at her heart. The emotional turmoil a demon could inflict was truly horrible. Another attack of Nevin's sent Quel plunging to his knees.

"Stop it!" she shouted at the demon.

Nevin sneered, turning back to her. *Remove the cross.*

"No."

I will take you, and you will like it. You will cry out in pleasure for him to hear.

"Fuck you, Nevin."

"Actually, I was hoping you would do that. You were always so good at it." His arm slid over her shoulders. He kept his chest away from the cross, she noticed. "Down in Hell, you were the butt of all the jokes. The demon who dreamed of being human." His laugh rang out in the square. "It's why Master never gave you the rank of high demon lord. He knew he couldn't trust you. He was right, of course. Look at you: weak, powerless. Pitiful. It seems you finally got your wish."

She took the cross and plunged it into his chest. It glanced off his ribs but sank deep enough. An unearthly shriek filled her ears. He hurled her to the ground, his hand pressed against the bubbling, ruined flesh.

"Mistake," he hissed, leveling an arm at Quel. Wave after wave of persuasion and dark energy flew in Quel's direction until the demon hunter writhed in agony.

"Stop it, Nevin!" Quel was suffering, and she was weeping. She couldn't bear to watch. Then again, Nevin knew that. He was torturing Quel for her benefit. He'd kill Quel, then her, but before he did, he intended to thoroughly enjoy the moment. With feline delight, he'd toy with his prey.

"Nevin, please." Choking on a sob, Shay reached for the hem of her blouse and lifted it. "I'll do it."

"Pretty water!" From across the square, a little figure in *Transformers* pajamas appeared. Dread pierced Shay at the sight of Damon Junior toddling toward the fountain, dragging his beloved "binkie" blanket behind him.

Nine

Little Damon stumbled once, landing on his padded bottom before righting himself. The town square looked like a battleground. The babe gave the remains of the subdemons little more than a passing glance. "Bad doggies," he muttered.

Nevin followed her horrified gaze. His lips slid back over his perfect teeth. It wasn't a smile as much as it was a snarl. "What is this?"

Pure, cold terror plunged down Shay's spine and slowed down her racing thoughts. Slowed down everything. *Protect the boy.* As if she were under water, she was flinging off her heels, tossing the pumps over her head. She was glancing in Quel's direction, seeing him pushing to his feet with shaking hands, his face pain-ridden but determined. Turning, she ran as Nevin lifted his arm to fire.

"No . . . !" Her voice was deep, drawn-out, as was each long stride that carried her ever so slowly away from Nevin and toward the approaching child.

Her focus had narrowed to one goal: reach the babe before Nevin attacked. *"No matter where you run, no matter where you hide, I will find you, and end you. You will never escape your fate."* Even as Lucifer's awful threat echoed in her mind, she focused outside herself, shoved aside her qualms. She did in fact no longer matter; what happened to her was irrelevant. Instead of the idea being frightening and terrible, it was freeing and wonderful. This was bigger than her, far bigger. Bigger than any of them. This little boy would save the world, and she would save him.

One last straining leap brought her to the boy. Sweeping him off the ground, she whirled, dancing on bare feet as she came face-to-face with Nevin. The demon's glowing eyes had narrowed, both of his arms rising, weapons to be used on her and the babe.

"Shay," the child said calmly, patting her arm. "Shay, good."

She'd already turned away from the imminent threat of Nevin, intending to flee across the square. Caught in the odd time warp of slow motion, she knew what she had to do. *Save the boy. At all cost, save him.*

"Bad man." Little Damon peered over her shoulder. His cherub mouth had screwed up into a frown. He pointed a chubby finger in Nevin's direction. "Bad man!"

Energy crackled, lifting her hair and blowing it in front of her eyes. It gathered strength and released in a resounding boom. Then a shout of outrage and pain came from Nevin's direction.

Shay turned to see what had happened, shoving tangled curls out of her eyes. Nevin clutched his chest with one hand, his other arm coming back up. Quel had risen to his feet behind him, raising his rifle as if it weighed hundreds of pounds.

Giggling, Little Damon clapped his hands together. "More!" Another pulse of energy lit up the night.

"More!" Lightning arced out from the babe's outstretched hand. Nevin lurched backward. Quel took aim and fired. The demon's eyes dimmed and grew bright again, like dying coals.

"Bad man!" Again and again the babe attacked, until Nevin's last cry drowned in a resounding splash. Then, it was silent, utterly silent.

Shay let out a startled sob. "Good Shay," she heard the boy soothe as he stroked her cheek. Everything seemed to speed up, the world returning to normal. Nevin was in the fountain, his feet hanging over the edge. Limping, Quel and now the town sheriff ran toward him.

Shouts sounded all around them. Drawn by the commotion, what looked like the entire town converged on the square.

Quel vaulted into the fountain and yanked the demon out of the water. With Quel's arm locked around Nevin's elegant neck, he wrenched him backward as Jeanie secured his hands behind his back with handcuffs.

"Damon Junior!"

"Mama!" Little Damon twisted in Shay's arms, straining to reach Harmony.

Shay was drawn into the family embrace, submitting to the hugs and kisses as the child was lifted from her arms. "He is an amazing boy," Shay said, breathless. "He saved my life, and Quel's. He defeated a demon lord. He's more powerful than we ever imagined." The estimations of her former master, Lucifer, included.

A familiar, foul odor filled the air. Harmony wrinkled her nose at the dirty diaper. "A shame my heroic son's superpowers don't extend any . . . lower."

They shared a teary laugh. "There's a lot more to tell you, Harmony," Shay confessed.

"I know." The woman's eyes revealed that she did indeed know. "For now, you belong somewhere else."

"With Quel . . ."

"Yes, honey." She smiled her knowing, enigmatic smile, the one that revealed her powers that she kept so well hidden. "Not everyone gets a second chance, Shay. Take it, and do not squander it."

"I won't," she whispered. It looked like Harmony would have to run another ad in the newspaper.

"Shay!" Quel was striding in her direction. Blood trickled from a cut above his right eye; bruises and dirty scrapes marred his knuckles. Their embrace was long and heartfelt. She breathed in his scent, willing it to stay inside her forever.

"Nevin?" she asked when they separated.

"He's being read his rights."

Sitting near the fountain, Nevin appeared decidedly unhappy as the sheriff angrily recited something to him. "Now I'm hauling your ass off to jail," Jeanie declared. "Get up and walk, pretty boy."

"I was sure you'd kill him."

"I thought about it." Quel's eyes narrowed at the departing demon. "Then I realized fate cooked up a worse punishment for the man."

"*Man?* You mean he's turned mortal, too?" The magic wishing fountain, she realized. Like her, Nevin had fallen in and come out with a soul. Unlike her, he'd never wished to be mortal. Or so she'd thought. "Just when you think you know someone . . ."

"My son Damon made that decision for him," Harmony said. "He wished it on the demon, not the other way around."

"Ha. Poor Nevin." Shay grinned and threw up her hands. Her giddiness reminded her of the postrace celebrations at Circus Maximus. "To Damon Junior, the new champion!" Everyone around them applauded and cheered. This was one victory she'd savor. Two ancient demons lost in the space of a week: Lucifer wouldn't be so eager to send another for quite some time to come.

"Now, I'd like to see you alone, Miss d'Mon." Quel grabbed her by the elbow, steering her away from the crowd.

"Both of you need medical attention," Dr. Fogg called out after them.

"Will do, Doc." Then Quel brought his mouth to her ear. "But first, we're gonna talk."

"I didn't mean it about not wanting to see you anymore." She assumed that's what he wanted to know. "I feared for your safety. I feared for your life."

"I hope you learned your lesson. I can take care of myself. And I can take care of you." His expression was fierce as he tugged on her hand. He found a quiet spot under a stand of fragrant conifers. There he stopped and turned to her. "From the very beginning, I knew you were lying to me."

Shay's heart sank.

"From the night you showed up, I was dead set on uncovering your little ruse, even if it happened *under* the covers. One thing was pretty damn certain: I wasn't going to fall for you in the process. No way in hell."

Shay bowed her head.

"I asked you out for a drink on your night off for investigative purposes. Then there was our hot little hookup afterward. I'd say that was 100 percent investigative, too, but I'd be lying."

He took her face in his hands, forcing her to look up at him. His eyes weren't angry, they were heartstoppingly tender. "The woman who started out as a she-demon turns out to be a virgin. Then she tells me we've got history I don't even remember but I sorta do, especially when we're kissing and I feel like I've been to that little corner of heaven before—so to speak."

"It *is* heaven," she whispered, imagining what God's domain would be like: all good, nothing bad.

"Shay, you've got me turned so inside out I can't think of anything else. I can't have that. No way. I'm a sixth-degree demon hunter, and I've got a job to do." He swept her into a passionate kiss. She could barely stand up when he was done. "How do you frickin' do that?" he said harshly against her mouth, sounding winded himself.

"Whatever it is, you do it to me, too."

"I'm thanking God it's mutual, because I wouldn't want to live knowing that it wasn't. I don't want to live without you at all. Angel, I know we're only getting to know each other again. I know you're just getting to live for the first time. What I need to know is if you wanna do it with me?" He pressed a finger to her mouth. "You're mortal now, so you have to think like one. That means waiting before you answer."

"Quel . . ." she mumbled, wanting to reply.

"Hear me out, woman. Life is short. That means you don't have to say yes to spending it with me." He stroked his knuckles down her cheek. "But you goddamn better."

"And I goddamn will." Smiling, she wept tears of joy that he gently wiped away.

Ten

The ring of a phone pierced the early morning silence. Shay's hand popped out from under a pile of blankets, hunting blindly for the contraption. For all she loved modern technology, there were times she despised its intrusions.

She found the phone and brought it to her ear. "Laredo and d'Mon," she answered. "Demon Hunters, Incorporated."

Quel's body was large and warm pressed to hers. His hand slid up her leg, then her thigh. Grinning, she stopped those clever fingers in their tracks so she could concentrate on the call. "Yes, we're available. Yes, we can fix your problem." Hanging up, she turned to scribble the information on a bedside memo pad.

"What do we have, angel?"

"Small town about a hundred miles north of here. Hellhole. Goblins have been disrupting the ski lifts."

"Sounds easy enough."

"Snow and goblins? I suppose. What I'd really prefer is another gargoyle-demon assignment. I loved New York City."

"Manhattan's better in the spring." He stroked his hand up

and down her leg. "We don't need an assignment for me to take you there."

He was right. Business was good if mostly uneventful. Neither one of them complained about the lack of challenge in most of their assignments. Someday, Lucifer might try to hit them harder. For now, he'd taken his defeat, and they'd take the respite. It left her with energy to spare for her charitable work with children from poor areas in New Mexico, where Quel had experienced his rough upbringing. Shame over her past deeds had initially driven her to help innocents, although Harmony assured her she'd been forgiven by "the Big Guy upstairs." The fact that she really did care about what happened to the kids had kept her involved ever since.

In Mysteria, she and Quel helped Harmony and Damon protect little Damon, planning to extend that assistance when the Faithfulls' second baby arrived in a few month's time. No one knew if the second child would have powers or if little Damon's amazing abilities were a fluke. The town's collective breath was held as everyone awaited the news.

Tossing aside the pen, Shay took refuge back under the covers in the rustic mountain cabin they rented every once in a while. Quel peered out the frosted-over windows. "It's a frickin' blizzard out there."

She sighed in bliss. "I know."

"You're crazy, woman, wanting to stay up here in a snowstorm. It may be why I love you."

She straddled him. "One of the reasons."

"I hear wind," he said. "And snow drifting up over my jeep. I hear my stomach growling for a cheeseburger and a beer, and my ass telling me it wants to be sitting on a warm couch watching the football game."

"I hoped you'd have a better time up here. I thought maybe it would jog your memory of when we used ride out the storms together. The first time."

"The first time," he muttered. "Angel, this is the first and definitely the last time we're camping in the middle of a blizzard—"

She silenced him with a kiss. "Swift River was never this cranky."

He slid his fingers behind his head as he sighed.

"Quel?" Shay asked, worried.

He sighed again and rubbed her back. "Look, Shay, I've never loved anyone—or anything—as much as you. Every day it gets better. But when you get to talking about our 'first time,' I get possessive, even though the man you're referring to is supposedly me."

"He is you . . ."

"No," Quel said. "He's not. I'm me."

In his voice and words, Shay sensed his disappointment and even jealousy. The mentions of Swift River had cast in doubt that what he shared with her was special between them, and only them. Shay ran guilty fingers over her lover's handsome face, hoping that what she felt in her newfound heart got through to him. "Quel, it's not like that. When I look at you, it's you I see. It's you I want. It's you I'm in love with."

"Yeah, I know." He smiled. That smile made her heart ache. He had the patience of a saint. She'd made a mistake waiting as long as she had to tell him those words. For as long as she'd walked the earth, she knew shockingly little of affairs of the heart. The past six months had been a learning experience for both her and Quel but most of all for her. She hadn't been capable of true emotions when she'd bedded Swift River. She was now, making her relationship with Quel a real one. Yes, there were moments she was sure Swift River and Quel Laredo were of the same, reincarnated soul, but the better she'd gotten to know Quel, the more the differences between the two men became apparent. For one, Swift River had been an open book, easy to read. Quel Laredo had been slow to give up his many secrets. Swift River had led a simple if not easy life, limited to the task of survival—his and that of his clan— whereas Quel's survival had been more complicated. His scars were mostly internal as opposed to Swift River's visible ones.

She shook her head. No more comparing. It was wrong. "I'm sorry, truly sorry. No more living in the past. From now on, I'm living for today and for however many tomorrows we're allowed to have." She poked him in the chest. "I intend to spend every last one of those days with you, Quel Laredo. In the future, when I ask you to camp in the snow, it's because

I feel peace here and want to share it with you, not because of Swift River."

"Then we'll continue to come up here."

"Camping doesn't have to be," her voice thickened with mischief, "burger-less."

"What?"

"Or—" Eager to reveal her surprise, she hopped out from under the covers. From under the bed she pulled a large box, then a small satellite TV. "Football-less!"

He coughed out a laugh of pure surprise. "When did you bring that shit up here?"

She joined him in laughter. "A girl can have her secrets, Laredo." Next, she pulled out a portable grill and a cooler full of chopped beef, all the fixings, buns, and beer.

Laughing, he watched her, love filling his eyes. Shay popped two of the cans, handing him one. "It's after five p.m. somewhere in the world," she reasoned, shrugging.

He raised his drink. "Here's to the good life."

"*This* life. The one we're going to concentrate on from now on."

Nodding, he touched the can to hers. "You got that right, angel. You got that right."

*And so it was that the little demon
who'd always dreamed of being human
got her wish and lived happily ever after . . .*

A
TAWDRY AFFAIR

Gena Showalter

To P. C. Cast, Susan Grant, and MaryJanice Davidson. Or, as we would probably be named inside of Mysteria: P. C. Sweetbottoms, Susan Buttercup, and MaryJanice Sugarlips. (Maybe I'd be Gena Dinglehop that's wait and see, though.) To Wendy McCurdy and Allison Brandau for putting up with me!

One

If Glory Tawdry discovered her sister, Evie, and Evie's vampire boyfriend going at it like wild cougars one more time—just one more!—she was going to throw up a lung, gouge out her eyes, and cut off her ears.

"You're disgusting," she grumbled, standing in Evie's *open* bedroom door. Her sister and Hunter must have severe discovery fantasies, because they always "forgot" to barricade themselves inside when things were getting heated.

They didn't even glance in her direction.

She coughed.

They continued.

Sadly, if Glory walked down the hallway of their modest little three-bedroom home, she'd probably hear her other sister, Godiva, going at it with *her* boyfriend, a werewolf shapeshifter. They, at least, liked privacy when they were screaming like hyenas.

Still. There was no peace to be found for Glory. Not even in town. Lately Mysteria, a place once known for its evil creature population, as well as a place she'd taken great pride in, had turned into a horrifying love fest of goo-goo eyes and butt pinching.

Except for me. No one makes goo-goo eyes at me. No one pinches my butt, even though there's enough for everyone to grab on to at the same time. She didn't care, though. Really.

Men and relationships were so not for her. Really.

"Hello," she said, trying again. "I'm right here. Can you stop for like a minute?"

Thankfully Evie and Hunter finished their show and collapsed side by side under the covers. Moonlight spilled from the beveled windows and onto the bed, painting them in gold. Both were panting, sweat glistening from their skin. Evie's dark hair was spread over the pillow and tangled under Hunter's arm. Vitality radiated from her.

Handsome Hunter looked exhausted and incapable of movement.

Score one for Evie, Glory supposed.

"Oh, Glory." Evie grinned, happiness sparkling in her hazel eyes. "I didn't see you there."

Ugh. Evie did everything happily now, and Glory was seriously embarrassed for her. Evie was the greatest vengeance witch ever to live in Mysteria. As such, she should scowl once in a while. *Glory* was the love witch, damn it, so *Glory* should be the happy one.

"Don't you know how to knock?" her sister asked.

Are you freaking kidding me? "Don't you know how to close a door? I mean, it's a difficult task to master, but with hard work and the proper training, I think you might be able to do it."

Hunter laughed, revealing long, sharp teeth.

"Ha-ha." Evie punched him on the shoulder.

When Evie said no more, Glory shook her head in disappointment. Used to, they would have argued and insulted each other, maybe yelled and thrown things. Now, she was lucky if Evie frowned at her.

A dysfunctional relationship it had been, but it had been *theirs*.

"I miss us!" she found herself saying. "You're a softie now, and it's killing my excitement levels."

Understanding dawned, and Evie scowled. Even pointed

an accusing finger at her. "Seriously, what's up with you, little sis? Every day I think you can't possibly get any bitchier, and then you go and prove me wrong."

Much better! Life was suddenly worth living again. "Lookit, you show pony, I need your help."

"Yeah? With what?" Unable to retain the harsh expression, Evie gave her another smile.

As always, that satisfied smile caused a deep ache to sprout inside Glory's chest. *When will it be my turn to fall in love, have great sex, and sicken the people around me?* The moment the thought drifted through her mind, she blinked in shock and revulsion. *Whoa, girl. That line of BS has to stop. Like, now. Before you crave more.*

She was a love witch, yes, but *she* didn't want to fall in love. Ever. People became slobbering fools when they succumbed to the soft emotion. Look at Evie! Proof right there in all her glowing splendor.

"I'm waiting," Evie said.

Glory opened her mouth to say . . . something. What, she didn't know. Great Goddess, how should she begin? She could *not* allow Evie to turn her down.

"Seriously. I want to bask in the afterglow." Evie rubbed her leg up and down Hunter's lower torso. "Hurry this along."

"I'm thinking."

Evie sighed. And yes, she was still smiling. "Go think somewhere else."

"You left your door open, so no afterglow for you. One year," she said in her best "Soup Nazi" impersonation. Glory tangled a hand through her hair, surprised as always that it was cool to the touch. Every time she saw the flame red tresses in the mirror, she expected smoke. *I can do this.* "Remember a few months ago, when Hunter was ignoring you—again—and you promised me a favor if I helped you win his heart? I told you that in return for helping you, I wanted you to give me something to ruin Falon's life, and you said okay, so I gave you a potion and you—"

"I know what I did. Jeez." Nibbling on her lower lip, Evie moved her hazels to Hunter.

He knew the full story, but Glory suspected Evie didn't like to remind him. He'd died because of Evie, after all,

killed by demons the lovesick fool had accidentally sum-
moned. *Then* he'd been turned into a vampire—a species
he'd once hoped to destroy. It had been difficult for him to
adjust to the change.

"You want to ruin Falon's life? Why?" Hunter's vampire-
pale arms tightened around Evie. Obviously no bad feelings
remained on his part. But he did frown over at Glory as if she
had sprouted a second head. With horns. Falon was his best
friend and right-hand man.

At least, Glory thought Falon was a man. In Mysteria, it
was sometimes hard to tell. He could have been a demon for
all she knew. Now that made sense. "Just . . . because," she
said, then squared her shoulders and raised her chin. She refused to say more about her reasoning. "Evie owes me. That
should be enough."

Evie threw up her arms and let them fall heavily onto the
bed. "Can't you drop this? I don't know what he did to
you . . ." She paused, probably waiting for Glory to pipe up
with the answer. When she didn't, Evie sighed again. "You
live in Bizarro World, little sis. You're supposed to be the
good witch, and *I'm* supposed to be wicked."

Glory arched a brow, her mind caught on the first part of
Evie's speech. "No, I can't let this go." The bastard deserved
to die. Slowly. Painfully. Eternally. "You reneging on me?"

Hot color bloomed in her sister's cheeks. "No. Of course
not."

"Evie," Hunter said.

"I promised her, baby."

Glory anchored her hands on her hips. "If it makes you feel
any better, Hunter, know that Falon brought this on himself.
He hurt me."

Hunter's green gaze sharpened. "Hurt you? How?"

Once again, she raised her chin and pressed her lips together. She hadn't planned on admitting even that much.

Realizing she'd say no more, he scrubbed a hand down the
harsh, rugged plains of his face. "You know I'll warn Falon,
right? I'll tell him what's going on."

"Like that scares me." Glory *wanted* Falon know she was
gunning for him. She wanted him to be scared, to tremble and
jump at every snapping twig in the night. Hell, maybe she *was*

a wicked witch, because she chuckled every time she thought of him dropping to the ground in a fetal ball and crying for his mother.

Sure, he was six feet four of solid—delicious—muscle. Sure, he'd kicked more ass in the few years he'd lived in Mysteria than the town's citizens were currently nailing. And sure, he probably made the creatures of the underworld pee their pants in fear of him. A girl could dream, though.

"Now." She rubbed her hands together. "Evie, my revenge, if you please. I've tried to bring it up several times, and you ignored me, ran from me, or let your boy toy sweep you off your feet. Literally. I'm not waiting anymore!"

"Whatever he did, I'll talk to him," Hunter said. "He'll apologize."

Glory shook her head, long hair slapping her across the face. It was too late for that. "*I'll* talk to him. Evie . . ."

"Fine." Frowning, Evie uncurled from her lover's body and rose from the bed, taking the sheet with her.

Cheeks heating, Glory quickly turned and faced the hallway. She so had not needed to see Hunter's crowning grandeur. Did she appreciate it? Yeah. Boy was blessed! Still. Her sister's boyfriend was not meant to be eye candy for her, and besides, she didn't need to add fuel to the fire of her constantly unsatisfied desires.

Behind her, she heard cloth rustling, the slide of a drawer, then things bumping together.

"Ah, here it is!" her sister said.

Footsteps sounded, then a delicate finger was tapping Glory on the shoulder. Heart pounding excitedly, she turned. Of course, her gaze flew to Hunter of its own accord hoping for another peek. He'd already tugged on a pair of jeans—jeans with a missing top button. Evie had probably bitten it off.

Glory's chest started hurting again.

Evie waved a black pen in front of her face. "Hello. You paying attention to me?"

Her gaze latched onto the pen, following its movements. Her frown returned. "You're giving me a pen? A *pen* to finally claim revenge against the man who savagely wronged me?"

"Yes. How did he wrong you?"

She ignored the question. "What, I'm supposed to draw a mustache on his picture? News flash. That's not going to leave him crying in his cornflakes."

"Why do you want him crying in his cornflakes?"

Grrr! "No matter how many times you ask, no matter how many ways, I'm not telling."

"Well, don't make him cry too hard. He's a good man and has always been nice to us."

Nice? Nice! Evie had no idea the cruelty that man was capable of. But revealing what he'd done to her would be more mortifying than, say, finding one of her sisters naked and in bed with a vampire, screaming his name as she climaxed.

"Pay attention, sister dear." Evie released the pen; it didn't fall. It hovered in the air between them, swirling, glitter falling like raindrops around it. "This little pen is magical."

"Rock on! What will it do?"

"Anything you write with it will come true."

Glory's eyes widened, the words sinking in. "*Anything* I write will come true?"

"Yes. Well, anything physical, nothing emotional. Just be careful. The more you write, the more ink you'll use, and there's no way to refill it. Also, the effects don't last forever, only for a few hours. For proper revenge, it's best to write about clothes disappearing right off a body in the middle of a crowd and—"

"Don't help her," Hunter growled.

"Yes, but *anything* I write comes true?" Glory asked again, just to be sure.

Evie rolled her eyes. "Physically, yes. I said so, didn't I?"

A laugh escaped her, her first true laugh in months. "Oh, this is classic. Truly perfect."

"I knew you'd appreciate the irony."

"What irony?" Hunter sat up and propped himself against the headboard.

"Can I tell him?" Evie asked her.

Why not? "Sure. He's almost family, and I've seen his goods."

"She's a novelist," Evie threw over her shoulder, "best known for bringing her heroes to their knees. Not always because they fall in love, but mostly because the villains always jack them up with a hammer to the tibia."

"Dear God," Hunter mumbled. "This is bad. Real bad."

Glory rubbed her hands together. Yes, it was. Falon the bastard was about to fall. Hard-core!

TWO

Anticipation hummed through Glory for the rest of the night and the following day, possibilities rolling continually through her mind. She'd hoped Hunter would tell Falon what was going on, Falon would rush to her and beg her to forgive him, and she would get to slam a door in his face, causing him to toss and turn for hours in fear.

But he never showed up.

So when the sun finally descended on the second day, she padded to her bedroom, wading through clothes, shoes, and donut wrappers, grabbed a notebook, and climbed onto the bed.

It was time to test the pen's powers.

Ever since Falon had—*Do not think about that right now! You know better.* Already, with that tiny half thought, her pulse had kicked into overdrive, and her stomach had clenched, sickness churning inside of it.

Think about your revenge. For this to work, she needed to be strong, unemotional. Otherwise, she'd do something mean, Falon would look at her with those otherworldly violet eyes of his, and she'd cave. Maybe even apologize. *He deserves to suffer.*

How best to torture him?

She thought about what she knew about him. She'd never slept with him, but she knew what he looked like when he experienced ultimate pleasure. She knew how he tensed, knew his voice dripped harsh and raspy. Knew he roared with the last spasm, pounding his big, hard body into his lover's.

Uh, not helping. Breath burned in her lungs, and fire rushed through her veins, but she couldn't stop her mind from traveling that road. One night she'd stumbled upon Falon in the woods, making love to one of his many women. Or, as Glory liked to call them, one of his many hookers. Anyhoodles, she'd been unable to walk away. He'd been unnaturally beautiful and darkly seductive, whispering the most erotic nothings in the hooker's ear.

Glory had suddenly understood why Falon could fight vampires and demons for hours and hours without breaking a sweat. He was total strength, inexorable stamina. *Nothing* tired him.

That night, she'd developed a tiny—enormous—crush on him. Even though he was way out of her league. Glory was a wee bit on the pudgy side, while Falon personified perfection. She exercised by riding her bike into town to buy a bag of Doritos; he worked out slaying his enemies without thought or hesitation. Men ignored her; women flocked to him. She spent hours in front of a computer, living life in her mind; he actually lived. Inside other people's pants, but whatever.

Rumor was he knew what a female craved before even she knew, and anyone who experienced the bliss of his sometimes gentle, usually savage touch was never the same again. Watching him, Glory had begun to believe that.

She'd fallen completely under his spell, haunted for days by his mesmerizing image. She'd yearned to have him in her bed. In her shower. On her floor. Wherever. She hadn't been picky. She'd just wanted him. Desperately and unequivocally. She'd wanted him naked, slipping and sliding into *her*, no one else, wrapped around her, cherishing her. She'd wanted her name on his lips, his taste in her mouth. Until . . .

Her hands clenched into fists. *You aren't supposed to think about this!*

The memories flooded her, anyway. A few months ago, she'd overhead him tell Hunter that one woman was the same as any other, and love was for idiots. Since they shared the same mind-set—love sucked giant elephant balls!—and he didn't care who he slept with, she'd decided to go for it and throw herself at him.

Pleasure was seriously lacking in her life, and she would have given all of her powers—well, rather, all of *Evie's* powers—to have him look at her with desire. Just once. That's all she'd needed, all she'd wanted.

So she'd gone to his house in nothing but a trench coat and heels. And yeah, she'd flashed him.

He'd taken one look at her and laughed. Laughed!

"Go home, little girl," he'd said. "You don't know what you're playing at."

"I'm twenty-three, not jailbait, and I'm anything but little, as you can clearly see. I'm here for a few hours of fun, that's all."

"Okay, let me put this another way. Get lost. You're not welcome here."

"I'm—I'm not your type, then," she'd stammered, mortified to her very soul. In that moment, she'd understood. Even though he'd said any woman would do, he'd meant any *pretty* woman would do.

His gaze had become hard as it perused her. "No, you're not my type."

He could have spared the remaining tatters of her feminine pride, but another woman had walked up behind Glory. Kaycee, a girl who had graduated a few years ahead of Glory, had obviously craved the same thing as Glory, despite the fact that she'd come with a basket of fruit to "sell." Just as she'd been in school, Kaycee had been tall and thin and pretty. And Falon had allowed that pink-skinned *married* fairy hooker inside before shutting the door in Glory's red-hot face.

Remembering, Glory gnashed her teeth together. "I will destroy his male pride," she said, determined. "I will teach him what it's like to feel unwanted and ugly."

But she spent the next hour staring at the notebook, mind blank. Shit! How did a girl teach a man that kind of lesson?

Just write something. Anything! Pretend this is one of your novels and test the pen's powers. Let's see, let's see. Roman solider? No. Falon didn't deserve to carry a sword. But she saw all kinds of possibilities in that time period. Gladiator?

Oh, yes, yes, yes. Gladiators were slaves, and she really liked the idea of Falon in chains.

Closing her eyes, she pictured Falon pacing the dirt floors of a barred cell, sweat rolling down the sculpted muscles of his bronzed stomach, pooling in his navel and dipping lower. Fresh from fighting, blood splattered him.

Licking her lips, Glory shifted against the covers. The scene continued to open up in her mind, painting her thoughts with its descriptions. She sucked in a deep breath and forced her hand to write what she saw . . .

Falon was lying in bed, cool, dry, staring at the ceiling of his bedroom one moment and inside a dirt-laden cell the next, pacing back and forth, sweat pouring from him. Shocked at the sudden change, he tried to stop. His feet kept moving as though they were no longer connected to his brain.

What the hell?

Moonlight slithered around him as he passed a crudely crafted bed, then an equally crude bench, kicking dirt with his sandals. *Sandals?* There was a metallic tang in air. The rustle of chains could be heard beyond the cell, as could moans of . . . injured men? Pleasured men?

Confusion slithered through him.

"Yo. Falon."

Hearing the husky female voice, he spun and faced the cell's farthest set of bars. A lone woman stood behind them, shadows covering her face. Glistening white cloth draped her, and gold flowers glinted from her left shoulder and hem. A chain belt circled her waist, cinching the drape around her and revealing slender curves. The scent of pampered, eager woman and desire drifted from her, sweet and exotic.

His body hardened in hated desire. Hated, because only one woman had that effect on him lately.

"Glory Tawdry," he said through clenched teeth. "I should have known."

"Great Goddess, it worked!" She clapped her hands, and he could easily imagine her smiling that sultry, white-toothed smile of hers. "I hope you don't mind, but I decided to write myself into the scene."

"Scene What scene?"

"This one." As she spoke, she stepped into a ribbon of that golden moonlight.

He couldn't help himself. He sucked in a heated breath and drank her in. Long, red hair framed her pretty face—the most sensual face he'd ever seen. Her eyes were large emeralds flecked with gold. Her nose was gently sloped, her cheeks pink and perfectly rounded. Her lips were luxuriant and red, utterly magnificent—but they would have looked better moving over his body.

You know better than to think like that, you walking penis!
"What do you mean, you wrote yourself into the scene? What is this place? How did you get me here?"

Her sculpted brows rose. "Didn't Hunter tell you?"

"Tell me what? I haven't spoken to him in days." His friend had stopped coming to Knight Caps, the bar he owned and where Falon bartended, preferring instead to spend every moment with his revenge witch. Disgraceful, if you asked Falon.

"Evie must have distracted him," Glory said with a laugh. "Damn, but I do love my sister."

That laugh . . . God, it was magical. Almost melted his fury. Almost. His gaze circled the cell. "What have you done to me, Glory?"

"Nothing much. Yet. This is just a small taste of my revenge."

Revenge. He didn't have to ask why. The night she'd come to his house, flashed him every one of her spectacular curves, and nearly felled him, he'd resorted to the only thing capable of saving him: cruelty.

His gaze met hers, and something hot filled his veins. This time, it wasn't fury. She looked utterly pleased with herself, and the look was good on her. Good enough to eat. She must have sensed the direction of his thoughts because she backed up a step. A pause stretched between them, layered with awareness. Sizzling with need.

There was something about her that appealed to the beast inside him. Something dark, dangerous, and bone deep that awakened urges inside him he'd thought long dead. Tender urges, savage urges.

Do not think like that, idiot! He'd made the mistake of willingly dating a witch twice. Once because he'd wanted the woman, once because he'd needed the woman. Both experiences had scarred him for eternity. The relationship with the first, Frederica, had not ended well, and the damn woman had cursed him with impotence. And no amount of Viagra or stimulation had fixed the . . . limpness.

Falon had been forced to give up a year of his life acting as a slave to Penelope, the second witch, to win his freedom. In return, Penelope had challenged Frederica, who quickly lost and finally reversed her spell. Had the return of his manhood been worth it? He wasn't sure. Penelope had not been an easy mistress. He'd cooked, cleaned, run errands, supplied her with orgasms and massages, balanced her checkbook, punished her enemies, and fixed her TiVo. So yeah, he fucking hated witches! They always abused their powers.

That hadn't stopped him from wanting Glory, though—who was now in the process of abusing her goddamn powers! Yes, he'd hurt her all those months ago. But he'd had to push her away before he'd caved.

Still, he'd regretted it ever since and had even tried to make it up to her, acting as her protector on several occasions. "I don't desire this," he said.

"Yes, you do."

"No, the hell I don't! That night in the cemetery, I saved you from hungry corpses." He wasn't sure how or why, but since that night on his porch he always seemed to know when she was in trouble. A fierce surge of protectiveness would rise inside him, and the next thing he knew, he'd be rushing to get to her, wherever she was.

Maybe she'd cast a spell on him.

He bit the inside of his cheek until he tasted blood. That made sense. He should have realized it sooner, but he had been consumed with thoughts of her naked. He wanted to curse at her but held back the words. No need to provoke her. Yet. Damn, what should he do?

Before that fateful night, he'd always avoided looking at her and her witch sisters. Had left a building the moment they'd entered it. Because one glance at that sensual face of Glory's, and he nearly forgot his no witch rule.

Rejecting her that night on his porch had been one of the hardest things he'd ever done. Literally. She'd been naked.

But he'd managed to do it—and he'd done nothing but dream about her ever since.

"What kind of spell is this?" he demanded.

"Don't you worry your pretty little head about that," she said with a sugar-sweet tone. "You worry about the pain and suffering I'm about to rain upon your life."

"Glory—" He pressed his lips together. *Do not antagonize her, or she'll make it worse. Duh.* He raked his gaze over her, trying to decide what to do. Wait. She looked . . . different. His head titled to the side as he frowned. "What did you do to yourself?"

"I wrote myself in as a glorious one hundred and twenty—" Now *she* frowned. A moment later, she disappeared as if she'd never been there.

"Glory?" He spun around, eyes roaming. Where the hell was she?

A moment later, she reappeared in front of the bars. And she looked even thinner, the robe bagging over her bony body. He didn't like it. He liked her curves and the lusciousness of her breasts, hips, and thighs. Even thinking of them caused his mouth to water. Was his tongue wagging?

She smiled. "I wrote myself in as a glorious one hundred and *fifteen* pounds."

"You're skin and bones."

"I know. Isn't it great?" She didn't wait for his answer but twirled, her smile never fading. Material danced at her ankles like snowflakes. When she stopped, her eyes narrowed on him, and she added tightly, "What do you think of me now?"

He decided to be honest. "I liked you better the other way," he said, crossing his arms over his sweaty, bloody chest—still having no idea how he'd become so sweaty or so bloody.

At first, Glory appeared stunned by his admission. Then her eyes narrowed even more, becoming tiny slits that hid those beautiful hazel irises completely. "Yeah. Right. I've seen your harem. You always pick the skinny ones."

Actually, the skinny ones always picked him, and after a year without being able to get Little Fal up, he'd taken what he could get, when he could get it. Except for Glory. Why'd she have to be witch?

"Where are we?" he asked.

Her lips curled into a slow, sensual grin, and his stomach tightened. "This is your prison."

He ran his tongue over his teeth. "Why?"

"We already covered this."

Yeah, they had. "Look, I'm sorry about that night. I wish it had never happened."

"But it did happen. Makes sense, though, that you're sorry *now*." Rage crackled around her, lifting strands of her hair as if she'd stuck her finger into a light socket. A moment passed while she calmed herself down, and her hair smoothed out. "I should have written myself inside the cell with you so I could torment you with my superhot bod, but I didn't want you to have access to my neck."

"So that's how you plan to punish me, is it? Magically transport me into a cell and make me horny? By all means, keep at it." He could imagine worse things.

"Oh, no. I plan to do much, much more than that." She licked her lips and perused him, gaze lingering on his stomach, between his legs. That gaze devoured him, eating him up one tasty bite at a time.

Clearly, she still wanted him.

His first thought: *Thank God.*

His second: *Holy shit, this is bad!*

"Don't look at me like that," he growled, not caring if she tried to punish him further. He could not allow this witch to desire him like that. Not when his resolve teetered so precariously. Look what had happened already. Any more . . . No. No way could he allow himself to have her.

Glory's eyes snapped to his, embarrassed hazel against furious violet. "I'll look at you however I want! You're my property right now. I own you."

"Stop this, Glory."

"Make me."

Very slowly, purposefully, he moved toward her.

Approaching her is dangerous, common sense said.

No other way, Little Fal replied.

Glory's mouth opened all the wider with every step he took, but no sound emerged from her. When he reached the bars, he whipped out his arms before she had a chance to stop him and clamped his fingers around her wrists.

"What are you doing?" Her tone lacked any heat, and she actually pressed herself into the bars until her body brushed his. "I didn't add this to the scene."

The contact, though light, sparked a jolt of pure fire in his bloodstream. Up close, she was even lovelier. Freckles were scattered across her nose. Her pale skin glowed with health and vitality.

"You want me to touch you? Is that what it's going to take to get you out of my life?" He anchored her arms behind her back with one hand and traced his other down the front of her robe. How he longed to linger over the small mound of her breasts, the hollow of her stomach . . . the waiting valley between her legs.

If she'd possessed her usual curves, he knew he would not have been able to resist. Her desire to be thin was actually a blessing. But even now, like this, his control wasn't what it should have been. He was trembling, for God's sake.

"Stop," she whispered. Her eyes said *more*.

All of his muscles bunched in reaction to that pleading tone, that needy expression, hardening, aching. He did not stop. He eagerly learned the length of her legs, her skin smooth and soft, like velvet. By the time he finished the full-body caresses, sweat beaded over his face and dripped in rivulets down his chest.

"More." She closed her eyes, all pretence of resistance gone.

He pinched several strands of her hair between his fingers, enjoying the silkiness. He brought the tendrils to his nose and sniffed. Nearly moaned. A fresh, blooming garden. That's what her hair smelled like. He could have breathed in the scent forever.

"If you want me to fuck you," he said, deliberately cruel, just as before, "you'll have to enter the cell." *For the best.* It was better to be punished than to cave, he decided.

"Wh-what?" Her eyes blinked open. He saw the need burning there, the want. Her nipples were hard, visible through her robe. The scent of awakened passion wafted from her, blending with the flowery fragrance of her hair.

"You heard me."

"No, I hate you." The words were spoken on a breathless

sigh. Then she shook her head, eyes narrowing again, and backed away. "I'm going to make you want me, Falon. I'm going to make you crave me. But you are never going to have me. Do you understand? Never."

A moment later, she vanished. The prison shimmered before disappearing, too, and the next thing Falon knew, he was lying in his bed again. As the cool sheets met his clean, dry skin, he rolled from the mattress and stalked to his closet.

Fury, desire, and determination pounded through him. He strapped weapons all over his body, dressed, and stalked from his house. No way he'd allow Glory to use her powers against him. Not again.

He was going to find her. Whatever he had to do, he was going to stop her.

Three

Heart thundering in her chest, Glory kept her eyes squeezed shut and inhaled deeply. The first thing she noticed was how the air no longer smelled of decadent man, sweat, and dark spice. Now she caught the faint drift of powdered sugar and jasmine incense.

Who would've thought she'd mourn the loss of sweaty-man air?

Time to check out the rest. Slowly she blinked open her eyes. Her notebook came into view. Everything that had happened was right there, the words staring up at her. She quickly looked away, not wanting to be reminded of her near capitulation. All Falon had done was touch her, for love of the Goddess, and she'd forgotten her need for revenge. The feel of his hands on her body, exploring . . . the sound of his rough voice in her ear, whispering . . . the desire blazing in his eyes, beckoning . . .

Her stomach tightened, and the ache she'd experienced inside the prison renewed between her legs. *Keep looking.*

Her flat-screen computer came into view, followed by the wall of magazine pictures she used for references and her *Hunks of the Month* calendar. Trash and dirty clothes were scattered all over her carpet. She hadn't cleaned since that terrible night; she didn't know why.

"It worked," she said, just to break the silence. "It really worked."

She'd actually sent Falon to an ancient prison, *then* she'd actually followed him there. *Oh . . . my.* She sagged against the mattress and closed her eyes again. Falon's image filled her mind. His eyes, an exotic, come-to-me violet fringed by thick black lashes. His dark hair, a little long. The shadowy stubble that dusted his jaw. The bronzed skin and body-builder muscles she'd almost held.

The man had exuded a potent animal magnetism; it had oozed from his pores.

What was he doing right now? Cursing her to the heavens? She laughed, delighted by the thought. He might even be tugging on his clothes, determined to race over here and punish her.

She stopped laughing.

Having trouble catching her breath, Glory scrambled out of the bed. Her jeans and panties floated straight to her ankles. What the hell? Frowning in confusion, she grabbed them, jerked them up, and launched forward. Almost tripped as the clothes tumbled again. Growled. She needed to leave the house, like, now, and the wardrobe difficulties weren't helping. As she bent to retrieve her stuff, the notebook slid out of her fingers and onto the floor.

She released her clothes and reached out. Her eyes widened as she caught a glimpse of her hand. She was so . . . skinny. Her arm was slender, the bones fine. Her fingers were elegant. Wow. No wonder her jeans no longer fit.

Why hadn't her slenderness faded with the scene?

The answer hit her, and she grinned. She'd written it a little later. For the next few minutes, she'd be a total babe.

Seriously, she'd never looked hotter. Maybe she should wait here. Maybe she should allow Falon inside. Maybe, as she'd hoped, he would be overcome with lust for her and the real revenge could begin. He would beg her to sleep with him, and she would say, "Hell, no."

And what if you plump up right before his eyes, huh? What then?

Shit! Glory's heart jolted into hyperdrive, and she raced throughout her room, kicking off the too-big jeans and panties and jerking on a nightgown. The silky pink material bagged on her, but it was the only thing that would cover her *and* stay put.

Why was she so nervous, anyway? There was nothing Falon could do to her. Not while she owned the pen. *Uh, he could steal it and use it against you.*

A knock sounded at the front of the house.

Her mouth fell open, and she straightened. No way. No damn way he'd made it here so quickly. She looked at her bedroom door, turned, and craned her neck to see out the room's only window. A black SUV sat in the driveway. Damn! He had.

"Glory, Falon's here to see you," Godiva called a moment later, only sounding the slightest bit confused.

"Tell him I'm not here." Glory propelled herself over her bed and to the window. She shoved the glass up and out of the way, never letting go of the pen. Cool air wafted inside, ruffling the thin, gaping gown against her skin as she climbed out. The grass was soft against her bare feet.

Maybe she'd go to Candy Cox's, she thought, racing through the night. No, no. Candy's sister was in town or due to arrive in town, and rumor was the woman negated powers of every kind. Worse, Candy's shape-shifting werewolf boyfriend would be there, which meant more sickening PDA.

She could go to Pastor Harmony's. Ugh, no, she decided next. Harmony was now a mother. The Desdaine triplets, then? No. The brats were likely to welcome her inside and secretly call Falon and alert him. So where did that leave her?

"Oh, no you don't," a male voice boomed behind her.

She gasped, panic infusing her every cell. Goose bumps broke out over her skin. One backward glance—*Shit!* He'd jumped out her window and was now moving toward her, menacing purpose in his every step. His eyes were narrowed on her.

The forest was a hundred feet in front of her. If she could just—a rock cut into her bare foot, and she fell. Grass padded her landing, but the hard impact still managed to shove the oxygen from her lungs.

"Glory," he said, sounding concerned.

"Go home." She grabbed a long, thin stick as she jumped

to her feet. Ouch, ouch, ouch. Might come in handy. She jetted forward, taking stock. Heart: still beating. Pen and stick: still in hand. Legs: workable. Aching, but workable. Twigs and rocks continued to scrape into her feet. *Worry about the pain later.* She just needed to get far enough away from Falon to write him into chains. If not . . .

"I called Hunter," Falon shouted, closer to her.

She yelped but didn't allow herself to look back. Already, his masculine scent wafted around her. *Faster, woman!*

"I want that pen, Glory."

Shit! He was even closer now. There was no time to hide. As she ran, branches slapping at her, stinging, she began writing on her arm. *Twigs reached out and grasped at Falon.* The words were barely legible.

Behind her, Falon growled. The rustle of trees echoed through the night.

Was it working?

Several of those twigs caught him and jerked him to a stop.

An animalistic snarl erupted. "Glory!" This time, Falon's voice carried on the wind. He sounded a good distance behind her. "Stop."

Glory slowed her steps. Panting, she tossed a look over her shoulder. Her eyes widened, and she ground to an abrupt halt. Limbs had indeed caught Falon. They were wound around him like bands of indestructible silk, anchoring him to the base of a tree. His lips peeled back from his teeth, and he scowled over at her.

"Come here," he shouted. "Now."

Despite her wheezing, she was feeling very smug. She turned away from him. One push of her fingers, and she broke the stick she'd grabbed when she'd fallen in two.

"What are you doing? Get over here!"

She gripped the hem of her nightgown and tied the pen inside it. Hopefully, if Falon managed to escape, he would confiscate the stick, thinking it was the pen. That done, she turned back to him and approached, waving the stick smugly.

Her muscles were sore from that run, and as she walked, her arms, legs, and waist began to fill out, the weight returning. Her breasts swelled, stretching the fabric of the nightgown. At least the pen stayed in place.

Still, some of her smugness disappeared. She didn't want Falon to see her like this, but she wasn't going to waste any ink making herself skinny again. Not now, at least. Right now he was too furious to experience desire, no matter what she looked like.

When she reached him, she hid her arms behind her back, as if keeping "the pen" out of his reach. Strands of her red hair blustered forward, stroking his face.

His pupils dilated, black swallowing violet. "You can escape tonight, but I *will* find you. And when I do, I'm going to take that goddamn pen and make you wish you'd never met me."

She leaned forward, as though she planned to reveal a big secret. "I already do wish I'd never met you." His warm breath fanned her cheek, a tender caress, and she had to jerk away from him before she did something stupid. Like suck on his earlobe.

Their gazes locked together, a tangle of emotions.

"Look at you," she said and *tsked* under her tongue. "At my mercy."

He raised his chin. "It won't always be this way."

"Like I want to keep you in my life that long. *Always*. Please." She snorted. "A few weeks should do it."

"You think I'll pretend it never happened? Leave you alone afterward?"

"Well, yeah." She arched a brow. "Unless you want more of me."

His eyes narrowed to tiny slits. His features were calm, but the pulse at the base of his neck hammered wildly. "More of you . . . interesting choice of words." Wind danced between them as his gaze perused her.

Her nipples hardened, and she barely restrained herself from covering them with her hands. Instead, she raised her chin and dared him to say something about her weight. She was surprised when he bit his lower lip, as though he was imagining her taste in his mouth—and liked it.

"Witches should have a code of honor, preventing them from hurting others," he said softly.

"Here's an idea. I'll draft up a witches' code of honor, and you draft up a how to reject a woman nicely code of conduct. Sound good?"

Shame colored his cheeks.

Gold star for me. Now drive the point deeper. "Let me tell you a little something about me, Falon. I have never had much self-esteem. My sisters are tall and slender, and men have always drooled over them. But not me. Not chubby Glor." She laughed bitterly. She loved her sisters more than anything on this earth, but they were so perfect, so pretty, that she, who was already vapor, became *nothing* in comparison. "In the span of five minutes, you managed to destroy what tiny bit of feminine pride I had."

His shoulders flattened against the trunk, his eyes closed, and he drew in a breath. "I admit it. I handled the situation wrong."

"Yes, you did. You didn't have to laugh at me. You could have simply said, 'No, thank you.'"

"I wasn't laughing at you. Not really. I just wanted to ensure you never came back. Wait. That sounds just as bad. Look, the truth is, sending you away had nothing to do with your appearance."

"Oh, please."

"It didn't." His lids popped open, and he was suddenly staring at her with such intensity she had trouble breathing. "You're a witch."

There was so much hatred in his voice, she stumbled back. "Yeah. So?"

"So, let's just say I'm not very fond of witches."

She snorted, refusing to believe him. "You've always been nice to Godiva and Genevieve."

"I wasn't . . . attracted to them." The admission was snarled, more an accusation than anything.

"That's—" Wait. What? He was attracted to her? Pleasure zoomed through her with such potency she almost fell to her knees. But the sensation lasted only five seconds before common sense reared its ugly head. *He'll say anything to soften you. Even a humiliating lie.* Pleasure morphed into searing fury.

Why, that . . . that . . . bastard! Her fingers tightened around the stick, and she had to fight the urge to grab the pen and write a hungry lion into the scene. "So you were attracted to me, were you?" she asked as calmly as she was able.

"What do you think?" he muttered, motioning to his dick with his chin.

She dropped her gaze, staring between his legs with wonder. Okay. Maybe he hadn't been lying. He was hard, his erection straining against his jeans. "Th-that's not because of me." Was it?

"Your nipples are hard, and I can see the outline of fine red hair between your legs. Obviously, you're not wearing any panties. So yeah, it's because of you."

Her mouth floundered open and closed. "Only because I'm the only woman present and you're probably in heat." Warmth bloomed in her face as she finally covered her breasts with one arm and between her legs with the other. "So you can just look away!"

"Make me."

"I'll take away your sight. Just see if I won't."

Finally his gaze snapped back up to her face. "Are you truly that cruel?"

Damn him! He'd zapped her anger with those words, making her feel like the wicked witch Evie had teased her about being. "No. I won't go that far," she whispered, as shamed as he'd been a moment ago.

"How far *are* you going to take it, then?"

She peered down at her bare feet—*Ick, time for a pedicure*—and kicked a rock with the tip of her toe. "I honestly don't know."

Falon clenched his jaw, cutting off any words that might try to escape his mouth. A mouth currently watering for a taste of the woman in front of him. Her curves were a thing of beauty. And with ribbons of moonlight seeping from the canopy of treetops, paying her flawless skin absolute tribute, with that flame red hair dancing like naughty nymphs around her shoulders and her lips glistening from the sting of her teeth, his beast wanted to tame her beauty.

Except, she now appeared defeated.

He hated seeing her like that almost as much as he hated being bound. Almost. Right now, however, he was too primed to feel anything more than desire. He wanted her to reach out, to touch him, kiss him. Suck him.

He was hard as a damn rock and needed to come.

"The night you came to my house in that trench coat," he said.

Her attention suddenly locked on him and the fire blazing inside him. "The night you screwed that fairy hooker? *That* night?"

Surprisingly enough, her waspish tone delighted him. "Jealous?"

"As if!"

He hadn't invited the fairy, whatever her name was, to his house. He'd met her in town earlier that day, had talked and laughed with her, but hadn't meant to take it further. She was married, for God's sake. Had Glory not been standing in front of him, he would have sent the fairy away. He liked sex, yes, but he'd never allowed a woman inside his home. They tended to linger, and he liked to do the deed and move on.

In fact, the moment Glory had taken off, he'd sent the pink-skinned fairy packing. Despite the fact that she had offered him apples—off of her body. He hadn't even touched her. Had just stood at the window, peeking out the blinds like a criminal, hoping for and dreading a reappearance from Glory.

He'd been hard then, too, so maybe he should have slept with the fairy. But it had been flame red hair his hands had wanted to tangle in, hazel eyes he'd wanted to stare into, and a soft, plush body he'd wanted to penetrate.

No one else would have done.

Maybe that was why he hadn't been able to have sex these past few months. He felt guilty for how he'd hurt Glory, so his body would no longer allow him to respond to other women. Maybe he needed to sleep with her once—or twice—and build up her self-esteem. She'd feel better about herself, he'd stop feeling guilty for the way he'd treated her, and they could both go on with their lives.

Are you kidding? Are you so hard up you've got to bed a witch? Think of the consequences, idiot! She's nuts now, so how much worse will she be after you've slept with her? What if she didn't want things to end after the sex was over? What if she tried to punish him again?

"Uh, hello?" she said, exasperated.

"What?" he asked more harshly than he'd intended.

She crossed her arms over her chest, drawing the material of her gown tight over her breasts. And nipples. Which were still hard. She was killing him. He could make out the edge of the pen between her fingers, but he couldn't make himself care.

"You mentioned the incident," she said. "Well, what about it?"

He'd had a point, hadn't he? Oh, yeah. "You were aroused when you came to me."

A huffy gasp left her. "No, I was not! I was going to give you a *chance* to arouse me. That's all."

"Please. You flashed me, and baby, you were already glistening."

Her cheeks heated to the same shade as her hair, making her all the lovelier. "You are very close to losing your favorite appendage." Scowling, peering at him hotly, she jerked the hand holding the pen forward and poised it just below his nose.

"Wait, wait, wait," he rushed out. Damn her and her powers! He lost his erection as every reason he hated witches flashed through his mind. "I'm sorry." *But not as sorry as you'll soon be.* "You were cold as ice that night." *You nearly singed me.* "You weren't turned on at all." *The scent of your desire is still imprinted on my brain.*

Slowly, she lowered her arm, expression mollified.

The limbs binding him began to loosen their grip, and he blinked in surprise. Was it possible? With a twist of his wrist, he was free. That easy, that simple, as if he'd never been bound. *He* had to hold on to the limbs to keep them upright. He blinked again, doing his best to hide his elation.

Glory was going to pay. Oh, was she going to pay. First, he had to claim that fucking pen!

"Com'ere," he said as gently as he was able. "Please. I want to tell you a secret."

She shook her head, red curls flinging in every direction. "What kind of secret?" Suspicion danced in her eyes.

He tried to look troubled.

"Tell me like this. No one can hear us."

"I don't want to say it aloud. It's . . . embarrassing."

Several moments ticked by, and she remained in place.

Then she sighed and stalked to him, hands fisted on her hips. She was so sure of her prowess—and his weakness. She'd learn . . .

"What?" she said.

Her feminine fragrance wafted to his nostrils, the same aroma she'd emitted that night on his porch. In the cell. She still desired him. He took a moment to simply enjoy. Savor. Crickets chirped a lazy song, and locusts rattled an accompanying, faster rhythm. In the distance, a dog barked. Around them, pink flower petals floated through the air, warm and sweet, each laced with a strong aphrodisiac. He'd heard that Glory had cast a love spell over the entire town, and since that day the petals had fallen from the sky like summer snow.

"What?" she demanded again.

"This." He grinned, and snapped his arms closed around her waist.

She yelped.

"Got ya," he said.

Four

Shock coursed through Glory, and it was mixed with an insidious thread of desire. Falon had her locked against his hard, hot body so tightly she could feel the frantic beat of his heart. Or maybe that was *her* heartbeat. Her breasts were mashed into his chest, her nipples like hard little points, and every time she breathed, she sucked in the scent of strength and soap and dark spice.

"Nothing to say?" Falon asked smugly.

"Let me go. Now." Trying not to panic, she attempted to lift her arms, attempted to flatten her palms against his chest and push him away from her, but her arms were glued to her sides.

"None of that," he said, latching onto her wrists with one hand and shoving them behind her. With his free hand, he grabbed the stick. Clearly, he assumed it was the pen, because his grin widened.

"Mine now," he said, and stuffed it into his pants pocket.

Do not smile. "Give it back."

"Make me."

Not knowing how to respond, she ran her tongue over her teeth.

His gaze followed the movement, his pupils dilating.

"What are you going to do with me?" she demanded. Or rather, meant to demand. Her voice was breathless. Again. Her body was trembling—and not with fury. How did he do this to her? Make her want him despite everything that had happened between them?

"I don't know," he answered honestly. "I need to think about it, consider my options. Because I can't allow you to run wild, using your powers against everyone who pricks your anger."

"Yeah, well, before you, I didn't use my powers for bad things."

"So I'm just special?"

"Of course you'd think so." Good. Her voice had substance now. "But the real answer is that you're simply the most irritating person I've ever met." *Kiss me. Let it be a terrible experience so that I never crave it again.*

He leaned down and traced the tip of his nose along the curve of her cheek, leaving a trail of decadent fire. Glory tried not to arch her hips and rub against his erection, but she did and, oh, Goddess, was he ever erect. Long and thick, hard and smoldering.

He groaned, his eyelids fluttering closed. "Again," he commanded.

Stop. Don't do this. Don't travel down this road. A kiss is one thing. But this. . . Ceasing her gyrations was the most difficult thing Glory had ever done, but she did it.

And suddenly he was eyeing her again, lashes casting menacing shadows over his cheeks and electric gaze piercing her soul. "I'm going to kiss you." It was a promise. "And you're going to kiss me back." It was a rough demand.

"No, you're not." *Please, please, please.* "And no, I'm not." *Impossible.*

"Yes, we are. We have to do something to end the madness."

"Fine. Whatever. Do what you want."

"This doesn't change anything."

"I'm glad you understand that."

"Try to take the pen, and you'll regret it."

"I'll regret it anyway."

He arched a brow. "Do you always have to have the last word?"

"Why, yes, I—"

His lips smashed into hers. Her mouth opened automatically, welcoming him inside. He thrust deep, and his flavor filled her mouth. Drugging, addicting. White-hot. A tingling ache sparked to life in her stomach, then spread to her chest, her limbs. She melted into him.

The iron lock on her wrists loosened. Rather than shove him, she wrapped her arms around him, pulling him closer. Her fingers tangled in his silky hair. His hands were free now, too, and they fastened on her waist, urging her forward and backward, mimicking the motions of sex.

Waves of pleasure constantly speared her. This was what she'd dreamed of since going to him that night, so long ago. His mouth on her, his hands all over her, his body straining against hers.

"More?" he whispered.

She nibbled on his bottom lip. "More."

He reached between them and palmed one of her breasts. His fingers plucked at the hardened nipple. "So perfect."

Moaning, she arched her hips. Exquisite contact. Her head dropped backward, and her long tresses tickled her overheated skin. Had Falon not been holding her up with that arm around her waist, she would have fallen.

No, wait. She was gripping spikes of his hair, tugging them. Hard. A few had already ripped from his scalp and were wrapped around her fingers.

He didn't complain.

She eased closer to him, relaxing her clasp. Her mouth found his neck, and she licked. His skin was a little abrasive, but perfect.

"You're so hot," he said.

"On fire," she agreed. She licked the seam of his lips.

He captured the tip of her tongue and sucked. The hand on her waist slid down . . . down . . . and cupped her ass. As he'd correctly guessed earlier, she wasn't wearing any underwear, and the tops of his fingers teased her most feminine core. She was so wet, she practically dripped between her legs.

"Shit. You're killing me." One of his fingers stroked her clitoris.

A tremor rocked her. *Shouldn't be this good. Not with him.*

Before the thought finished whispering through her mind, her entire world spun. Then cool bark was pressing into her back, and Falon was searing her front. He pinned her arms over her head with one hand and palmed her breast with the other.

"I knew you'd be this good," he growled, not sounding the least bit happy about it.

"Wh-what?" Trying to find her common sense, she blinked open her eyes. When had she closed them? Falon loomed over her. His features were harsh, lined with tension, his gaze a swirling sea of blues, purples, and pinks. How odd. They'd never looked that way before.

His shoulders were so wide, his body seemed to engulf her. Sweat beaded over his sun-kissed skin. He was like an animal whose stomach was rumbling—and he'd just spotted his prey. "Knew it," he finished. "Feared it."

What was he talking about? Feared what? And why wasn't he kissing her? "Falon, I—"

"I want this nipple in my mouth."

"Yes." Please, yes. That still qualified as kissing. "Hurry."

He ripped her nightgown down, revealing both mounds of her breasts. They were large. Overflowing. The nipples were pink, the hardened tips desperate. For a long while, he simply stared down at her.

Glory's cheeks began to heat, and not with desire. Did he like what he saw? He was used to slender women, had once turned Glory away because she wasn't his type. How could she have forgotten?

Embarrassed to her soul, she jerked at his hold, meaning to slide the nightgown back in place. He held strong.

His lips curled in a frown. "What are you doing?"

"Ending this," she said, unable to look at him.

"Be still."

"No."

He increased the death grip on her wrists, and his other hand cupped her chin, forcing her to face him. "Why do you want to end it?"

"Because." Like she'd say it aloud. But maybe that's what he wanted. Maybe that's how he meant to punish her.

Punishment. Of course. How could she have forgotten?

You brought this on yourself. Tears burned her eyes, and her chin trembled.

"What's wrong? You look ready to cry."

"Let me go," she commanded brokenly, focusing on his nose so that she wouldn't have to see those amazing eyes of his and whatever emotion was now banked there.

A moment passed in silence.

"Glory," he said.

Do it; look at him. Get it over with. See his disgust and start to hate him again. Slowly, her gaze lifted. When their eyes met, she gasped. There was a fire raging there. Tension still branched his mouth, and sweat still trickled down his temples. He looked on edge, aroused to the point of pain.

"I think you are the most beautiful creature I've ever beheld. And, like I said, I want your nipple in my mouth, and I think you want it there, too."

She gulped, unable to speak past the sudden lump in her throat.

"I'm going to release your arms. You can push me away or you can urge me closer. The choice is yours."

And just like that, she was free. Her arms fell to her sides. She gripped the tree, and jagged bits of bark cut past her skin. The sting did nothing to dampen her desire. He was so hard and hot against her he was like a brand. The pulse in his neck galloped fiercely. His lips were red and glistening from the kiss.

His chest had stopped moving, she realized. He was holding his breath. Waiting. The knowledge . . . softened her. Was he afraid she'd leave him?

With a shaky hand, she reached out and palmed his erection. He hissed in a breath.

The tip of his penis had risen well above the waist of his jeans. Actually, the material was so strained, the button had snapped open on its own.

"Trying to torture me?" he croaked. " 'Cause it's working."

Was it? She moistened her lips and released him. Was bereft without him in her hand.

Now he moaned.

Despite the warnings trying to slither into her mind, she cupped her breasts and lifted them. "Touch me."

His eyes widened in surprised delight. A moment later, he dipped down and flicked his tongue against one pearled nipple, then the other.

She'd experienced pleasure before, but that had been nothing compared to this. There was an invisible cord from each of her nipples that lead straight to her core, as if he were actually thrumming her clitoris while he licked her. This was Falon, the man she'd fantasized about for years. The man's whose strength and heat and raw intensity destroyed her defenses and made her crave . . .

Soon she was writhing, couldn't have remained still if the plan had been to pretend she felt nothing for him to undermine his confidence and try to convince him he was lacking. He was not lacking.

He scraped her with his teeth, and she groaned. His fingers caressed a path down her stomach. Her muscles quivered when he paused. Glory felt as though she stood on a precipice, waiting to be pushed over. Would he delve lower, like before, only . . . deeper?

"How did I ever find the strength to send you away?" he asked hoarsely.

Some of the flames inside her dwindled to a crackle, and she almost screamed in frustration. If he kept talking, kept reminding her of their painful history, she might lose her pleasure buzz. "No more talking. You'll ruin it."

A soft chuckle rumbled from him. The tip of one finger traced a circle around her navel, then dipped again, lower this time. Dabbling at the small triangle of hair, tickling. "Nothing could ruin this. You're perfection."

Her? Perfection? Entranced, she parted her legs, giving him all the access he could possibly need.

Through the material of the nightgown, he circled her clitoris next. Again. Finally. He pressed.

"Oh, bright lightning," she gasped.

"Like that?"

"Yes. More."

He didn't give it to her but continued to play with her,

revving her to that sense of uncontrollable desire again. "You're so wet," he praised. "For me."

"Yes. You." She tried to arch into his touch, tried to force his fingers to press harder. "Falon."

"Oh, but I like the sound of my name on your lips." His tongue glided up to her collarbone, his teeth nipping along the way. She turned her head aside, and he sucked at her pulse.

"I want to get on my knees. I want to taste between your legs. Say yes." He gripped the hem of her nightgown, slowly lifting.

"Ye—" *Red alert!* blared inside her mind, shoving past her need to scream *yes*. If he touched the knot in her gown, he would discover the pen. He would realize he'd taken a stick from her instead.

His knuckles brushed her thigh, and her knees almost buckled. "All you have to do is say *yes*, and my tongue will be inside you . . ."

His dark head, buried between her legs . . . one of her knees, draped over his shoulder . . . his tongue, stroking her to orgasm . . . She yearned for it so badly she had tears in her eyes. But she forced herself to say, "No," and at last to shove him away.

The action was puny, really, but he released her. He was panting, eyes narrowed. She was panting, eyes still burning.

"Things have already gone too far," she managed to get out. *Do I sound as breathless to him as I do to myself?* "This ends now."

He scrubbed a hand over his mouth, his gaze never leaving her face. "Oh, I get it. Punishment received."

He turned and stalked from her, and she wanted to shout that this hadn't been a punishment, not for him, but the words congealed in her throat, and then it was too late, anyway, because he disappeared from view.

Five

Falon fumed for the next three days. For three reasons. (Three must be his new lucky number.) One, Glory had outsmarted him, leaving him with a magicless stick rather than the revenge pen. Two, he hadn't gotten nearly enough of her and had thought about her constantly. And three, she was now ignoring him, as if he didn't fucking matter to her.

He should be happy about that last one.

He wasn't. Damn it, he wasn't!

Motions clipped, he paced through his living room, trying to decide what to do. Like his lack of happiness, this *should* have been a no-brainer: stay out of her life. Never antagonize her again. She'd had her revenge. She'd made him burn, desperate for her, and then had rejected him. They were even. There was no reason they had to deal with each other again. Most likely, bad, magical things would happen if they did.

"As well as hot and sweaty," he muttered. Her passion had been a thing of beauty. She'd writhed against him, her lush body flushed, her hazel eyes blazing. Her breasts had overflowed in his hands. Her skin had been the softest he'd ever caressed. Her long red hair had tumbled down her shoulders and arms, the perfect frame for her exquisite loveliness.

What would have happened if she'd have let him strip her? What would have happened if he'd spread her legs and pounded inside her?

"Heaven, that's what." *But what about afterward?* Would she have wanted more from him or been done with him? Would she have used her naughty magic against him again?

Falon scrubbed a hand over his scalp, nails raking. He was—or rather, had been—crown prince of the Fae. Women had thrown themselves at him, hoping to be queen. None had captured his interest. Then he'd meet Frederica, the witch, and had been entranced. Now he thought, perhaps, she'd used a love spell on him and there at the end it had worn off. But even still, he hadn't hungered for her the way he hungered for Glory. Glory challenged him in every way imaginable.

"Not hard, nowadays," he muttered.

To serve Penelope for the required year in order to gain his freedom from Frederica's impotence curse, he'd had to relinquish his crown. His brother, Falk, had then taken over. Falk was a good king, respected, admired, and loved. Falon didn't have the heart to take it from him when the year ended. *What kind of king would I make, anyway?* Not a good one, that was for sure. He'd always been too wild.

Besides, over the years he'd managed to carve out a decent life for himself. He didn't need money, but he worked with Hunter at the bar. Amusements abounded, and there was never a dull moment. Brawls, seductions. Plus, it was a hub of information. When people were drinking, they tended to spill their deepest secrets. A few months ago, Falon had overheard three female fairies planning to poison Falk. He'd passed the information on, and the women had been captured in the act, Falk saved.

Falon sighed, his gaze traveling through his home. To thank him, Falk had sent him gifts. Lots and lots of gifts. From plush crimson couches to thick obsidian rugs. From jeweled goblets to a tiered chandelier. While the outside of his modest house might look ordinary, the inside was like a sultan's palace. White lace even hung from each of the doorways. Not his doing. Falk had also sent a decorator.

Falon stopped in front of the velvet sapphire lounge. He pictured Glory splayed across it, naked, her little pink nipples hard. The lamp resting on the marble table beside the seat would be lit, and she would be bathed in a golden glow. She would nibble on her bottom lip, her eyes closed, lashes casting shadows on her cheeks, hand delving down her soft stomach, fingers sinking into the red curls between her legs.

Just like that, he was rock hard. Again.

"Damn it!"

He needed to bed her. Just once. Otherwise, he'd never be able to get her out of his head.

Growling low in his throat, he stalked to the emerald-studded phone. He'd kind of liked his old one, plain and tan, but oh, well. He dialed Glory's number. *This is dumb, this is so damned dumb.* His blood heated at the thought of hearing her sultry voice. What would she say to him?

One of the Tawdry sisters answered on the third ring. "Yeah, hello." She sounded breathless.

"I need to speak with Glory."

"Falon? Is that you?"

"Yes, who's this?"

"This is Genevieve."

"Hey, Evie. I really need to speak to Glory." Before he came to his senses and took matters into his own hands. Literally.

"Is something wrong?"

He closed his eyes and prayed for patience. "Look, is she around?"

"Well, yeah, but I don't think she'll want to chat with you, and maybe that's for the best. She's in a mood."

Evie sounded like that was newsworthy. When *wasn't* Glory in a mood? "Is something wrong with her? Is she okay?"

"Meaning, did someone physically hurt her? No. You know they'd be dead by my magic if they did."

A warning? "Emotionally, then."

"I don't know. You tell me. Did you kiss her?" Evie asked.

"Who you talking to, baby?" Falon heard in the background.

"Let me speak with Hunter," Falon said.

Crackling static, and then his best friend was saying, "What's going on?"

"Glory okay?"

"Oh, man. She's been stomping around the house for three days, muttering about a stupid kiss, a stupid man, and stupid revenge. She write you into another scene or something?"

"No." But she could do so at any moment, which made him all kinds of an idiot for making this call. And why was she angry? *She'd* rejected *him*. He'd done nothing but try to pleasure her.

"My advice, bro, is to just leave her alone. She'll calm down, and then she'll forget all about you."

That was the problem. Falon didn't want her to forget him. Shit. *He* seriously needed to forget *her*.

"Uh-oh. Here she is," Hunter muttered.

"I'm going for a run," Falon heard her grumble.

"You? Run?" Shock dripped from Evie's voice.

"Well, no one in this household can seem to master magical weight loss, so I'm running the pounds off. You got a problem with that?"

"You don't need to loose weight," he wanted to shout. Then he thought, *She'll be out of the house. It'll be the perfect time to search her room and snatch that pen.* Once the pen was out of her possession, seduction wouldn't be so dumb. A lie, but he didn't care. "Talk to you later, Hunter," he blurted. "Don't tell her I called." He hung up, grabbed his car keys, and stalked into the waiting daylight.

Glory ran until her lungs felt like they'd caught fire. She ran until her body was shaking from exertion. She ran until her mind was mush. Sadly, none of those things shoved Falon from her mind.

Him and his too-soft lips, his decadent, drugging taste. His hardness, his sweet hands. His final request to taste her. She'd stayed away from him, hadn't even tried to punish him again.

Sweat poured from her as she stumbled up the porch

steps and into her house. Cool air kissed her skin. She propped herself against the nearest living room wall and hunched over, trying to catch her breath. It had taken her a few hours after leaving him in the forest to deduce exactly how he'd convinced her, even for a second, that he truly desired her.

Good thing she'd stopped him. Only two other outcomes had been possible: *he* would have stopped before actual penetration, leaving her gasping and desperate, or, if they'd actually gone all the way, he would have told her how bad she was afterward. He might have laughed at her again

Her teeth ground together as she straightened. He'd told her she would regret using the pen against him. Now she did. She needed a distraction.

The living room was empty. "Evie," she called. "Godiva." No reply.

Had they left, or were they in their rooms, getting it on? Glory rolled her eyes and pretended there wasn't an ache in her chest. Probably the latter, the disgusting witches. Did they ever take a break? Legs screaming in protest, she lumbered forward, using the wall as a prop.

Down the hall she maneuvered. When she reached her bedroom door, she waved her hand over the knob, magically unlocking it. The door creaked open, and she stumbled inside, forced to kick past the clothes and food wrappers still scattered across the floor.

"Hello, Glory," a strong, male voice said.

She gasped, frozen in place, gaze searching. Her heart pounded in her chest, nearly cracking her ribs when she spotted the intruder. Falon was splayed out on her bed. His dark head rested on her pillow, his arms propped behind his neck.

He wore a clinging black T-shirt that veed at the neck and jeans that showed off the muscles in his thighs.

"Wh-what are you doing here? And how did you get in?" No. No! He'd seen the national disaster state of her bedroom. Seriously, a bra hung from the lamp beside her bed. Sadly, she looked worse. "Don't look at me," she said, wanting to turn away as his eyes drank her in.

"Why? You're beautiful. I *like* looking at you. Just as you are," he added.

She rubbed her damp palms against her thighs. "What are you doing here?" she repeated, because she didn't know how else to react to his praise. The pleasure she felt was unacceptable.

"I would have pegged you for a neat freak," he said, ignoring her question. Again.

At least he didn't sound disgusted. "So?"

"Where's the pen?" he asked conversationally.

She raised her chin. "Like I'll tell you."

"You haven't used it against me since our . . . the . . . our time in the forest." Had he just stammered? Had his voice dropped with desire?

"Maybe I just haven't thought of the appropriate punishment yet."

One of his brows arched, and he sat up slowly. "Punishment for what? Making you feel good?" Now his voice was dry. "Or not taking you all the way?"

"Just get out." She pointed to the hallway.

He flattened his palms at his sides, his gaze roving over her. That white-hot gaze lingered at her breasts, between her legs, reminding her of everywhere he'd touched—and everywhere he'd wanted to touch. She gulped. She was wearing a white tank top and sweat shorts, and sweat still poured down her flushed skin. She probably looked ridiculous and frumpy.

"Your skin is glistening," he said, and there was enough heat in his eyes to keep her warm all winter. If Mysteria ever got cold, that is.

"Sweat does that to a girl."

"I wish I had been the one to make you sweat."

Now her heart skipped a beat. "What do you want from me, Falon? An apology? Well, you're not going to get one. We're even. I'm done with you."

His eyes sharpened. "You're not done with me. Not until you destroy the pen in front of me."

"No. There's ink left."

"So you plan to use it against me again? You just said we're even."

"We're even *now*. I destroy it, and you're free to torment me for the rest of your life."

He leaned forward, and she caught the scent of soap and dark spices. Shivered—then shuddered. What did *she* smell like?

"I'll swear not to hurt you," he said.

"And I'm sure you'll mean it. Today. What about tomorrow?"

Growling, he fell back into the mattress and scoured a hand down his face. She noticed he did that a lot when he was frustrated. "I came here to find the pen, but do you know what I really wanted to do?" He didn't wait for her to reply. "I wanted to follow you on your run, make sure you were safe."

Really? How . . . sweet. Some of the ice around her heart melted. *Don't believe him, stupid!*

"I wanted—want—to strip you, make love to you. Finish what we started. I can't get you out of my mind. You're the last person I should want." Now he seemed to be talking to himself. "But want you I do. Maybe if I have you, I can stop thinking about you."

Oh, how she wished. He'd consumed every corridor of her mind since their kiss. Always she craved him. Always she dreamed of him, hungered. Sometimes she was even willing to toss caution aside and go to him, beg him to take her. But . . .

What would happen afterward?

She had several strikes against her. She was a witch, and he hated witches. He was perfection, and she was the epitome of *im*perfection. She'd spent the last week torturing him.

Three strikes. You're out, girl. Glory sighed. She was afraid she'd already fallen for him, though. He was strength, and he was courage. He hadn't backed down from her once, even though her powers were considerable, and she could do major damage to him. His kisses were the best thing to have ever happened to her. His touch, electric. Finally she'd gotten a glimpse of what Evie and Hunter, Godiva and Romeo must experience every night. And different hours through the day. She'd liked it, wanted more.

Wanted him.

"No response?" he said, cutting through the silence.

She shook her head in hopes of clearing it. "You're willing to have me now?"

"I was willing before. I just fought against it."

"But you're not fighting now?"

"No. I can't." He rolled to his side and stared over at her. "I'm helpless. Did you cast a love spell on me?"

"No!"

"I didn't think so," he muttered. "Hoped, but didn't think."

"Why not?"

"Because a witch did it once, and this isn't the same."

Her shoulders sagged. No love for her, he meant.

"It's more intense," he grumbled, surprising her.

Her legs began shaking more forcefully, and any moment she feared she would collapse. Somehow she managed to stumble to the chair in the corner and plop atop the many T-shirts heaped there. Falon's gaze never left her. She felt it boring past her skin and straight into her soul.

"You want me, too," he said. Hard, flat. "Don't try to deny it."

As if she could. "Who tried to deny it?"

His lips formed a thin line. Almost a smile, but not quite.

"Look, I came to you once offering the same thing. One night. You rejected me."

"Yes, and it was the biggest mistake of my life."

"Because you were made to suffer for it," she said. A statement rather than a question.

"No. Because I crave you."

Truth or lie? She dared not hope. "Now you're out to protect yourself from me, and that's perfectly understandable, but—"

"I don't need protection from you," he snapped.

"Falon, we'll never be able to trust each other. We'll always suspect each other's motives."

"We can call a truce. I'm not asking for a lifetime. I'm asking for a night. And when you came to me that night, that's all you wanted, too."

"I—I—" *Wanted to say yes,* she realized. Wanted it more than anything. After his kiss, though, she couldn't delude herself and hope the sex would be so bad she'd never desire him again. The sex would be great. At least for her. She *would* want more than a night; she knew that now. He . . . affected her. "I can't," she finally said.

"Damn it. Why?" He shot up again, glaring at her.

If he approached her, if he touched her . . . Tremors racked her, part of her wishing he'd do it. Force her hand. "We bring out the worst in each other."

Surprisingly, that mollified him somewhat. "I don't know. I thought we brought out the best in each other while in the forest."

"That was a mistake."

"My favorite mistake, then."

Goddess, if he kept saying things like that, she'd cave. Already her defenses were cracked. Really, what would one time hurt? Sure, she might fall for him even more than she already had. Sure, she might crave more from him. Sure, he might compare her to every girl he'd ever been with, and she would definitely come out lacking. Sure, this might be a scheme on his part to castigate her for using that pen against him. But she'd have an orgasm, so what did those things matter?

And what if . . . what if he truly desired her? What if he enjoyed being with her?

What if: the most dangerous words known to man.

"I just can't," she forced herself to say. Her voice cracked, just like her defenses. She had to swallow a sudden lump in her throat. "My answer is and will always be *no*. Find someone else."

"You want me to sleep with another woman?" he gasped out, incredulous.

"Yes?" she replied, a question she'd meant as a statement.

"You won't care?"

"No." Her hands curled into fists as rage swam through her bloodstream. She'd destroy anyone he touched. Obliterate anyone he—*What are you doing? Stop thinking like that!* "I can give you a love potion for the woman if you think it'd help." *Idiot! What are you saying?*

I thought I was supposed to push him—oh, never mind. Damage done.

Scowling, he jackknifed to his feet. "You want me to be

with someone else, I'll be with someone else. I don't need a fucking love potion to do it, either. See you around, Glory."

Glory watched him stride from her bedroom, heard the front door slam. Her shoulders sagged against the chair, and she covered her mouth with a shaky hand. What the hell had she just done?

Six

He'd made the boast to see another woman. Now he had to see it through. *Shit,* Falon thought. But if he had to prod Glory's temper until she snapped and used that stupid pen, he'd do it. Do *anything* to have her in his arms again. *What's happened to me?* He'd gone from hating her powers to craving them. He just flat-out refused to be ignored by her any longer.

"I'll give you a love potion," he mocked. He'd seen the jealousy flare in her gorgeous eyes when they'd talked about him dating another woman. Glory hadn't wanted him to sleep with someone else; she just hadn't wanted to admit she desired him for herself. So he'd *make* her do it. Because he had to get his hands on her breasts, had to rub himself between her legs. Had to have her taste in his mouth and her pleasure moans in his ears. *Then* he could hate her magic again. Then he would go back to being a rational male who didn't need anyone in particular.

He massaged the back of his neck. Hopefully, if he worked this just right, he wouldn't earn himself another year of impotence. Hopefully, Glory would write the two of them into a

sensual scene, and he would be able to finally, blessedly se-
duce her.

Who would have guessed he'd be reduced to seducing a
witch? Not him, definitely. Yet here he was, at home again and
picking up the phone to dial an old lover who was still a
friend.

When she answered, he said, "I need a favor. And before
you say yes, you should know we'll be dealing with a very
powerful and somewhat insane witch."

And then, when he hung up with Kayla, he called Hunter.
His best friend answered, and he said, "Look, I need a favor,
and you owe me, so don't even think about saying no."

"Hurry, up, Glor!"

"I'm hurrying, swear." The moment Glory had sailed
through the front door of their home, her sisters had rushed
her into the shower. They'd thrown a tight black dress and lacy
lingerie at her when she'd emerged.

Now she was in the process of fitting her body into the
sheer clothing. She should use the pen to make herself slender
again but didn't want to waste the ink for some silly dinner.

Hunter was taking them to the Love Nest, a five-star restaurant that catered to the affairs of the heart. Gag. She'd rather
vomit than go, but Godiva had batted those sweet hazel eyes at
her, and she'd found herself agreeing.

Unfortunately, the shower had failed to wash away the trials of the day. Glory had spent six hours in town, hawking
her love potions for a little extra spending money. A few
times, she'd wondered what she would do if one of the
women who'd purchased a vial of Number Nine used it on
Falon. Then she'd thought, *If he truly loves someone, no potion will sway his heart.* Then she'd thought, *If he doesn't
love anyone, he's fair game.* Which basically meant Falon
was fair game.

The knowledge had settled uneasily inside her, made her
twitchy. She'd always considered her powers a blessing. For her,
for others. Perhaps Falon was right, though. Perhaps she was a
danger to everyone around her. But it wasn't like she could
forsake her powers. They were a part of her.

"We're going to be late," Evie said, drawing her from her musings.

"So? I think the restaurant will survive."

"So Hunter is a vampire and only has a limited amount of time to play. Hurry."

Glory sighed. "You're right. I'm sorry. Maybe I should stay home. I'm in a terrible mood. Besides, I should be working. I have a book due in a few months, and I haven't written a word."

Now *Evie* batted hazel eyes at her. "You can put it off for another night. Please. For me."

She had no willpower when it came to pleasing her sisters. "Fine. I'll go. What are we celebrating, anyway?"

"The anniversary of the first time Hunter said he loved me."

Trying not to grimace, Glory spun and faced her sister. "Are you freaking kidding me?"

Clueless, Evie shook her dark head. "No."

The two lovebirds celebrated everything! The anniversary of the first time they had laid eyes on each other. The anniversary of the first time they had made love. The anniversary of Hunter's change from human to vampire. It was truly sickening. "Isn't that something the two of you should celebrate alone?"

"We will." Evie's lips curled slowly, suggestively. "Later."

Godiva peeked her pale head around the door. "Ready, sister dear? Oh, my." Her body rounded the rest of the corner, and then she was walking forward, expression warm. "You look gorgeous."

There wasn't a single malicious cell in her oldest sister. The woman was pure gentleness and had always been that way. "I feel silly," she admitted. She faced the full-length mirror.

The black dress flowed gracefully over her hips, gossamer, like a butterfly's wing. But with her arms stretched down at her sides, the hem did not even reach her fingertips. Thin straps held the material in place on her shoulders. A beaded empire waist cinched everything in just under her breasts, before flaring and floating free.

Overall, the dress was a naughty version of a Grecian toga.

On her feet, she wore strappy black sandals. Her toenails were painted a vivid shade of emerald.

"You've always been the most beautiful of us," Godiva said.

"Hey." Evie frowned at their oldest sister. "I'm standing right here. What am I, dog food?"

Godiva waved a hand in dismissal. "You've always been the firecracker."

"You've always been the peacemaker," Glory said, "and let's be real. I've always been the—"

"Nope," Godiva interjected, gripping her shoulders and spinning her. "I'm not going to allow you to put yourself down. You are an amazing woman, and it's time you realized that."

Fighting tears, Glory kissed her sister softly on the cheek. "I love you."

"Love you, too."

Evie threw her arms around them with such force, they gasped. "I love you guys, too. Now let's haul ass! And, Glory, bring your pen. You know, just in case."

Everything inside of her froze with dread. "Just in case what?" Each word was punctuated with warning. Had Evie done something?

"Who knows? It's a beautiful night. Anything can happen."

"I never thought I'd see you like this."

Falon eyed Kayla Smith from across their candlelit table. She was a beautiful woman with pale hair, bright blue eyes, and legs that went on forever. Sadly, she did nothing for him. Not anymore.

She was cousin to Candy Cox, the infamous high school teacher now dating a werewolf; was fully human; and had lived in Mysteria so long she found nothing unusual about vampires, goblins, fairies, or witches. They'd dated on and off for a few months, realized they were working themselves into a relationship, and had backed off. Neither of them had wanted to be tied down. He'd always liked that about her. She was fun and playful and never took anything too seriously. Even men.

But he found himself wondering how Glory had been with

past boyfriends. Fun and playful, which he decided he no longer liked? Hopefully, Glory had been miserable with other men. Or had she been serious, which for some reason he liked even less. Fine. He just didn't like the thought of Glory with another man, period.

More, he found that he didn't like the fact that he didn't know everything about her. Suddenly he yearned to know what she ate for breakfast, what her favorite song was, what she dreamed for her life, if she liked to snuggle and watch movies in bed. And if so, were they romantic comedies or action adventure? Probably slashers.

"Are you listening to me?" Kayla asked him.

No. What the hell had she just said? Oh, yeah. She'd never seen him like this. "Yes, of course I was listening. What way do you think you see me?" he asked, his gaze immediately straying back to the restaurant's front door. Where was Glory?

"On edge for a specific woman." There was laughter in her voice. "By the way, you missed a very scintillating conversation I just had with, apparently, myself about a hot tub."

He waved the hot tub away with a dismissive hand. Although, Glory, wet and naked . . . "I'll get her out of my system." He hoped. "Don't worry." With every minute that passed, he just wanted her more.

How would she react when she saw him with Kayla?

Hopefully—how many things was he hopeful about now?—her sisters had convinced her to bring the pen. Hopefully, she would write them into a bedroom. Maybe chain him to the headboard. Yes, chains could definitely come in handy.

The front door to the restaurant opened. He stiffened, poised on the edge of his seat.

Godiva strolled inside, directly behind her was her boyfriend, Romeo, tall and muscled and very wolfish. Falon's stomach rolled into a thousand different knots. Evie walked in, saying something over her shoulder. A moment later, Glory came into his sights. Finally!

Breath congealed in his throat. Dear God. She was . . . magnificent. Like the goddess she worshipped. Her long red curls tumbled down her back, and the sheer fabric of her dress swayed over her lush hips and thighs.

Hunter stepped in behind her and approached the hostess.

The group was led to a table directly across from Falon's. The closer she came, the hotter his blood flowed. *See me. Want me.*

It was as Glory was helped into her seat that she spied him. Her hazel eyes widened with shock then narrowed with fury. Or arousal. She licked her lips. Spotted Kayla. Gripped the edge of the table so tightly he feared it would snap in half.

"Wow," Kayla said. "I don't have to ask which one is yours."

His. He liked the sound of that.

"She's the one shooting daggers at us. Or rather, me."

"Right."

He should take Kayla's hand, perhaps kiss it. But he couldn't bring himself to do it. The only skin he wanted to kiss was Glory's.

Her sisters took their places at her sides, and he heard her bark, "Did you know about this?"

Both women nodded guiltily.

"Traitors! Why not ask him and his date to join us, then. I couldn't possibly feel any more uncomfortable."

"Hey, Falon," Hunter called. "Glory would really love it if you and your date joined us."

Glory's mouth fell open. "I was joking. I didn't—"

"We'd love to." He was on his feet a second later, jerking Kayla to hers.

Kayla chuckled softly.

Deep down, he didn't think Glory would turn the heat of her anger on the other woman. After he'd foolishly turned her away that night, she hadn't gone after the fairy he'd allowed inside. Only him. Clearly, she was a smart woman and knew where to properly lay the blame.

A waiter dragged two extra chairs to the table, positioning him and Kayla directly across from Glory. He wanted to be closer but would settle for simply looking at her.

You have it bad, man. You've gone from hating witches to being desperate for one in less than a week.

Strangely, he didn't care anymore. Not while he was soaking her in.

"Since the big guy isn't going to introduce me," Kayla said, breaking the silence, "I'll introduce myself. I'm Kayla Smith."

Everyone introduced themselves. Except for Glory. When it was her turn, she motioned the waiter over and ordered a glass of flaming fairy. Falon nearly choked on his sip of water.

"You know I'm of the Fae. How?" he asked her. Not many people did. He was too big, too much a warrior compared to the usually party-loving race.

Her eyes widened. "You're Fae?"

Okay, so she hadn't guessed. He didn't mind that she now knew; he wanted her to know everything about him. "Yes."

"Why didn't you tell me?" Hunter asked, incredulous.

"No one's business."

Awkward silence followed.

"Well, this is fun," Evie said, probably to break the tension.

"A blast," Kayla agreed. She tossed her hair over one shoulder, revealing sun-kissed skin.

Glory saw the action and popped her jaw.

"I've always had low self-esteem," she'd once told him. Oh . . . shit. Bad move, bringing the ex, he realized. He didn't want Glory to feel bad about herself or think he found Kayla more attractive. "You're the prettiest woman here, Glory," he said honestly.

Her drink arrived, saving her from replying. But her eyes had met his over the candlelight, soft and luminous. Her lashes cast dark shadows over her cheeks. Shadows he wanted to trace with his fingertips.

Menus were thrust at them. Falon didn't bother opening his. He didn't care about the food. He continued to watch Glory, couldn't stop himself. He was entranced. She opened her menu, though she didn't read it. She still watched him, too.

Her cheeks flushed to a rosy pink. She was clearly having trouble drawing in a breath, her chest rising too quickly and too shallowly.

"Hungry?" he asked her in a low, raspy voice.

Her gaze dipped to his lips. "A little."

"I'm starved."

"Why do I get the feeling they're not talking about food?" Evie muttered.

"Because they're not," Hunter told her, "so hush."

The table fell quiet, all eyes glued to Glory and Falon.

Get your pen, he mentally willed. *Write us away from here.* But she didn't. She finally looked away.

His teeth ground together. He'd just have to push her harder, then. *God, I'm pathetic.*

"I decided to take your advice," he said.

Fury curtained her features a split second before she blanked her expression. What thoughts tumbled through her mind? "Is that right?" The words were precisely uttered, as though shoved through the crack in a steel wall and ironed out.

"That's right."

The waiter came to take their order, but Kayla shooed him away. Hunter, Evie, Godiva, and Romeo propped their elbows on the table, unabashed by their staring.

"Funny that it wasn't too long ago you *protested* taking my advice," Glory said.

"Isn't it?"

"It is. I'd like to say I'm surprised, but I can't." She tapped a nail against her glass, and the red liquid swished. "Not if I'm being honest."

His lips pursed. Did she truly think so poorly of him? Of course she did, he thought in the next instant. He'd once told her that he hated witches. He'd once told her that he would pay her back for all she'd done to him.

Worry about that later. When she's naked and under you. Or over you. Right now, you have to push her. "I'm thinking about showing Kayla my favorite . . . gladiator costume. Does *that* surprise you?"

Hunter choked on his water. Romeo nodded encouragingly. Evie, Godiva, and Kayla leaned forward, obviously intrigued.

Glory gasped at the reminder of the night she'd written him into a slave's cell, splattered with blood and fresh from battle.

"I'm learning things about you I wish you'd kept hidden," Hunter muttered.

"Shut it," Falon told him.

"Why don't you show her your jackass costume?" Glory asked through clenched teeth. "Oh, wait. You're already wearing it."

Okay, he'd walked into that one. Had she been talking about

anyone else, he would have laughed. He loved her wit. And she must love warriors. Why else would she have written him into such a situation?

He racked his brain for things he knew about ancient Rome. Not much. Everything he knew, he knew because of Russell Crowe. "For the woman I desire, I would be willing to do anything." The words were dare, a challenge.

"A few flicks of my wrist, and I can make you prove those words. Violently."

Do it. "Please." He snorted. "You've run out of ink, and we both know it."

She leaned forward, curls spilling onto the table. God, she was lovely. "Do you *want* to die?"

"Yes. Of pleasure."

Her pupils dilated, and her nostrils flared. Just then, she was like a living flame, fury crackling over her skin. *I'm close. So close. Just a little more.*

"Maybe you'd like to visit a village of Vikings? Or maybe you'd like to come face-to-face with a Highland chieftain and his sword?"

"If that turned you—her on, then yes."

Glory ran her tongue over her teeth. Every muscle in his body jerked at the sight of that pink tongue. Oh, to have it on *him.*

"It would," Kayla said. "It really would. What do I have to do to get in on this action? I'd prefer a Viking over a chieftain, but will graciously accept whichever you give me."

Slowly, Glory eased back in her seat. Slowly, she grinned, though the expression lacked any type of humor. "I think something can be arranged. For you," she added, eyeing Falon, "not her."

"Please," Kayla said at the same time he said, "Fine. I understand." He was thinking, *Finally!*

As she reached inside her purse, Falon added, "Oh, and Glory?"

"Yes?" Grin feral, she lifted the pen and tapped it against her chin—to taunt him, he wouldn't doubt. Fire still raged in her eyes.

Are you really going to do this? He peered at her heaving chest, her dilated pupils, her lush, red lips. *Hell, yes.* "Since

I'm doubting you have the courage to write yourself into the scene, I guess I'll see you when I get back."

Her eyelids narrowed, and she lost her grin.

He barely stopped himself from laughing. *See you there, baby.*

Seven

❋

He wanted her to write them both into a scene, an oddity on its own. He hadn't seemed to mind the thought of his precious Kayla being given to another man; he had seemed more interested in Glory. Glory knew all of those shocking things, but she didn't understand them.

Why had he fought for magic to be used against him? Why had he antagonized her?

Did the reason matter? she thought next. She was at home, alone in her room, and she was going to use the pen. Not to punish Falon—though she wanted to do so. He'd taken another woman to dinner. A beautiful, slender woman. No, Glory was doing this to be with him, to have him to herself. She'd simply used punishment and anger as an excuse.

When will I learn?

She'd tried to stay away from him. She'd ignored his phone calls, hadn't ventured near his house. She'd even walked out of a room anytime he had been mentioned. She feared falling so deeply in love with him, she'd never recover. As she'd once told him, they could never trust each other. But she was still going to do this. She craved him, and the craving wasn't going away.

Despite all of her reasons for avoiding him before, she couldn't stop herself now. She needed to shove him from her thoughts and dreams, and nothing else had worked. Why not give this a shot and experience another dose of that heady pleasure while she was at it? She'd do her best to guard her heart. Oh, oh. Maybe she could take an antilove potion.

She was nodding as she popped to her feet. Antilove. Of course! There was nothing she could do about the emotions she harbored now. Once there, they were immune to magic. But she *could* prevent herself from falling for Falon completely.

Clothes and trash soared through the air as she crouched on the floor and rooted through them. Every vial she found, she set aside. Love potion Number Nine. Love potion Number Thirteen.

A magic suppressor. A magic unleasher. Ah, finally.

Straightening, she raised a tiny bottle of swirling, azure liquid. There was a warning label in the center.

"Take with food," she read. "May cause dizziness. If you become sick, consult your nearest witch."

She'd given the potion to hundreds of women but had never sampled the goods herself. There'd been no need. The recipe had been designed by her great-grandmother and was now used in every spell book she'd ever encountered. It had to work. No one had ever complained.

"Here goes nothing." Glory popped the cork and drained the contents. Tasteless but smooth. A minute passed. Nothing happened. Another minute. Still nothing. She tossed the empty bottle over her shoulder. Maybe she wasn't supposed to feel anything.

Frowning, she swiped up the pen and a notebook and plopped onto the side of her bed. What was Falon doing right now? Was he at home with Kayla? Waiting for Glory to act?

What was the couple doing to pass the time?

"Grr!"

Unable to wait any longer, Glory began writing: *Falon is alone in his house, unable to leave.* That took care of Kayla. Glory's frown faded. She wouldn't make him battle anyone like he'd suggested. That would make her admire him more.

Even the image was dangerous. Falon. With a sword. Her mouth watered.

She'd get straight to the sex. Do him and forget him. *His clothing suddenly disappears, leaving him naked.* As the ink stained the paper, she had trouble drawing in a breath. Her hand was shaking.

Glory appears—

No. She scratched out those two words. Falon was now alone and naked. She couldn't just appear in front of him looking like this.

Glory weighs one hundred and fifteen pounds and is wearing a lacy, emerald green bra and panty set.

One moment she was draped in the black dress her sister had given her, the next, cool air was kissing her bare skin. Glory looked down. Sure enough, her *small*, perky breasts were pushed up by emerald lace. Her stomach and legs were thin and glorious. She grinned and kept writing.

Falon is chained to his bed, and Glory suddenly appears in front of him, pen and notebook in hand.

Glory's messy bedroom faded to black, and then Glory was lying against cool, silky sheets. Cold metal anchored her wrists and ankles in place, her pen and notebook gone. A white chiffon flowed overhead, like a cloud descending from heaven.

"What the hell?" She tugged at her arms. The chains rattled but didn't budge.

Suddenly Falon approached the side of the bed, the pen and notebook in his hands. He looked at Glory, and his eyes widened. He looked at the contraband he was holding, and he grinned.

"It worked," he said, shocked. "It really worked."

Her struggles increased. "What worked? What happened? What did you do to me?" What the hell was going on?

He was naked, and his tanned body was magnificent. Rope after rope of muscle, traceable sinew, and a long, hard erection. A glittering necklace hung from his neck.

She looked away from the sheer majesty of him, struggled some more.

"Be still," he said.

"Go to hell!" The metal began to cut into her skin, drawing warm beads of blood.

Falon *tsked* under his tongue. He strode out of the bedroom, leaving her alone.

"Falon!" she cried. Panic infused every corridor of her body. "Don't leave me like this! Come back."

He returned a moment later, the pen and notebook gone. In their place were strips of cloth. "Be still," he ordered again, sharply this time.

She obeyed. She was panting, skin overly hot. At least he'd covered himself with a robe, blocking all that male deliciousness from her view. "What's going on? How did you do this? You don't have any powers."

He eased beside her, and the mattress jiggled. She tried to scoot away, but the chains didn't allow her to go very far. "No, I don't have powers. But I do have a friend who is dating a witch who wants her sister happy."

Her jaw went slack. "*Evie* helped you?"

Leaning forward and wafting the scent of man and dark spice to her nose, Falon began wrapping the cloth underneath the chains, protecting her skin. *Do not soften.* She'd taken the antilove potion. She shouldn't have to warn herself to remain distant, but the potion wasn't freaking working.

"Hunter questioned Evie about the pen," he finally explained. "Apparently, Evie failed to tell you that she had a charm to counteract the effects of it."

"I don't understand." *Come closer, keep touching me.* She had to bite her lip to keep the words inside.

"Anything negative you wrote about the person wearing the charm would be done to *you* instead."

Shock sliced through her, as hot as he was. "That's—that's—"

"What happened. Hunter also emptied out your potions and replaced them with colored water. Just in case you tried to feed me one."

So that was why . . . "That little jackass!" No wonder the antilove potion hadn't worked. Now she was helpless, on her own. The knowledge should have panicked her all the more. Instead, she found herself praying his robe would split, and she would be able to see his nipples. Maybe lick them.

"I had wondered what kind of scene you would write, and must admit I'm surprised by what you chose. I expected hungry lions or a raging, bloody battle and thought I would have to pluck you from its midst. I'd even draped myself in armor, just in case. Then that armor disappeared and I began to hope . . ."

Her cheeks flamed; they were probably glowing bright red. She tried to cover her embarrassment by snapping, "Why didn't my clothing disappear instead? Since you have the charm and all."

"The removal of clothing isn't negative." His head tilted to the side, and his gaze roved over her. He frowned. "Why do you write yourself like that?"

"Like what?"

"So . . . thin."

"Because," was all she said. *Because I want to be pretty for you.*

"I like you better the other way."

"Liar. Now write me out of this scene!"

He shook his head. "Hell, no. I've got you right where I've always wanted you. And I'm not a liar. In fact, I refuse to touch you while you're like this. When you're back to normal, *then* the loving can begin."

A tremor rocked her. She didn't dare hope . . . "The chains will disappear by then, too, and if you think I'm staying here, you're crazy."

"You can be rechained."

Good point. "The pleasuring will never begin, because I've decided I don't want you."

"Now who's lying?" He pulled a plush lounge next to the bed and sat, gaze never leaving her. "I'll make a pact with you. I won't lie to you, if you won't lie to me. From now on, we'll be completely honest with each other. Okay?"

"Whatever you say," she said in a sugar-sweet tone.

"So what do you think of my bedroom?"

"It's—" She'd been about to say something mean, but then her sights snagged on the crystal chandelier, dripping with thousands of teardrops. On the intricately carved dresser, orchids spilling from vases. A bejeweled tray provided the centerpiece. "Unexpected," she finally finished.

"Everything inside the house was a gift from my brother."

Her head snapped toward him. "I didn't know you had a brother."

Falon nodded, his hair dancing over his cheeks. "There's a lot you don't know about me, but that's going to change. We're going to get to know each other, Glory."

"No." That would defeat the purpose of loving and leaving. If he continued this, she would leave, but she would not be unscathed.

"Oh, yes," he insisted. "And every time you reveal a fact about yourself, you'll earn a reward."

Goose bumps spread over her skin. "And if I remain quiet?"

Slowly, he grinned. "You'll earn a punishment. I have the pen, after all."

This is not fun. This is not exciting. I am not turned on. "Fine. Tell me how many women you've had in here." There. That should deepen—dampen—her terrible—wonderful—mood.

"You are the first."

She flashed him a scowl. "I thought we weren't going to lie to each other anymore."

"I spoke true. You are the first woman I've ever allowed inside this bedroom."

"What about the fairy? That night—"

He held up a hand for silence. "I sent her home the moment you were out of sight."

Seriously? Glory didn't know whether or not to believe him, but she adored the idea of his claim. "What about Kayla?"

"Sent her home, too. I didn't want her; I wanted you. As you might have guessed, I used her to get your attention."

"Well, you got it," she grumbled, then cringed at the admission.

"I noticed you the first day I moved into town, you know," he said.

He'd noticed her? In a good way? She shivered, feeling as if his hands were already on her, caressing, stoking her desire.

"Cold?" he asked.

She nodded, because she didn't want to admit his words had ignited a storm of desire inside her.

He rose, grabbed the black silk comforter, and tugged it over her. The material was cool against her skin, but damn it, it didn't dampen her need. No, it increased it. Every nerve ending she possessed cried for him.

Falon placed a soft kiss on her lips. Automatically she opened her mouth to take it deeper. He pulled away.

A moan slipped from her.

"Soon," he said as he reclaimed his seat. His voice was tense. "Now, back to the first time I saw you. You were outside with your sisters and selling your potions. At the time, I didn't know they were potions. I just saw a beautiful woman with rosy skin and hair like flame."

She gulped, couldn't speak.

"I wanted you so badly." As he spoke, his fingertip caressed her thigh. "I was making my way toward you when I heard the words 'potion' and 'witch,' and then I couldn't get away from you fast enough."

Maybe he *was* telling the truth about his desire for her. Maybe he did like her just the way she was. Maybe . . .

"I never tortured anyone until I met you," she admitted softly.

His head tilted to the side, and he studied her intently, violet eyes blazing. "Why me?"

"Because," was all she said.

"Glory."

Just tell him. She sighed. "Because I wanted you, and I knew I couldn't have you."

"You wanted me?" he asked huskily.

"You know I did." She watched him from the corner of her eye. He leaned back and stretched his legs out and up, the robe falling away and revealing his strong calves. There were calluses on the bottoms of his feet, as if he often ran through the forest without shoes on. Made her wonder if he wore any clothes at all. Her stomach quivered with the thought.

"Tell me about the first time you noticed me. Please."

Like she could deny him anything now. She thought back to that fateful day, and the quiver in her stomach became a needy ache. Well, another needy ache. She was consumed with them. He'd been moving boxes into this very house. She and her sisters had walked here to welcome him to town. When he spotted them, he'd frozen. Introductions had been made, and he'd smiled coolly but politely at Evie and Godiva. Glory, he'd simply nodded at before looking hastily away.

"I thought you were the most beautiful man I'd ever seen. The sun was shining over you lovingly, and you were sweating. Glistening. You'd taken off your shirt, and dirt smudged your chest."

His lips twitched. "I've noticed you have a thing for manly sweat."

"I do not."

"You placed me in a gladiator cell straight from battle, woman. You like men who do physical labor. Admit it."

"So what! There's nothing wrong with that."

"No, there isn't. It's cute." He didn't give her time to respond. "So why did you want to place me in chains tonight?"

She fought for breath. "You know why."

"Tell me. Say the words aloud."

"I—I'd decided to be with you. Just once. You know, to purge myself of you like you suggested before."

"And you thought you needed chains for that?"

"No. I just . . . I wanted to be in control of everything."

"I don't think so," he said with a shake of his head. "In the forest, you almost came when I pinned your wrists over your head and took control *away* from you. Right now, your nipples are hard, and your skin is besieged by goose bumps. You like where you are."

Her mouth dried as the realization settled inside her. He was right. She loved where she was. She loved that he could do anything he wanted with her, and she couldn't stop him. Didn't want to stop him.

Would one night be enough? She couldn't possibly learn all there was to know about his body, his pleasure . . . her own.

Oh, damn. Already she was doing what she'd sworn she wouldn't: falling deeper, wanting more. Fear dug sharp claws inside her. "Maybe this isn't a good idea," she said, squirming. "Maybe we should stop here and now and part. As friends. I won't hurt you again. You have my word. And you even can keep the pen."

"Oh, I'm keeping the pen," he said darkly, "but I'm not letting you go." He pushed to his feet. He was scowling.

"You're angry. Why? I'm setting you free from our war."

"I hate the thought of you walking out of this house—ever—and I don't understand it." The robe fell from his shoulders and onto the floor, pooling at his feet. She sucked in a breath and simply drank in his magnificence. He was harder than before, his erection so long it stretched higher than his navel.

He grabbed the pen and notebook and started writing. Before she could ask what he was doing, the chains fell away from her. Tentative, she eased up. But she didn't leave; she couldn't make herself, though common sense was screaming that she do so inside her mind. This was what she'd asked for.

"Thank you."

Fight for *me*. Wait. What? No.

"Not yet." He continued writing.

Quick as a snap, her weight returned, her bra and panty set nearly unraveling from the sudden excess. She gasped. Falon finally paused, his electric violet eyes all over her, eating her up.

Never taking his gaze from her, he locked the pen and paper inside a drawer on the nightstand, and then he was on the bed, crawling his way toward her.

Eight

Falon had never wanted a woman the way he wanted Glory.

What was it about her that kept him coming back for more, despite her origins? Despite her actions and her words? She was exquisite, yes. Lush and soft, panting with arousal. She smelled of jasmine and magic, which was a feast to his senses. She was vulnerable yet courageous, daring and volatile. She had never and would never bow to him. She would fight him if he wronged her and always demand the very best from him.

He liked that. Liked who he was when he was with her. She made him be a better person. Honest and giving. Hopeful. And now that he thought about it, everything she'd done to him with that pen hadn't been malicious, it had been . . . foreplay.

His skin was nearly too tight for his bones as he stopped, his palms flattened beside Glory's knees. "Still want to leave?"

"No," she said breathlessly. She leaned back, propping her weight on her elbows. The plump mounds of her breasts strained beyond the bra. God, her curves were lovely.

"Want me?" He barely managed to work the words past the lump in his throat.

"Yes." No hesitation. "Maybe I'm crazy, but yes."

"Good, because I want you. All of you, this time." Fingers sliding under her knee, he lifted. His lips met the inside of her thigh, the cool stone of his necklace brushing against her, and she gasped.

He kissed again, his tongue stroking closer . . . closer . . .

Another gasp from her, followed by a shiver. "Hot," she said, trembling.

"Good?"

"Very."

"Hunter told me you write romance novels."

"Sometimes. Kiss again."

Grinning, he obeyed, running his tongue to the edge of her emerald panties.

"Oh, Goddess." She fisted the sheets. He wanted those hands in his hair, holding on, holding forever.

She was perfect for this bed—his bed—he thought, staring down at her. A bright flame against black silk. "Have you ever thought of me when writing a love scene?"

"Yes." As though she'd read his mind, she gripped his head and pulled him down for another intimate kiss.

His cock throbbed at the thought, at the sight of her, at the taste of her, and he bit the inside of his cheek. Never had a woman appealed to so many of his senses. "What did you fantasize? What did I do to you?"

"Consumed every inch of me," she said, back arching, silently begging for more.

The best kind of answer.

Then she added, "We have one night together. I want everything I fantasized about."

One night. A muscle twitched underneath his eye. He didn't like the time limitation reminder but let it pass. For now. "Did it turn you on, what you wrote? Did you touch yourself?"

"Yes." Reaching up, she thrummed her nipples. "Like this."

"No. Between your legs. Show me."

She lifted her head, her eyes wide and focused on him. Her hands ceased moving on her breasts. "Wh-what?"

"Show me." Desperate for another taste of her, he kissed the center of her panties. They were wonderfully damp. He groaned, his mouth watered. "I want to see what *I've* been imagining."

"Oh." Slowly, so slowly, her hand slid down her stomach. "Like this?"

Licking around the seam of her panties, he fisted his cock. "More."

Slowly, so slowly, her hand circled the apex of her thighs, teasing. "Better?"

Down, he stroked. Up, squeezing tight. "Not yet."

He straightened; their gazes met again and held. "How about this?" Her fingers delved under the emerald lace. Her knees fell apart, and her lashes lowered. She cried out, hips undulating.

Shit. She *looked* like magic just then. Magic he craved. Down and up he continued to work himself, the sight of her so erotic he knew it was branded into his mind for eternity. *Touch her. Learn her.* He'd never wanted anything more.

"Stop," he commanded.

She stilled. Her eyes opened.

He released himself and latched onto her wrist, drawing her hand away from her body. She moaned, bit her bottom lip. "My turn." Leaning down, he lifted her fingers to his mouth and sucked one, then another inside. Her taste coated his tongue. "Like honey." And he needed more.

He laved his tongue inside her navel, gripping her panties and urging them from her legs. He thought she must have kicked them aside, because the bed bounced as he straightened.

"I've wanted to do this for a long time," he said, fingers parting her wet folds. The thin patch of curls shielding her femininity were as bright a red as the hair on her head. Beautiful.

"Do it. *Please.*"

The desperation in her voice mirrored what he felt. He pressed her legs farther apart, spreading . . . spreading . . . God, so pretty. Pink and glistening. He lowered his head and stroked his tongue up the center.

"Falon," she cried.

He circled her clitoris as he sank a finger deep inside.

Her hands fisted in his hair just as he liked. "More."

Another finger joined the first, stretching her. All the while, he sucked and nipped at her. Had he ever tasted anyone so sweet? So addicting? Having her once wouldn't be enough, he realized. He'd need her over and over again. In every way imaginable. He just had to make *her* crave more.

As he licked her, he told her everything he wanted to do to her, how beautiful she was, how he needed her. Soon she was writhing, her head thrashing from side to side. He wanted to see her come. Had to see it, would die if he didn't. And then she was. Her inner walls clamped down on his tongue as she gasped and cried and even screamed.

He pulled from her, his gaze devouring her. Her eyes were closed, her teeth chewing on her bottom lip. Her skin was flushed. So quickly her chest rose and fell, lifting those rosy nipples like berries offered to a god.

A long while passed before she stilled. When she did, her eyelids cracked open.

He stayed just where he was, kneeling between her legs, cock rising proudly. "Like?"

"Like." She reached out and circled it with her fingers. "More."

A moan burst from his lips. "Glory."

"My turn," she said, squeezing him tighter. "I want to taste *you*."

He shook his head. "I don't want to come that way this first time, and if your mouth gets anywhere near my cock, I'll come."

She urged him forward, and he was helpless to do anything but follow wherever she led. "I'll stop before you come."

He found himself on his side. "No, you won't."

She grinned slowly, wickedly and rolled him to his back. Like a sea siren, she rose above him. "Okay, I won't. But you can try to force me to stop like the he-man you are."

God, the thought of her mouth on his shaft, hot and wet . . . her hair spilling over his thighs . . . His head fell back onto the pillow. "All right. But only because you insist."

She chuckled. "Such a martyr."

His cock twitched against her leg, her laughter as arousing as her touch.

Now she gasped. "Mmm, what was that for?"

"I like the sound of your laugh," he admitted. He wanted to hear it. In the morning when he woke up, at lunch, at dinner. Just before bed.

"Sometimes you're as sweet as candy." She crawled down his body until her lips were poised over him. Just like he'd feared, his already intense sense of pleasure revved to a new level. "Probably taste like it, too."

He hoped so. He wanted her to like him, this.

"Tell me what you've fantasized about." Her warm breath stroked him, teased him.

He had to grip the sheets or he would soon be fisting her hair, and then there would be no stopping himself from coming in her mouth. "You. Doing this."

"What else?" She licked the tip, lapping up the glistening moisture already beaded there. "Mmm."

Shit. "Me, inside you."

Her teeth scraped the head, and he groaned at the delicious sensation. "What else?" she demanded. "Tell the truth, and you'll be rewarded. Isn't that how you like to work?"

"Pounding, hot, hard, wild, screaming, you bent over, me taking you from behind. My fingers on your clit, working it. You coming over and over."

As he spoke, she sucked him down, up, down. Taking him all the way to the back of her throat. He barely managed to get the words out, but he kept talking. Anything to continue that delicious pressure. One of her hands kneaded his balls, the other glided up his chest and flicked his nipple.

He felt attacked at every pleasure point, and he loved it. He was bucking, unable to slow his movements, close to the edge. If she kept this up, he really would—*Shit, shit, shit.* Falon grabbed her shoulders and jerked her up. Her lips were swollen and wet, she was panting, her desire clearly renewed.

She moaned in disappointment. "I wasn't done."

"Condom," he said, the word more a snarl. "Now."

Her pupils were dilated, her cheeks flushed as she gazed around wildly. "Where are they?"

Damn, where had he placed them? He searched, saw two silver packets resting on the floor. He'd thought ahead, thank God. He reached out, way out, grabbed one and ripped it open with his teeth. Motions jerky, he straightened and worked it over his length.

His hands settled on Glory's thighs and spread them as

wide as they would go. Her wet, needy core was poised over his cock, just like her mouth had been. "Ride me."

"I thought—you said behind."

"Next time," he said, and then she was pressing, he was arching, and he was all the way inside her, surging deep, taking all of her that he could get.

Her head fell back, her hair tickling his legs. Her breasts arched forward, and he cupped the small of her back, jerking her forward. When those hardened buds abraded his chest, he growled out a, "Fuck yes."

"Feels so good."

"Kiss."

"Please."

He pounded in and out of her as their lips met. His tongue thrust inside, and she eagerly welcomed it, rolling it with her own. Their teeth clashed together once, twice, but that didn't douse the intensity.

Every other woman he'd ever been with faded to the back of his mind as if they'd never existed. There was only Glory. There was only here and now. Eternity—with her.

"Falon," she gasped, and he knew she was close.

He reached between them and thrummed her clitoris. That was all she'd needed. She came in a rush, squeezing at his cock, crying his name again and again, nails raking his chest.

He, too, fell over the edge. And when he came, it was the strongest of his life. Every muscle he possessed locked and released, spasming. Blood rushed through his veins, so hot it blistered everything it touched.

"Glory," he chanted, and it was a prayer for more. More of her, more of this.

Now I've gone and done it, Glory thought. She was snuggled into Falon's side, warm and sated—more so than she'd ever been before. He was asleep, his breathing smooth. Even in slumber, his hand traced up and down her spine as though he couldn't stop touching her.

I love him.

There, she'd admitted it. She did. She loved him. Would

have liked to spend forever with him. Making love, talking, laughing. Impossible.

She was a witch, and there was nothing she could do about that. She possessed magic powers. That wasn't something she could switch off. Not for long, anyway. And Falon would always fear her because of it, no matter what he claimed.

All these months, she'd gagged every time she'd seen her sisters with their boyfriends. Her chest had ached, and she'd assumed the ache was from disgust not love. Now she was experiencing the emotion for herself. The ache for what could not be.

Her eyes filled with tears. She loved Falon, but she couldn't have him. Even though he thought he wanted more from her. He'd said as much before falling asleep. She hadn't answered, hadn't known what to say. But she could just imagine him cringing during their first fight, suspecting her of evildoing. She could just imagine the accusations he'd hurl at her every time something went wrong in his life.

That would destroy her. Better to walk away now, as planned. It was the only way her heart could survive.

Gingerly, Glory slipped from his body, from the bed. Her legs were so shaky she almost fell. Since she'd written herself here without any real clothes, she borrowed a pair of sweats and a T-shirt from Falon.

Before she put them on, she held them to her nose and inhaled deeply. They smelled of him, like soap, dark spices, and strength. A tear fell. Once dressed, she walked to the edge of the bed. Still he slept soundly. Must not have gotten any rest these past few days. He'd probably feared she'd attack with her pen at any moment.

What if things could be different? What if there was a chance they could make it work?

He looked so peaceful. His dark hair was in disarray against the pillow. His face was flushed with lingering pleasure. The sheet had fallen, revealing the entire expanse of his mouthwatering chest.

Who are you trying to fool? Make it work? Please. Those silly tears began falling in earnest. She was going to miss him. Taunting him, being with him, sparring with him, had been fun. He was witty, and he was warm. He was wild and protective and a lover who cared more about her pleasure than his own.

His fingers flexed over the part of the mattress she'd occupied.

Her heart stopped beating. One step, two, she backed away from the bed. Any moment, he would probably wake up. What would he say to her? What would he do?

Doesn't matter.

Glory pivoted on her heel and stalked quietly from his house. They only lived a mile apart, and she'd traveled the forest many times before, so she entered the night without hesitation.

She left her heart with Falon.

Nine

When Falon woke up alone, he was not happy.

When he rushed to Glory's house and discovered she had packed a bag and taken off, telling no one where she planned to stay, he was angry.

When he drove around town, asking if anyone had seen her and found that no one had, he was beyond furious!

Why had she left him?

To punish him? He didn't think so. They were past that point now, he knew it, and she wasn't the type to do so without gloating—something he loved about her. Loved. Yes. He loved her. She was his woman, the other piece of him. He knew that now, and so there would be no more denying it. The fact that she was a witch didn't matter anymore. He'd rather have her and her powers than be without her.

Had she left because she was . . . scared?

Yes, he thought. *Yes*. Well, he was scared, too. New relationships were always scary, but this one more so than most. They'd been at odds for a while. But they'd also just had the best sex of his life. Addictive sex. He'd just have to prove they could be together, that he wouldn't hurt her, wouldn't stop loving her. But how?

You still have the pen.

The thought slammed into him with the force of a jackhammer, and he grinned. He rushed back home.

Glory was inside her Ford Taurus one moment and back home the next. Brow puckered in confusion, she gazed around. "What the hell?"

Her sisters were sitting in the living room, reading *Witch Weekly*. They glanced up at the sound of her voice.

"Oh, there you are," Godiva said.

"Where have you been?" Evie asked. "Falon's been desperate to find you."

She gulped. Rubbed her stomach. Falon. The pen. Damn it! He was using the pen. Why, why, why? She'd almost made a clean getaway. Had almost given them a clean break. Clean. Yeah, right.

A knock sounded at the door.

She whipped around, eyes wide. Oh, Great Goddess. Was it Falon?

Another knock, this one harder.

"Well, aren't you going to answer it?" Godiva asked.

"Open up, Glory. I know you're in there. I made sure of it."

Falon's deep, dark voice filled her head, and she almost fainted. He'd truly come here. Why? He could have written her anywhere, but he'd written her inside her own home and knocked on her door.

"Glory!" Evie laughed. "Don't just stand there."

If he was going to ask—again—for more from her than one night, she wouldn't be able to turn him down. She'd sobbed like a baby the entire drive away from town. In fact, her face was probably swollen and red even now. Where she'd been headed, she hadn't known. She'd just needed to put distance between them, or she would have forgotten all the reasons to stay away and gone to him.

"Please," he said, and he sounded tortured. She could very easily imagine his hands resting on the door, his forehead pressing into the wood.

Shaky legs walked her to the entrance. Her palm was sweating so she had trouble twisting the knob. What was she going to find? Slowly, she pulled open the only thing blocking the man she loved from her view.

Falon stood there, wearing a trench coat and nothing else. Not even shoes. She blinked in surprise. *So* not what she had expected.

"What are you doing here?" she managed to get out.

Her sisters crowded behind her.

"Looking good, Falon," Evie said.

"Nice," Godiva said.

His cheeks bloomed bright red, but his attention remained focused on Glory. "I want you in my life."

Her stomach twisted painfully. "That wouldn't be smart. We'd fight, you'd hate me, fear my powers."

As she spoke, he was shaking his head. "You're different from the other witches I knew, I know that deep down. Even though you had every right to be angry with me, you were never malicious."

"You think so now, but what about tomorrow? Or the next day?"

Again he shook his head. "Not gonna happen."

"You can't guarantee that."

"But I *can* guarantee that I love you."

Her eyes nearly bugged out, his words echoing inside her brain. "Wh-what?"

"I love you."

Godiva gasped. "Oh my Goddess. Did you hear that, Evie?"

"I'm standing right here. Of course I heard. Glory, what do you have to say to him?"

"Give me a chance," he begged. "I don't deserve it, I know I don't, but I'll do anything to get it. I need you in my life."

She covered her mouth with a shaky hand. This was too much, too good to believe.

He forged ahead. "You once came to my door, wanting a night with me. Now I've come to your door, wanting an eternity with you. I'm here, just as you were, in nothing but a coat. My heart is yours."

Okay, now the trench made sense. Dear Goddess, that

meant he was naked underneath. Her blood heated with the knowledge.

"Please don't send me away. I need you. You're a witch, yes, but I don't fear your powers. After last night, I'm grateful for them."

"Oh, Glory!" Godiva brushed away her tears. "This is the most romantic thing I've ever seen. Don't send him away!"

"If you don't take him," Evie said, "I will."

"Hunter," was all Glory managed to get out.

"He's only good for the night. Maybe I'm looking for a day man."

Glory elbowed her sister in the stomach.

Evie backed off, taking Godiva with her. "Come on. Let's give the lovebirds their privacy and listen from the kitchen where Glory can't assault us." Footsteps echoed.

"I love you, Glory." He dropped to his knees. "Please, say something to me. Anything."

Could he truly love her? Her? Could he live with a witch and not fear for his life? She studied his face. Lines of tension edged his eyes and mouth. His lips were drawn tight. He was pale. His hair looked as if he'd plowed his hands through it for hours.

He really was worried she'd say no.

"Last night wasn't enough," he rushed on. "Forever probably won't be enough. You're all I can think about, all I crave. I'm addicted to you. I know you're scared, but I vow to you, here and now, to protect you, cherish you, trust you. I know you aren't evil. That's something you don't have to fear. I know you're good and pure and—"

"I love you, too," she finally said. Making a leap, trusting him like he was trusting her.

He was on his feet in the next instant, jerking her into his arms. "Thank God. I would have had to write you into another scene if you'd rejected me." He placed little kisses all over her face. "Not that I would have minded."

She laughed as she wound her arms around his neck. "Are you sure about this?"

"I've never been surer about anything in my life. You're *my* witch, and I love you. I can't believe I was stupid enough to ever push you away." Grinning, he spun her around.

Her head fell back, hair flying, and she laughed again, joyful, content.

He stopped, peered down at her, his grin melting away, burned as it was by desire. "Okay, now I'm turned on. That laugh of yours . . ."

"Come on," she said, leading him to her bedroom and earning winks from her sisters, who stood in the kitchen entry. "I have the perfect spell for that." She shut the door, then proceeded to work her magic all over his body.

IT'S IN HIS KISS ...
(Title hummed to the tune of Cher singing 'The Shoop Shoop Song')

P. C. Cast

*To Gyna Snowater
with love from P. C. Castwater.
We rock when we team up, baby!*

One

"All right, we're going to start a new unit, so get out your fold-
ers and get ready to take notes," Summer said in what she
liked to hope was her best Teacher Voice.

"What's the new unit, Miss S.?" called a male voice from
the rear of the class.

Summer frowned. Was it disrespectful to call her Miss S.?
Oh, Goddess! Another question she'd have to ask her sister on
the phone tonight. She cleared her throat and tried to look severe and ten years older. "Shakespeare's *Romeo and Juliet.*"

The girls in the class sighed and looked dreamy. The boys
groaned.

"Hey, I hear there's sex in that play," came the same voice
from the rear of the class.

"Well, yes. Actually it's a play about star-crossed lovers
whose families won't let them be together," said Summer.

The girls smiled. The boys rolled their eyes.

"So that means there's sex in it. Lots, actually," Summer
said before her mind caught up with her mouth.

"Cool!"

"Of course, it's all written in Elizabethan English," she

hastily amended, reconnecting with the excellent control she usually had over everything she said or did.

"Sucks fairy butt," said a surly voice from the other side of the room.

"So we won't get it?" asked a cute blonde in the front row who wore a short, pink cheerleading uniform with FIGHTING FAIRIES emblazoned across her perky bosom.

"Don't worry. I'll make sure you get it," Summer said.

"Awesome!" chorused several annoying male voices, accompanied by giggles from the girls.

"Hey, Miss Smith, can we watch the movie?" asked the cheerleader.

"The one that shows Juliet's boobs!" called the irritating male voice. Which kid was that, anyway? Maybe she should move him up closer. (As if she wanted the annoying child *closer* to her? Ugh.)

"I'll think about the movie," Summer said firmly. "What we *are* going to see is an art exhibit of Pre-Raphaelite paintings that features Ford Madox Brown's famous *Romeo and Juliet* balcony scene."

The classroom went dead silent. Finally a pleasantly plump redheaded girl who sat smack in the center of the class smiled up at Summer through extra-thick glasses and a face full of unfortunate zits and said, "You mean we're taking a field trip?"

"Yes, we're taking a field trip. Tomorrow."

There was a general class-wide sigh of relief and several high fives accompanied by murmurs of "Dude! That means no class tomorrow!"

"Okay, don't forget to work on the Shakespearian vocab I gave you at the beginning of class. It's due the day after tomorrow, and then we'll begin—" Summer was saying when—thank the blessed Goddess—the bell rang that signaled the end of the period as well as the end of the school day.

"High school sucks," Summer muttered to herself as the last pubescent boy filed out of her classroom, almost running into the doorframe as he tried to keep his eyes on her cleavage as long as humanly possible. When the coast was clear, she dropped her head to her desk, and with a satisfying thud began to bang it not so softly. "I'm not a fool for teaching high school. I'm not a fool for teaching high school . . ." she spoke the litany in time to her head banging.

"Oh, honey. Just give up. We're all fools. That's one of the things that makes a truly great teacher: foolishness. The second thing starts with a *W*."

Summer looked up to see a tall, slender woman dressed all in black. Her acorn-colored hair was shoulder length and wavy in a disarrayed I'm-so-naughty style. She offered her hand to Summer with a smile just as the door to her classroom opened again.

"What?" The tall, slender woman whipped around, skewering the hapless teenage boy with her amber eyes.

The boy's eyes flitted from the scowling woman to Summer, and back to the scowler again.

"Mr. Rom? Isn't that your name?" asked the slender woman in a no-nonsense voice.

The boy nodded nervously.

"And what is it you wished to bother Miss Smith with?"

The boy's mouth opened, closed, and then opened again. "I have my journals to turn in. The ones that were due yesterday," he finally blurted.

The amber-eyed woman glanced down at Summer. "Do you take late work, Miss Smith?"

Summer swallowed. "No. I mean, isn't that the English Department's policy?"

"Of course it is." The slender woman raised one arched brow at the boy and trapped him with her sharp gaze. "No. Late. Work. Means no late work. Now, go away, child, before you truly anger me."

"Y-yes ma'am!" the boy's voice broke as he backed hastily from the room and then scampered away.

"How in the world did you do that?" Summer said, gaping at the tall, young woman.

She smiled and held out her hand. "I'm Jenny Sullivan, your across-the-hall neighbor and fellow English teacher, as well as a Certified Discipline Nymph. Sorry, I would have introduced myself last week at the beginning of the semester, but I was on that delicious staff development trip to Santa Fe."

Summer blinked blankly at her, so Jenny hurried on. "You know, Discipline in the Desert 101. Goddess! There are just so many applications for desert discipline in the high school classroom." She shook herself. "Anyhoodles, just got back today and heard that you'd taken your sister, Candy Cox's, place on our staff, and thought I better welcome you." She paused and glanced at the closing door after the student. "I see I arrived just in time."

"What's the thing that starts with a *W*?" Summer asked.

"Whips?" Jenny said hopefully.

"Whips? We can use whips here? Candy never told me that."

"Wait—wait. I think we're having a communication difficulty. You asked me for a *W* word and, naturally, I thought of whips."

"Okay, no. Let's start over. You said foolishness and something that starts with a *W* make us great teachers."

"Oh!" Jenny brightened. "Sadly, the answer to that is not *whips*, though it should be," she finished under her breath.

"Then it's . . ." Summer prompted.

"Whatever."

"Pardon?"

"The other thing. It's the Whatever Factor. Honey, I can already tell that your problem is you give a shit too much about what the hormones and germs are thinking."

"The hormones and germs?"

"Aka teenagers."

"Oh."

"Darling Summer, you need to understand that teenagers rarely think." Jenny patted her arm. "Come on, let's lock up, and then I'll treat you to a drink at Knight Caps."

Summer started to grab her keys and her purse, then her eyes flitted to the clock on the wall. "Uh, Jenny. It's barely three. Isn't that too early to drink?"

Jenny hooked her arm through Summer's and pulled her toward the door. "When you teach high school, it's never too early to drink. Plus, rumor has it you ate lunch in the vomitorium. You'll need a good healthy dose of martini to cleanse your system of those toxins."

"Vomitorium?" Summer asked as Jenny took her hand and led her toward the door.

"Just another word for the cafeteria. And, yes. You should be afraid. Very afraid."

"Wow. Teaching is so not like I imaged when I was in college."

"Darling, nothing is like you imaged in college. This is the real world," Jenny paused and then snorted. "Okay, well, Mysteria isn't actually part of the real world in the *real*ity sense, but you know what I mean. College is college. Work is work. Teaching is work."

Summer sipped her sour apple martini contemplatively. "Teenagers are a lot more disgusting than I thought they'd be."

"Preaching to the choir here," Jenny said.

"I mean, Candy told me to change my major to anything that didn't involve teaching, and I just thought she was, well . . ." she trailed off, obviously not wanting to speak badly about her sister.

"Here, let me help you. You thought Candy was just old, burned-out, and disgruntled. And that you, being twenty-some-odd years younger and ready to take on the world, would have an altogether different experience with *touching the future*." Jenny said the last three words with exaggerated drama while she clutched her bosom (with the hand that wasn't clutching her martini).

"Yeah, sadly, that's almost exactly what I thought."

"Until your first day of real teaching?"

"Yep."

"And now you want to run shrieking for the hills?"

"Yep again."

Jenny laughed. "Don't worry. A few short lessons in discipline from an expert—that would be *moi*, by the by—and another martini or two, mixed with one of Hunter's excellent five-meat pizzas, which I'll split with you, will fix you right up."

"Okay, except I never have more than one martini, and, well, I'm a vegetarian."

"One martini? Sounds like you're a little tightly wrapped, girlfriend."

"I like to think of it as maintaining a healthy control."

Jenny rolled her amber eyes. "In my professional Discipline

Nymph opinion, I might mention that 'healthy control' is often an oxymoron. And you're a vegetarian? Really?"

Summer chose to ignore Jenny's comment about control and said, "I'm really a vegetarian. I don't eat anything that had a face. Makes me want to throw up a little in the back of my throat even to think about it. So get my half with cheese and veggies."

"Cheese and veggies on your half it is." She motioned for one of the fairies to come take their order and then frowned when the pink-haired, scantily clad waitress ignored her and instead giggled musically at something a werewolf at the bar had said. Jenny lifted one perfectly manicured finger and started swirling it around in the air. "Looks like girlfriend over there needs a little discipline lesson. She needs to learn it's best not to ignore me when I—"

Summer grabbed Jenny's finger. "Do. Not. Use. Magic!"

Jenny yelped in surprise and put her finger away. "What gives?"

"Did Candy never mention what kind of, ur, *magic* I have?"

Jenny's frown deepened. "Well, no. Candy didn't have any magic, or at least she didn't until she hooked up with that handsome werewolf of hers. I think she felt kinda weird that everyone else had some sort of magic, so she didn't talk much about it. Plus, you know school's supposed to be a Magic Free Zone. There was no need to go into it much. Why? What's your magic?"

"Opposite."

"Huh?"

Summer sighed. "My magic is opposite magic. Any spell worked around me instantly turns opposite, or at the very least becomes totally messed-up and twisted around. That's another reason I decided to teach."

"To really fuck with the teenage mind by screwing up all the furtive little magics they attempt at school?"

"No, though that does sound like it might be a fun by-product. The truth is that I wanted to get a job back home in Mysteria. I really like it here. While I was in college, I missed . . ." She hesitated, trying to decide how much to say. "Ur, I uh, missed the people who live here," she finally decided on. And it was true. She had missed the people—some of them more than others. Actually, one of them more than others. "Anyway, I wanted to live in Mysteria, but I didn't want to constantly be messing up people's magic."

Jenny's expression said she knew there was more to the "Ur, I uh, missed the people who live here" nonsense, but the only comment she made was, "Oh, I get it. So working in the high school, a Magic Free Zone, sounded perfect."

"In theory," Summer said, mournfully sipping her martini.

"Hey, cheer up. It could be worse."

"How?"

"You could be teaching at the grade school. At that age they touch you *and* pee in their pants." Jenny shuddered. "Yeesh!"

Summer sighed. "This might fall under Emergency Procedures and require one more drink."

"Of course it does, and of course you do. I'll get it and order our pizza." Jenny slid her lithe body from their booth. "I'll go to the counter and order it. Although I do wonder what would happen if my kick-the-flirting-waitress-fairy-in-her-lazy-ass spell went opposite."

"You don't want to know. It's always a true mess and—"

A gale of giggles and the door opening caused Summer to lose her train of thought and glance over her shoulder at the entrance to the bar. Then she sucked air. Her face blanched white and then flushed a bright, painful pink.

"Oh, Goddess!" Summer whispered. "It's Kenneth."

TWO

"Yeah, it's Kenny the Fairy. So? What's the big deal?" Jenny was saying when the gaze of the tall, blond, male fairy in the middle of the new group of laughing girl fairies lighted on Summer and, smiling, he hurried over to their table.

"Hey, Summer! You're back!"

"Hi, Ken," Summer said, managing to stiffly return his hug. "Yeah. That's me. Back. For a week." And she blushed an even hotter shade of pink.

"Come on Kenny-benny! You promised to buy us mushroom pizza and those fizzy blue hypnotic drinks," pouted a pair of identical twin sliver-haired, gold-winged fairies.

Kenny gave Summer an apologetic smile. "Sorry, gotta go. I'll call you later, okay? Is your number still the same?"

"Yeah. The same. Still." Summer tried to smile, but her face ended up looking more like an enthusiastic grimace.

"Oh, no no no. This is so damn sad. You have a crush on Fairy Kenny," Jenny said when they were alone again.

"Shhh!" Summer hushed her. "He might hear you."

"Oh, please. He's too busy with the slut sisters and their trampy friends. Hang on." Jenny turned, faced the counter, and nailed the giggling pink waitress with her stern gaze. Her voice carried easily across the bar, slicing through the chattering fairies like a saber through a butterfly-infested flower garden. "Esmeralda, we need another round of martinis and a veggie pizza. Now. And do not make me repeat myself." The waitress gulped, nodded, and scampered off to place their order. Jenny briskly brushed her hands against one another, as if pleased at a job well done, then she sat back in the booth, turning her full attention on Summer. "Okay, give. Why did you turn into the Incredible Cardboard Woman the instant Kenny-benny spoke to you?"

"I like him," Summer whispered, upending her martini and patting on the stem as she tried to coax the last of the liquid from the glass.

"Yeah, so? That doesn't explain the stiffness."

Summer sighed. "He and I grew up together. We were best friends, or at least we were until we hit puberty and I realized how gorgeous and perfect he is. Since then things have been kinda awkward between us."

"Kenny's been through puberty? Who knew?"

"Stop it! He's cute beyond belief. Don't you think he looks just like Legolas?" she said, shooting furtive glances at Ken.

"I guess so, only gayer. If that's possible." Jenny shrugged. "But whatever floats your boat."

"He definitely floats my boat," Summer said.

"Does he know that?"

"Huh?"

"You said you guys grew up together, and then things changed when you started crushing on him. Maybe you should let him know why things changed."

"Oh, I don't know about that. I'm not very good at—"

"Here are your drinks, ladies. Your pizza should be right out," gushed the waitress as she sloshed their new martinis down on the table in front of them.

"Thank you, Esmeralda. How kind of you to finally show us special attention."

"I—I just didn't realize it was you, Jenny," the fairy said. "Discipline Nymphs always get special attention at Knight Caps."

"As well they should," Jenny said smoothly, bowing her head in gracious acknowledgment of the fairy's apology.

The waitress hurried away, and Jenny turned her gaze back to Summer. "So, you need to let Kenny know you have the hots for him."

"Ack!" Summer sputtered, mid–martini sip. She swallowed, coughed, and said, "Jenny, like I was saying, I'm not good at, well, the guy-girl thing. It's just so—I don't know—unpredictable."

"Oh, please. Kenny-benny isn't a guy. He's a fairy. And they're really predictable. They frolic—they flirt—they scamper."

"I happen to think there's more to Kenny than that, but as I said, I'm not good at the social interaction thing."

"You have issues with guys."

"No, just with guys I like."

"Okay, fine. Just with guys you like. What are you going to do about it?"

"Huh?"

Jenny snorted. "Darling, you're definitely old enough to take the bull by the horns. Figuratively and literally."

Summer took another drink of her martini. "You're right. I know you're right. But knowing and doing are two different things."

"Look, you don't seem especially tongue-tied right now. Actually, you've been rather amusing, so you're definitely not conversationally impaired. Just talk to the fairy."

"I'm only conversationally impaired when I have to talk to someone I want to sleep with. I like you, and you're attractive and all, but I definitely don't want to sleep with you."

Jenny preened. "Nice of you to notice I'm attractive." Then her arched brows went up. "Hang on—you want to have hot, nasty sex with fairy boy?"

"No, I'd like him to make tender, slow, amazing love to me," Summer said, blushing again.

"Are you sure?" Jenny studied her carefully. "I'm getting the need-to-have-it-uncontrolled-and-hot-and-hard vibe from you, and I'm rarely wrong about my vibes."

"Jeesh, I'm sure. I don't do uncontrolled. Enough already."

"Okay, okay. You two are friends, right?"

"We were."

"You can still play off that. Hey, aren't you living in your sister's cabin at the edge of the woods?"

"Yeah."

"So, invite fairy boy over for dinner. You know," she winked, "for old time's sake. Then jump his bones," Jenny paused, rolled her eyes, and added, "slowly and tenderly."

Summer chewed her lip. "I don't know . . ."

"Take it from me. When dealing with men, fairy or otherwise, it's always best to be in charge and direct. Plus, you like control, and you'll definitely be in control if the date's on your turf."

"I'll think about it," Summer said, her eyes moving back to where Ken was perched in the middle of the group of fawning fairies at the bar.

"What you should think about is taking another gulp of that martini, putting on some of this nasty red lipstick, fluffing your hair, and marching yourself right over to that bar and extending the big invite to fairy boy." Jenny fished in her purse until she pulled out a tube of lipstick called Roaring Red and tossed it to Summer. Then she gave the giggling fairies a contemptuous glance. "You're cuter than those pastel pansies; don't let them intimidate you. Female fairies would lust after a snake if you put jeans on it and called it Bob. Everyone knows how easy they are, and no one takes them seriously."

"I guess I could." Summer gnawed her lip again. "I mean, we are old friends."

"Exactly."

She took a big drink of her martini, letting the alcohol burn through her body. Another gale of giggles erupted from the fairies, and Summer seemed to shrink in on herself. "I can't. I just can't. It's so . . . I don't know . . . *unplanned.*"

"Girlfriend, life is unplanned. Get used to it. Okay, how about this deal: if you ask Kenny-benny over for dinner, I'll take my class on the field trip to the gallery with you tomorrow and be sure the hormones and germs act right."

Summer sat up straighter. "You'll come with me?"

Jenny shrugged. "I'm getting ready to start *Romeo and Juliet* with my freshmen, so I might as well. Plus, your students will probably behave dreadfully and need an ever-so-firm disciplinary hand," she finished with a gleeful smile.

"Promise?"

"That I'll jump squarely into your students' shit? Absolutely."

"Not that. Do you promise you'll come with me if I ask Ken out?"

"Yep."

"Even if he says no?"

"Don't put that negative energy out there. Of course he'll say yes, and of course, regardless of the fairy, I'll go with you tomorrow. Now gird yourself and go ask him out."

"Fine. Okay. I can do this." Summer gulped the last of the martini, ran her fingers through her curly blond hair, and in two quick swipes of Jenny's lipstick completed the transformation from Nice New Teacher into tipsy Discipline Nymph Trainee.

Just before she stood up, Jenny motioned for her to lean across the table. "Here, this will help." She deftly unbuttoned the top two buttons of Summer's blouse. "That's better. I'd do a quick make-your-nipples-hard spell, but what with your opposite magic, I'm afraid of what would happen."

"Don't even think about it," Summer said. She stood up and tossed back her hair.

"You are beautiful and powerful and desirable. Just keep telling yourself that."

"Okay. Okay. Okay." Nodding woodenly, Summer made her way to the bar.

"Kenny-benny, sweetie-weetie! You have a glob of cheese on your lip. Want me to get that for you, baby?" One of the twin fairies cooed.

"No, let me!" said her sister, using a tip of her wing to push her sibling out of her way so she could angle her lithe body closer to Ken.

"Girls, girls—settle! I can wipe my lip myself," Ken said, laughing.

"We know you can, honey-bunny!" said one twin.

"But it's so much more fun if we help you!" trilled the other twin.

None of them noticed Summer. At all. So she drew a deep

breath, closed her eyes, and told herself, *When I speak, I'm going to pretend to be Jenny.* She opened her eyes, lowered her voice, and said, "Excuse me, I need a word with Ken." Summer almost jumped at the strong, stern tone she had (somehow) used. All of the fairies, including the ditzy waitress who was carrying their veggie pizza from the oven, turned to stare at her. *I'm Jenny . . . a Certified Discipline Nymph . . . beautiful . . . powerful . . . desirable . . .*

"Hi, Summer," Ken grinned at her. "Do you want me?"

"Y-yes, I do," Summer stumbled briefly, but then she straightened her spine and lifted her chin. "Could I speak with you? Privately?" She didn't let herself look at the scantily clad, beautiful fairies.

"Okeydokey!" Ken said. "Hang on, girls. I'll be right back." He took Summer's elbow and moved her to an unoccupied spot down the counter. "What's up?"

"Ken, I'd like to . . . um . . ." She swallowed the lump that had suddenly risen in her throat and made another attempt. "What I mean is would you want to—" Thankfully, a fit of ridiculously loud coughing from Jenny interrupted Summer's babble and gave her a chance to pull herself together. "Ken, would you like to come over tomorrow night and have dinner with me?" she finally managed to say.

"Yeah, sounds cool. Are you living at your sister's cabin?"

"My sister's cabin. Yes."

"Great. So, I'll see you about eight?"

"About eight. Yes."

"Want me to bring something to drink?"

"Something to drink. Yes."

"Okay, see you tomorrow at eight!" He smiled again and went back to his seat at the bar.

"Okay. Yes. Yes. Okay," she told the air as she moved back to their table.

"Here, have the rest of my martini. You look shell-shocked. Are you okay? What did he say? How did it go?"

"Yes. He said yes." Summer said and then gulped Jenny's martini.

Three

✳

"Hangover. Ugh, I sooo have a hangover." Summer shakily sipped the sludge that almost passed for coffee she'd gotten from the teachers' lounge.

"I'm usually not a big proponent of control, but three martinis was probably one and a half too many," Jenny said. She studied Summer with a critical eye. "Good thing you're young. Only the very young can still look as good as you do this morning *and* deal with a wicked hangover."

"You keep talking like you're so much older than me, but you can't be over thirty," Summer said irritably.

"Oh, girlfriend, don't be silly. I'm two hundred and thirty-five. And a half."

Summer choked on her coffee.

"Discipline Nymphs are some of the most long-lived of the nymphs. It's because discipline is good for body and soul."

"I had no idea," Summer said.

"Well, girlfriend, you do now."

"Hey, speaking of stuff I'm confused about, would you please explain to me why a Certified Discipline Nymph is so roll-your-eyes about my control issues? Isn't control pretty much just another word for discipline?"

"Oh, my poor, deluded young friend. Let Ms. Sullivan help you. Discipline is what you have to be good at so you can release control. Girlfriend, you're too tightly wrapped. Flex those discipline muscles, relax that snoreable übercontrol you carry around with you, and you'll be amazed at the results."

"I dunno . . ." Summer said doubtfully. "But I can tell you I never thought of discipline as the antithesis of control before."

"Gives you a whole new outlook on discipline, doesn't it?"

"You're right about that. I can tell you that I'm going to start flexing my discipline muscles with the hormones and germs in my class. Like you said last night, I'm only going to call them by their last names, miss or mister whoever. It's much more formal; much more *disciplined*."

"Well done, you!" Jenny smiled encouragement. "I knew you'd be a quick study. Speaking of the germs and hormones, let's round them up. I do believe I see the field trip bus waiting for us out there." As they herded the students onto the bus, Jenny called, "You did clear this with Barnabas, the gallery owner, didn't you?"

"I sent him an e-mail saying that I'd be bringing a busload of kids to view the exhibit today. I got a reply saying that would be fine."

"Good. I was worried for a second, because I thought I heard that Barnabas had left for a vacation to France. The nymph gossip said that the poor gay vampire took off to France because he was inconsolable about Hunter Knight falling for Evie Tawdry instead of him."

"But Hunter's not gay," Summer said as they followed the last student on the bus and took their seats near the front.

"Moxie, we've got them all," Jenny called to the short, squat, green-haired bus driver.

"Moving out, Ms. Sullivan," Moxie growled, let loose the emergency brake, and pulled the bus out onto the street.

"What is she?" Summer whispered. Eyes focused on the back of Moxie's green hair, she was sure she saw one of the thick strands move of its own accord.

"Mox? She's a troll. They make the best bus drivers. They

234 • P. C. Cast

don't put up with shit." And then, as if she literally had eyes in the back of her head, Moxie's head turned almost all the way around and she barked, "Sam Wheeler! Get your big, nasty boots off my bus seat. You are not at home. Put them up there again, and I'll take those feet off at the ankles. I'd much rather clean up blood than pig crap."

"Yes ma'am," Sam said sheepishly.

"See? Trolls know their discipline. Anyway, where were we? Oh yeah. No, Hunter's definitely *not* gay, as everyone, including Barnabas, knows. But I feel kinda sorry for the poor gay vamp anyway; unrequited love gets me right here." Jenny fisted her hand over her heart.

"Really? I wouldn't have pegged you for the sentimental type, Ms. Discipline."

"I'm not sentimental. I'm romantic."

"A discipline romantic?"

"Girlfriend, you have so much to learn. Romance is best with a healthy touch of discipline. Especially if it involves whips and handcuffs. And since we're on the romance subject, what's on the menu tonight with Kenny-benny?"

"I really wish you wouldn't call him that."

"Sorry. I'll be good. Promise."

Summer noted that Jenny's sparkly eyes said she was the opposite of sorry, but she decided not to say anything. Plus, she really did want to go over what she was going to cook for Ken. *She was going to cook for Ken!* Just the thought had her stomach rolling with nerves. She cleared her throat. "Okay, I thought I'd make a nice salad, with lots of lovely greens, and then have spaghetti with tofu and, of course, garlic bread, and maybe finish up with a big slice of peach cobbler. What do you think?"

"I think I was asking about your lingerie and not about dinner."

"But you asked me what was on the menu tonight."

"Yes, and I expected you to say something like, 'Why, Jenny, me and my lovely black panty and bra set are definitely the first three courses.'" At Summer's blank look, Jenny's eyes got big and round. "Oh, Goddess! When you asked him over for dinner, you *really* meant dinner."

Summer frowned. "Of course I did."

"Oh, um. Okay, well, tofu spaghetti sounds just dandy then."

Summer seemed not to have heard her. "Ohmygoddess! Do you think Ken thinks *I'm* on the menu, too?"

"Let's hope so," Jenny said.

"No!" Summer gasped. "That's not what—I mean, I wasn't thinking that. Exactly. Or at least not on our *first* date. That's isn't in accordance with my plan. We weren't going to have sex until the third date." She chewed her bottom lip. "Jenny, have I messed up?"

"Are you kidding? Kenny-ben—ur—I mean, Kenny isn't exactly Mr. Forceful. If he comes on to you, and you don't want to do him, just say no."

"I might want to do him," Summer whispered.

"Okay, then just say no nicely."

"But that wasn't what I was planning."

"Oh, please! Would you loosen up? If you want to have sex, then boink the fairy. If you don't, then wait until the third or even the thirtieth date. Whatever."

Summer fanned herself. "I'm never going to be able to do this."

Jenny peered down her nose at her as if she were an unusual specimen under a magnifying glass. "Darling, didn't you date at all in college?"

Summer's cheeks flushed pink. "Yeah, of course I did."

"And?"

"And nothing. If I liked the guy, I decided when we'd, well, *do it*, and then we did it."

"Always according to your well-controlled plan," Jenny supplied.

"Always."

"Oh my Goddess! You've really never been swept off your feet by hot, sticky, steamy, raunchy sex."

When a couple of the kids sitting closest to the front of the bus gasped and laughed, Jenny turned her narrowed eyes on them, instantly quieting their tittering.

Summer frowned and lowered her voice. "No, and I don't think I'd like what you just described. It sounds so . . . so . . ."

"So out-of-control?"

"Yes. Exactly. And I'm not particularly good with out-of-control."

"That is shameful," Jenny said.

"Well, it's the way I am. And there's nothing wrong with the way I am," Summer said, more than a little defensively.

"Oh, girlfriend, I don't mean to make you feel bad about yourself. It's just that you're missing so much."

Summer shrugged. "I don't know. I had fun in college."

"I don't mean frat banging and one-night stands. I mean love."

"Huh?"

"Girlfriend, don't you know that love can't be controlled and planned and prepackaged or hermetically sealed to be taken out when it fits into your schedule?"

Summer chewed her lip and thought about Ken. When she spoke, her voice was so soft that Jenny had to tilt her head toward her to hear her. "I was kinda thinking that Ken would be the guy I let myself fall in love with. You know, college is over. He's here in my hometown. He's literally the boy next door."

"I don't know. It just sounds so clinical. And love is definitely not clinical." Jenny shook her head. "No. This will never do." She tapped a long, manicured red fingernail against her skintight black slacks. "What if I did a spell on you—one that I meant to be the opposite of what I really cast?" Before Summer could protest, she hurried on. "I could cast a control spell on you. That should get zapped by your opposite magic and allow you to relax with him tonight. Then what happens between you can at least happen naturally. Right?"

"Jenny, you can't ever, *ever* cast any kind of spell on me. It won't work like you expect. I guess the opposite magic isn't exactly the right way to describe what I have. It's more like opposite squared. It doesn't *just* make the spell reverse; it also makes it wacky."

"Define wacky."

"Okay, here's the perfect example. When I was in high school, Glory Tawdry thought she would help me out. It was right before our senior homecoming dance, and I didn't actually have a date with Ken, but I'd told him that I'd meet him there and would save all the best dances for him."

Jenny shook her head. "This has been going on between you two for years, hasn't it?"

"This?"

"Waffling. Unfulfilled romance. Missed opportunities. All because of your insane need for control."

"Yes. And my need for control is not insane. Anyway, as per usual for my high school days, overnight I grew the biggest, nastiest zit right in the middle of my forehead. No amount of makeup would cover it. It was like I had a third eye."

"Yuck."

"Yeah. So I asked Glory to cast a zit spell on me."

"Goddess! There's such a thing as a zit spell?"

Summer nodded. "She got the spell from her sister, Evie. You know she's a vengeance witch."

"Oh, that's right. Okay, go on."

"Well, it should have been simple enough. I wanted the zit gone. I have opposite magic. Glory casts a spell to fill my face with zits, which should have totally *cleared* my face of zits."

"It does sound simple enough."

"It didn't work out that way."

"What happened?"

"It cleared my face. Of everything."

"Everything?"

"Absolutely everything. I had no gigantic zit, but I also had no eyes, nose, or mouth."

"Shit! What did you do?"

"Freaked out. I knew it was bad, because I couldn't see anything, but when Glory started screaming, 'Oh great Goddess help! Her face is gone,' I lost it. I tried to scream with her, couldn't, so I did what any normal girl would do when scared shitless and utterly blind."

"You ran?"

"Yep. And promptly fell over my cool fuchsia beanbag chair, smacking my head on the corner of my very large and very metallic stereo cabinet, which negated the spell. Thank the Goddess."

"So your face came back?"

Summer nodded. "Along with the Cyclops zit. See, that's what happens when I think I'm smart, take a chance, and let my opposite magic do its thing. It never works exactly opposite. It's more like sideways, around-the-corner, upside-down magic. And the spell only goes away if something major happens to me."

"Like smacking your head."

"Like smacking my head."

"Okay, I get that that was bad, and your control issues are making more and more sense, but have you ever tried to control your *magic* instead of controlling yourself?"

"Huh?"

"Think about it. You have weird magic, fine. Besides that, you have strong weird magic. How you've dealt with it is to clamp down major control over everything else in your life, but maybe all you have to do is to take control of your magic—you know, show it who's boss—and make it act right."

Summer shook her head. "You're nuts."

"I'm just sayin' discipline can be a good thing."

"Sure, for someone who is comfortable with it," Summer said.

"So get comfortable with it."

"Easier said than done."

"Maybe you just need the right incentive," Jenny said. "Want me to give you a quick dominatrix lesson or twelve? It'd be fun."

"Thanks, but no thanks. I think I'll just bumble along as I am, which means no 'helpful' magic spells from you or anyone else. Okay?"

Jenny held up her hand like she was taking an oath. "Promise." Then she added, "Guess it looks like you're going to have to get a handle on your übercontrol issues and your bizarre magic."

Summer sighed. "Sadly, it looks like it."

"Well, never fear. You have a Certified Discipline Nymph on your side. Plus, Kenny-benny may surprise both of us and take forceful control of your date tonight and ravish you properly." Jenny giggled and then, at Summer's frown, cleared her throat and sobered up. The bus lurched to an awkward halt in front of Dark Shadows, Mysteria's only art gallery. "But before anyone gets ravished, we will edify and educate the masses." She winked at Summer, stood up, smoothed her hair, and faced the bus full of teenagers. "Touch *anything* and you will have to deal with me—before school in the boy's restroom with a toothbrush, a can of Comet, and a collection of Shakespearian sonnets."

"What're the poems for?" whispered a voice from the silent, staring students.

"To clean your minds out while your hands—your *glove-less* hands—clean out the urinals," Jenny said sweetly. She turned around and, to a chorus of gagging sounds from the students, grinned at Summer. "Let's go, shall we?" Jenny sashayed from the bus, leading the way into the gallery with Summer and the well-disciplined students following close behind her.

Summer thought entering the gallery was like leaving one world for another. Inside the spacious building it was cool and dark. Even from the foyer she could see that instead of the usual plain white expanse of gallery walls, Dark Shadows had been painted in unyielding black, broken only by spotlights trained on each painting so that the entire exhibit gave the impression of floating dreams poised on the surface of a dark, sleeping sea.

"Wow, it's been years since I've been here, and I'd forgotten how dramatic the black walls make this place," Summer told Jenny in a hushed voice.

"Yeah, Barnabas told me that he hadn't planned the effect. He'd painted everything black only because it's easier on his vampire senses. The weirdness of it was just a happy by-product."

"Well, vampires gross me out with their definitely non-vegan diet, but there's something about this place that I like, even if it is a little creepy and—"

"Ladies, how may I help you?"

At the sound of the deep voice, Summer jumped guiltily and looked up . . . and up . . . and up into the face of a god of a man. He was standing just inside the shadowy entrance of the gallery, and even though it was dark and cool within, he was wearing mirrored sunglasses. As she blinked at her own reflection in those glasses, the man slowly reached up and removed them, revealing eyes so dark they looked black. His gaze locked with hers. *Gorgeous, dark, dangerous* were the descriptive words that flitted through her mind. "You're not Barnabas," she said abruptly.

One black brow lifted. "Astute observation, ma'am."

"Oooh, you must be Colin, Barnabas's older brother. Tell

me I'm right, handsome," Jenny demanded, flipping her hair coquettishly.

"You're right." His eyes sparkled playfully when he turned to Jenny. "And you must be a Certified Discipline Nymph."

"Smart and handsome—my second-favorite combination," Jenny said.

"Your first favorite?" Colin asked with a sexy smile.

"Smart, handsome, and bound by the wrists," Jenny said.

Summer felt the urge to roll her eyes. Instead, she cleared her throat and said, "High school field trip—students—right behind us. Remember?"

Jenny shrugged, barely glancing at the wide-eyed students. "I'm just being friendly. But you're right. We should get down to business." The purr in her voice said that she'd rather go down on Colin than get down to any other business.

Summer frowned at Jenny and then stuck her hand out to Colin. "Hello, I'm Miss Smith. I sent the e-mail several days ago reserving the gallery for the field trip this morning. I'm assuming that's still okay, even though your brother isn't here?"

Colin took her hand in his, and Summer had to force herself not to gasp. His grip was strong, but she'd expected that. He was, after all, a *very* big man who had *very* big hands. It was the temperature of his skin that shocked her. Being touched by him was like being touched by an awakened statue. His hand was smooth, hard, and cool. Their eyes met again, and Summer was jolted by the dark intensity with which he was studying her—as if she was, at that moment, the most important thing in his universe. She'd only known of one species of Mysteria's creatures who could spear someone with such intensity and whose skin felt like molded marble . . .

"You're a vampire!" she blurted, pulling her hand free of his firm grip.

His smile was slow and knowing, not in the least bit ruffled by her statement. "I am. Both of my brothers and I are vampires. It runs in the family, you know," he said smoothly.

"Does it?" Summer made herself not wipe her tingling palm down the side of her slacks.

"It does when you're all bitten by the same master vampire," he said.

Summer noticed that when he spoke to her, the playful

sparkle that Jenny seemed to automatically evoke in his eyes changed . . . darkened, and even though he was no longer touching her, he was still studying her with that uncomfortable intensity. Feeling weirdly light-headed, Summer spoke more briskly than she'd intended. "That's interesting. Maybe we can talk about it later. Right now I think we should start our field trip. If that's okay with you—or your brother. Is Barnabas really not here?"

Colin cocked his head and looked down at her, a small curve of amusement shadowing his full lips. "Barnabas is in Paris drowning himself in wine and young Frenchmen so that he can forget being jilted by Hunter Knight." The vampire shrugged one of his broad shoulders. "Foolish of him to become so obsessed with a straight guy. I tried to tell Barnabas that Hunter's as gay as I am."

"Which is to say not at all," Jenny chimed in.

Colin's grin was almost a leer. He answered Jenny, but his eyes stayed on Summer. "Yes, ma'am. You're right about that."

"So, does that mean the field trip is off?" Summer said, wondering why Jenny's flirting with Colin should annoy her.

"Not at all. The reason I moved to town temporarily from my ranch is because Barnabas asked me to babysit this special exhibit. The field trip is definitely on. Besides, you just got here, Miss Smith. I'd hate for you to leave until we've gotten to know each other better." Colin's dark eyes trapped her gaze, and she felt her breathing deepen.

Is he making me dizzy? Is he working a vampire mojo on me? Summer mentally shook herself. She was being ridiculous. Magic didn't work on her. Or if it did, it went way wrong. Her overactive imagination and hormones were the only things working on her. What was probably happening was she was displacing her excitement about the impending dream date with Ken. No way was she interested in this vampire! He definitely didn't fit in with her well-thought-out plan for her future. "Excellent. Let's get started. The students have really been looking forward to this field trip," she lied.

"I hadn't been thinking much about this field trip at all." Colin lowered his voice so that it seemed to brush against Summer's skin. "At least not until I saw who was leading it. Now I do believe it's going to be a very interesting experience. It is good to meet you, Miss Smith." He tipped an imaginary hat to her in a cowboylike move that appeared to be second nature to him. Then he raised his voice so that the waiting students could hear. "Come on in and check out the art. And, yes, there are some nudes."

There were spontaneous high fives given in response as the students filed into the gallery.

"Ladies, if you'll follow me, I'll give you a more personal tour," Colin said. Though he spoke to both women, his eyes rested on Summer's face hungrily. He strode into the main gallery, giving Summer plenty of time to take in the faded jeans that snuggled his firm ass and the broad shoulders that strained the fabric of the black, long-sleeved shirt he wore. And were those cowboy boots? On a vampire? Sweet Goddess, gay Barnabas's brother was a sexy cowboy vampire!

"Damn, Summer! Are you secreting some kind of come-fuck-me! hormone? Tall, dark, and vampire is clearly hitting on you."

Summer pulled her eyes from Colin's muscular body and managed to scoff. "Oh, please. I'm so not interested in him."

"Really? That's not what your nipples are saying. Better check your control, girlfriend."

Horrified, Summer glanced down to see the outline of her very obviously aroused nipples pressing against her cream-colored blouse. Hastily she crossed her arms over her chest and muttered, "It's just cold in here," as she hurried into the gallery with Jenny's knowing laughter following her.

Four

✳

"All right! Move away from the nude, and no one gets hurt!"
Jenny snapped, and the group of gawking teenage boys shuf-
fled reluctantly away from the full frontal nudity of George
Wilson's *The Spring Witch*.

Colin waited until the three of them were alone before saying, "Wilson was a big fan of Dante and William Blake, so he
liked the poetic and romantic subject here."

Summer blinked in surprise up at Colin. The tall vampire
actually seemed to know something about art.

"Huh!" Jenny snorted a little testily. "I don't see anything
terribly romantic about witches. Sexy—maybe. Wanton—for
sure. Romantic? Nah."

"The subject isn't a witch as we know them in Mysteria,"
Colin explained, his eyes on the nude painting. "It's actually
Persephone as she emerges from the underworld. See the
pomegranate in her hand?"

"Oh, well, that makes more sense. Goddesses are definitely
romantic," Jenny admitted.

"What do you think of her, Miss Smith?"

Colin's question, as well as the intense gaze he shifted from the painting to her, caught Summer unaware, and she automatically said what was foremost in her mind. "I think I like her body better than most of the other women in the exhibit. They look too manly."

Colin's brows lifted. "I agree with you, Miss Smith. The Pre-Raphaelites tended to give their female models masculine characteristics. I like my woman to look like a woman, and not like a man in drag."

"As if that matters to the germs and hormones," Jenny said, eyes lighting on a group of laughing, jostling teenage boys clustered around the huge, colorful, and seminude painting of *Toilette of a Roman Lady.* "Excuse me for a sec. I'm going to kick some boy butt."

As she hurried toward the students, Summer called, "Herd them back into the main gallery in front of the Romeo and Juliet painting. I'm going to give them their topic for the essay assignment."

Jenny's teeth flashed white as she grinned over her shoulder. "Oh, good. They'll hate that."

And, just like that, Summer and Colin were left completely alone for the first time.

She didn't have to look up at him to know his eyes were on her. Again. She could feel his gaze—against her skin, inside her blood. It heated her body, arousing her nipples and making her inner thighs tingle, and her woman's core became hot and wet and needy . . . needy for his touch, which wouldn't be sweet and gentle and loving, as she'd fantasized about Ken's touch being. Colin's touch would be like his body: hard and strong and sexy. No, Colin was nothing like Ken.

"What are you thinking about?"

His deep voice came from very close to her. *When had he stepped into her personal space?* She looked up at him. *Those eyes! They're so intense—so sexy.* He was close enough that his scent came to her, and it, too, was a surprise. Instead of smelling like the grave or worse, like a carnivorous, bloodsucking monster, Colin smelled as sexy as he looked. His scent was man mixed with something spicy, like cinnamon or even more exotic, like cloves and darkness and cool nighttime breezes sifting over love-dampened skin.

She stared at him and breathed the unique scent that was

Colin distilled by his own skin. *Nothing like Ken, who smells like lemons and laughter, and who I'm supposed to be having a dream date with tonight!* "My date tonight," Summer finally managed to answer.

Colin's dark eyes narrowed dangerously. "You shouldn't lie to me. You know vampires can smell lies."

Summer took a step back and put up her chin. She was damn sure not going to let this overbearing, way-too-masculine creature intimidate her, no matter how yummy he smelled. She was a college graduate and a professional teacher!

"Then you should sniff again I was definitely thinking about Ken," Summer said with finality.

"Ken?" his dark-chocolate voice was heavy with amusement. "As in Barbie's boyfriend?"

"No. Ken, as in *my* boyfriend."

With a movement too fast to follow with her eyes, Colin grabbed both of her arms and lifted her so that he only had to bend a little to fit his face into the soft slope of her neck. He inhaled deeply and then let his breath out slowly, caressingly, so that it brushed against her sensitive skin and caused her to shiver.

"You may have been thinking, *briefly*, of him. But you do not have a boyfriend."

"What makes you say that?" she asked breathlessly.

"If you belonged to a man, I could scent him on you, and you smell only of yourself: sunlight and honey and woman."

He let her go as abruptly as he had grabbed her, and Summer stumbled back a couple of steps.

Her head was spinning, and her breath was coming short and hard. It was like he'd filled her mind with the white noise of the inside of seashells. All she could think to say was, "I smell like sunlight and honey?"

"Yes." Colin ran one cool finger down her heated cheek and the side of her neck. "Warm honey on a golden summer's day. You draw me to you like a field of lavender draws bees. Will you let me taste you?"

"Hey, Miss Smith! Miss Sullivan says we're all waiting for you, and we need you now. Uh, you better come, 'cause she seems kinda pissed."

Colin's hand fell away from her face, and Summer turned

to see the little blond cheerleader standing in the doorway to the main gallery.

"Y-yes. Okay. I'm coming. Now." Without looking back at Colin, Summer hurried from the room.

She could feel him following her. She thought it was like having a dangerous but darkly beautiful panther stalking her. He wanted to taste her! Summer shivered and crossed her arms concealingly over her breasts. Again.

"There you are, Miss Smith. The students are ready for their essay assignment." Jenny told her, then her eyes snapped over the group of milling students. "I said get your notebooks out. Now."

Book bags exploded as kids hurried to do her bidding. Summer could only watch in awe. How the hell did Jenny do that? She hadn't even raised her voice. Soon the entire room (which included one dark and brooding vampire) was looking expectantly up at her.

Summer cleared her throat. "The topic of your essay is this: a Pre-Raphaelite art critic wrote that this painting of Romeo and Juliet by Ford Madox Brown was 'splendid in expression and fullness of tone, and the whole picture is gorgeous in color.' I want you to be a modern art critic and tell me in your essay what you learned about Romeo and Juliet from Mr. Brown's painting." Summer paused, narrowed her eyes, and did what she hoped was a believable impression of Jenny's firmness, then added, "No, that does *not* mean that I want you to tell me Romeo is wearing a gay-looking red outfit, and Juliet's boobs are showing. What I want you to tell me is what this painting says about them as a couple. Questions?" She didn't give them time to ask any but hurried on. "Good. I'll let you have about fifteen more minutes here in front of the painting to take notes and start getting your ideas on paper."

A hand went up. It was one of Jenny's students, so she said, "What is it, Mr. Purdom?"

"Does your class have to write the essay, too?"

"Yes. I suggest you get busy," Jenny said smoothly.

There were a few muffled groans, but most of the kids settled down to studying the painting and taking notes.

"I'm going to go tell Moxie to bring the bus around. Do you think you can handle *it* by yourself?" Jenny's tone made the pronoun semi-suggestive. The sultry glance she sent Colin made it fully suggestive.

"Yes, definitely. No worries here," Summer said.

Jenny met her eyes before she left the room and blinked a couple times in surprise before her face practically exploded in a smile. "You like him!"

Summer felt her cheeks warm. "I don't like him. I don't even know him," she whispered.

"Okay, maybe I should have said you're hot for him. Well, go ahead, girlfriend. He's clearly more interested in you than me." She winked at Summer and disappeared out the front door.

Summer sighed and turned back to the room of sullenly writing students. Thankfully, Colin was on the far side of the room standing close to the painting. She could see that he was busy answering questions about it for some of the students. Good. That should keep him occupied. It also gave her an opportunity to study him. Goddess, he was handsome, but not in a typical fashion. What was he like? He reminded her of someone, and she couldn't quite—

Then, with a little jolt she did remember who he brought to mind. Her favorite fictional hero, Mr. Rochester from *Jane Eyre.* Yes, that dark, powerfully masculine look of Colin's would definitely fit in as master of Thornfield. *You know you think Rochester is the sexiest of all fictional heroes, as well as your favorite,* her mind whispered. *No,* she told herself sternly, *Ken is really my type—all blond and sweet and gentle. He's what I planned for my future. The Rochester type needs to stay where he belongs—in the pages of fiction.*

But she was still staring when Colin looked up from the student he'd been helping and met her eyes.

Come to me . . . The words filled her—mind, body, and soul. Before she realized what she was doing, she was making her way around the group of students and heading for the vampire.

Summer was only a few feet from him when she stopped and shook her head, breaking the stare that had locked their eyes together and getting control of herself. Oh, hell no! What was she doing? Imagining his voice in her head and then obeying that imagining? Had she lost it? Had the stress of trying to teach teenagers cracked her already?

And then, not far behind her, she felt a too-familiar prickle up her spine. She knew even before she heard the whispered singsong words of the quickly uttered spell that one of the asshole teenage sorcerers-to-be had thought he'd be clever and whip up a little magic to see if he and his girlfriend could skip out of the assignment. Summer whirled around in time to hear the last stanza of the incantation. She opened her mouth to yell, *No! Stop!* Backing as quickly as she could away from the kids—and right into an impossibly hard, cold body she knew had to be Colin. She wanted to warn him. She wanted to do something—anything. But instead, the magic was already grabbing her, robbing her of speech.

> *Me and my bitch get in the picture, yo!*
> *Somewhere our teacher can't go!*
> *Where school and stupid essays ain't no mo'!*
> *And it's cool to get with your ho!*

Completely helpless, she did the only thing she could do. Summer closed her eyes, wrapped her arms around the pillar of strength that was Colin, and held her breath as she felt their bodies being wrenched, lifted, and tossed.

When everything was still again and the nauseating sensation of wobbly, opposite magic lifted, Summer slowly opened her eyes.

And looked straight into Colin's dark gaze.

"What the—" he began, and then his eyes widened in sudden fear. "The sunlight! I have to get out of . . ." The vampire's words trailed off as he realized he wasn't bursting into flame. Completely confused, Colin gazed down at Summer. "What's happened to us? It's day. I'm outside in the sunlight, and my skin is not burning."

"It's, well, because of my magic and that kid casting a spell. If I'm close enough to magic, it always messes up, and—" she began, and then her words broke off as what her eyes were seeing caught up with her mind. They were, indeed, outside. Actually, it wasn't full daylight, just a lovely morning dawning in the east. They were on a balcony, surrounded by a perfumed profusion of flowering rose vines. Colin was there with her, but he wasn't dressed in his jeans, black shirt, and cowboy boots.

Here he was wearing an amazing crimson-colored outfit, rich as a king, or maybe even a god. She glanced down at her own clothes and gasped. She had changed, too, and was wearing only a soft, transparent chemise, which was cut low to expose her breasts to the nipples. She could feel Colin's eyes on those nipples as she looked up at him. "Uh-oh," she said. "I think we're inside the Romeo and Juliet painting,"

Five

"By the Goddess, I think you're right! How could this have happened?" Colin said, gazing around them while he shook his head in disbelief.

"It's me," Summer said miserably. "It's because of me that we're here."

His dark eyes rested on her. "How could this possibly be because of you?"

"It's my magic. Or maybe my nonmagic would be a better way to explain it." Summer sighed. "One of the students cast a spell in the gallery—something about getting inside the Romeo and Juliet painting so that he and his *ho*," she wrinkled her nose in distaste at the word, "could get out of the essay assignment."

"But what does that have to do with you? Other than it being your assignment?"

"I was close enough to the stupid teenager when he cast the spell to have my own magic work on it. And my own magic is opposite magic—kind of. Actually, it's more like sideways, opposite, totally screwed-up magic. The bottom line is that my magic messes up all other magic around me. So here"—

she made a sweeping gesture, taking in the balcony and the pearly morning—"we are."

"In the Romeo and Juliet painting."

She nodded. "In the Romeo and Juliet painting." Summer smiled sheepishly. "Sorry."

Colin shook his head in amazement and lifted his hand so that the red velvet sleeve slid back to reveal his muscular arm all the way to mid-bicep. The morning light gilded his skin so that for that moment he looked tan and unexpectedly young.

"Incredible!" he said. Then he bared his other arm to the morning light, threw back his head, and laughed. "Do you know how long it's been since I've felt the sun on my skin?"

Summer couldn't answer him. She could only watch as he transformed from intense and brooding to vibrant and amazing. He laughed again and, with one swift motion, ripped open the buttons on his linen undershirt. Colin faced the rising sun, arms spread, face open. He'd been handsome before—all Rochester-like and mysterious. But here he'd transformed into a man whose beauty went beyond his height and hair and bone structure. This new Colin was so incredibly full of life that he seemed to vibrate with it.

"You did this?"

He turned the force of his full smile on her, and Summer thought that the heat he radiated would melt her. She nodded a little weakly and managed a "Yes."

With another laugh, he lifted her in his arms and spun her around the balcony. "I knew you were special from the moment I touched you."

"It's just my weird magic. I've been wishing I could figure out how to get rid of it or control it for years," Summer said a little breathlessly as he finally released her.

"Get rid of it? No way! And, take it from me, control is overrated. No! You're perfect just as you are—and so is your magic." He took her hand in his and, with dark eyes sparkling mischievously, he bent gallantly over it. "Thank you, my lady, for granting me a reprieve from unrelenting night and bringing me sunshine again."

Colin kissed her hand. As his lips met her skin, Summer felt a jolt of sensation that rushed through her body. His lips weren't the cool marble of a vampire! They were warm and soft and very, very much alive. She gasped, "You've really been changed. You're not a vampire here."

He didn't release her hand. Instead, he lifted it and slid it inside the open front of his shirt so that it rested over his heart. Summer could feel the beating of that heart under the warm, pliant skin of his chest.

"I don't know how long this magic will last, but I'm going to enjoy every moment of it."

"You're . . . you're so different here," Summer said, having difficulty concentrating on words with her hand pressed against his bare chest.

"Different?" Colin smiled and shrugged. "I suppose right now I am more like I used to be." He looked from her to the morning sky. "I think I've lived so long in darkness that I'd forgotten what it is to feel really alive." His eyes met hers again. They were full of the emotion reflected in the deepening of his voice. "You brought me the sun."

"On accident," Summer whispered. "I didn't really mean to."

"I smelled it on you when we met. Remember? I said you reminded me of sunlight and honey."

"I remember," Summer said softly, completely lost in his gaze.

"You drew me to you even then." He touched her cheek caressingly. "What is your first name?"

"Summer."

His smile was brilliant. "Summer! Perfect. Let me taste you, Summer. Let me breathe in your sunlight . . ."

Summer knew she shouldn't. She should step away from him and take control of this ridiculous situation and then fall on her head or whatever it took to break the spell. Instead, she felt her face tilt up to him as he bent to her lips. But he didn't kiss her—not at first. Instead, his mouth stopped just short of hers. She could feel his warm breath as he seemed to inhale her. Colin nuzzled her cheek and whispered into her parted lips, "You are sunlight and honey, *my* sunlight and honey."

Summer shivered. One of his hands still pressed hers against his chest. The other slid down her back, holding her close to him. She molded to him; only the transparent material of the thin chemise separated them, and she could clearly feel every part of his hard body.

"Do you want me to kiss you, Summer? Do you want me to taste you?" He breathed the words against her lips as he inhaled her scent.

"Yes," she whispered back. "Yes."

"Summer," he moaned, and then he claimed her mouth. His kiss wasn't gentle. It was rough and demanding. He possessed her lips, plundered her mouth, tantalized her tongue. His kiss engulfed her. It was the kind of kiss she'd always imagined she wouldn't like. It would be too filled with unbridled lust, too overwhelming and uncontrolled. So it was with a sense of utter surprise that Summer felt herself responding, body and soul, to Colin. She wrapped her arms around him and met his passion with her own. White-hot lust speared through her as the kiss deepened even more, as she gave herself completely over to him and—

—And Summer fell so hard on her butt that the wind was knocked out of her and she saw little speckles of light dance in front of her eyes.

"Thank the Goddess! You're back!" Jenny's hands were patting her as if she was checking for broken bones. "Are you okay? You had me so worried!"

Summer sucked air, blinked rapidly, and managed to nod.

"Is she hurt?" a deep voice asked.

"Colin? Oh, good. You're back, too," Jenny said briskly. "I think she's just had the wind knocked out of her. Here, help me get her to her feet."

Strong hands lifted her, and Summer realized that it felt familiar and somehow right that he was touching her again, even though his skin had lost the flush of sun-kissed warmth and was cool and marblelike again.

"Are you really all right?" Colin's voice came from close above her.

Summer looked up, finally blinking her vision clear. He was still holding one of her elbows, and he was watching her with the same dark intensity with which he'd studied her before they'd been magicked into the painting.

"I'm fine," Summer said. "At least I think I'm fine. I feel kinda—"

"Let's get you on the bus and back to school where the nurse can check you out," Jenny interrupted. "Colin, keep hold of her." And she marched off, leaving Colin to support Summer as they headed to the door.

Summer glanced up at the tall, silent vampire. He was Rochester again, with his broody expression and his dark intensity. Had it just been moments ago that he'd been laughing openly and so full of life and joy and passion? Especially passion.

"I'm sorry," she blurted, although she wasn't sure what it was she was apologizing for.

His gaze met hers as they came to the front door. "Don't apologize. I don't want to know you're sorry about what happened between us."

Summer frowned. Well, she was feeling dazed and confused, but she hadn't meant *that*. "No, I didn't mean—"

Jenny threw open the door, and a bright shaft of sunlight filled the entryway of the otherwise dark gallery. Colin dropped her arm and moved hastily back into the shadows, pulling his mirrored sunglasses from the pocket of his shirt and placing them on his nose so that he completed the metamorphosis from the charismatic man who had been seducing her on the balcony to the tall, silent vampire.

"Colin, I—"

"Come on. You still look terrible." Jenny's hand replaced Colin's on her arm, and the Discipline Nymph pulled her firmly from the gallery.

Over her shoulder, Summer could see Colin turning away as the door closed on the bright afternoon.

The kids were suspiciously quiet on the ride back to school. Jenny kept shooting them slit-eyed looks.

"Detention does not begin to describe what Mr. Purdom is going to be serving for a solid week," she muttered. Then her gaze shifted to Summer. "Do you think you're okay? You're still looking pale."

"I feel fine. I guess." She lowered her voice and tilted her head to Jenny's. "What did it look like to you?"

"Well, I was just coming back into the gallery when the girls were screaming bloody murder, saying you and Colin had disappeared. I was trying to figure out what had happened—by the by, Purdom and his buddy, McArter, were looking guilty as hell, so I knew the little turds had something to do with it—

when that damn nosy girl . . . oh, what's her name? You know, blond, chubby, thinks she's way cuter than she is, and her mom's a witch with a *B*?"

"Whitney Hoge."

"Yeah, that's her."

"So Miss Hoge was pointing at the R and J painting with her mouth wide open, unattractively, mind you. I took one look at the picture, saw you two in place of the originals, and hustled the kids out of the room. I briefly chewed out Purdom's ass—will do a more thorough job of that later—and ran back into the gallery at about the time you landed on your butt in the middle of the floor."

"So no one watched us inside the painting?"

"Nope. No one was inside the gallery." Her brows went up. "Was there something to watch?"

"Sorta."

"Oooh! Nastiness?"

"Kinda."

"*Sorta* and *kinda* are not answers. They are especially not answers with details."

"I know," Summer said, and closed her mouth.

A sly expression made Jenny's face look decidedly nymph-like. "If I remember correctly, and I have an excellent memory—it's part of the whole discipline thing—anyway, if I remember correctly, you said that the way your opposite magic gets broken is by you being shocked. Right?"

"Right," Summer said reluctantly.

"Okay, then what shocked you so much the spell was broken?"

Summer chewed her lip.

"Look, you can tell me. I'm a professional."

"A professional what?"

"Certified Discipline Nymph, of course. We wear many hats: classroom disciplinarian, workout disciplinarian—yes, I'm hell in the gym—and, most especially, *sexual* disciplinarian. So, give. Details, please."

"It was his kiss," Summer said.

Jenny blinked in surprise. "Colin's kiss shocked you so much that it broke the spell? Jeesh, was it that bad?"

"No," Summer said softly. "It was that good."

Six

"No, Summer, I don't have your purse. Sorry. I'll bet you dropped it when that kid zapped you into the painting," Jenny said.

"Ah, shoot. I must have left it at the gallery."

"Could that have been a Freudian slip? Perhaps something that would give you a reason to see Colin again? You know you could just cancel the date with Kenny-benny, and go back there tonight," Jenny said.

"First, stop calling him that. Second, no, I'm not canceling my date. I'll go get my purse tomorrow or whatever. As I already explained, this thing with Colin was just a fluke. He's not my type, and he doesn't fit into my plan." A vision of Colin on the balcony, arms outstretched, head flung back, laughing his full, infectious laugh flashed through Summer's mind, but she quickly squelched the memory. That wasn't really Colin. The *real* Colin was much more subdued and uncomfortably intense, not lighthearted, fun, and happy. "The whole Rochester thing doesn't work for me in the real world," Summer blurted.

"Huh? Who's Rochester?"

Summer sighed. "You know, Jane Eyre's Rochester."

"Oooh! He's yummy. What about him?"

"That's who Colin reminds me of, and he is definitely not my type."

"You, my friend, might be insane."

"There's nothing insane about wanting a guy who's light-hearted and happy and fun. And blond," she added.

"You forgot 'and easy to control,'" Jenny added, then she hurried on, talking over Summer's sputtering protestations. "Girlfriend, just because a man is intense doesn't mean he's not happy and even fun sometimes, too. Plus, you might want to consider that lighthearted could mean light-*headed*, as in the guy might not have enough sense to be serious," Jenny said. "And what the hell's wrong with tall, *dark*, and handsome?"

"Not believing you about the whole broody-could-equal-happy thing," Summer said stubbornly, completely ignoring the obvious reference to Ken's brains or lack thereof. "And I happen to prefer blonds, light*hearted* blonds in particular."

"Did you prefer them when Colin had you in a lip-lock?"

"Yes. I still preferred them. I was just surprised, that's all."

"Which brings us back to my main point. You were surprised because it was so damn good. If it's so damn good, you might want to consider revisiting the scene of the crime."

"You want me to get back in the painting?"

"No, I want you to get back on the vampire."

"Jenny, I am going to get ready for my date. With Ken. The guy I'm really attracted to. So I'm going now. Bye."

"All right, all right! I hope you have a good time, and I want all the details."

"Good-bye, Jenny."

"Jeesh you're grumpy when you're sexually confused. Bye."

"I'm not sexually confused," Summer told the dead phone. She glanced at the clock. "Shoot! I am late, though." Putting Colin out of her mind, Summer rushed into the kitchen and threw the tofu spaghetti sauce together to simmer.

She also put Colin out of her mind while she showered. The warm water running down her naked body did *not* remind her of the warmth of his hands through the ultrathin material of the chemise.

"His hands aren't even warm. Not really," she muttered as she put on just a hint of makeup.

And she definitely didn't think about him while she picked out the ever-so-cute peach lace bra and panties set and then slid on the breezy, buttercup-colored skirt and the creamy, V-neck pullover that made her look and feel like a fresh spring wildflower, basking in the sunlight, just waiting to be plucked by a tall, dark—

"No!" she told herself, and marched into the kitchen. Summer was stirring the pot of sauce when the jaunty *shave and a haircut, two bits* knock sounded against her front door. She patted her hair and hurried through the living room.

"Hey, Sum! I couldn't figure out what kind of wine to get, so I got, like, three colors. I figured the more the merrier." Ken grinned boyishly and presented the bag that, sure enough, held a bottle of cheap Cabernet, cheap Chardonnay, and cheap white Zinfandel.

Summer returned his smile and motioned for him to come in, squelching her disappointment that there wasn't a bottle of nice Chianti in the mix. It wasn't like Ken could have known they were having spaghetti and that she preferred Italian wine with it. She'd just let him know next time. "How about we open the red? It'll go great with the spaghetti," she said.

"You made spaghetti?" He took off his jacket and dropped it over the back of the couch before she could ask him for it.

"Yeah, I hope you like it."

"Spaghetti's awesome! Hope it's almost ready. I'm starving."

She opened her mouth to tell him all she'd have to do is to boil the pasta, but he didn't give her a chance to speak.

"Hey, want me to come to the kitchen with you and open the wine? A drink would be awesome."

"Sure, come on back," she said and then led him to the back of the cabin and her sister's spacious kitchen.

"Wow, this is a great kitchen," Ken said appreciatively.

"Yeah, Candice loves her gourmet cooking." She sent Ken a shy look as she handed him the corkscrew. "Hope you're not disappointed that she got most of the cooking genes in our family."

"Nah, as long as it's hot and full of meat, I'm cool with it."

"Uh, Ken, didn't you remember that I'm a vegetarian?"

He looked up from opening the wine. "Huh? A what?" Then he glanced at the simmering pot on the stove. "Oh, you're worried I won't like your spaghetti." Grinning, he grabbed the big stirring spoon and ladled himself a generous taste test. "Yum! You don't have anything to be nervous about. This sauce is awesome!" he said through a full mouth.

"Oh, uh, good." Summer stirred the bubbling pasta. *What he doesn't know won't kill him,* she decided. Or at least she didn't think fairies were allergic to tofu.

While Summer put the finishing touches on their meal, Ken sat on her sister's pristine butcher block island, drank wine, and talked. And talked. And talked.

"Hey, Sum, so you actually made it through college."

"Yeah. It's funny—I didn't think I'd like the academic part of it, but once I got into my lit major I—"

"Man, I don't know how you stayed away from Mysteria for four whole years. No way would I want to do that. The mundane world is no place for fairies."

"Well, I did miss Mysteria, and, well, lots of the people here." She smiled and felt her cheeks get warm when she added, "Especially certain fairies. That's one of the reasons I came back."

"Of course you missed fairies. The world just isn't the same without them!" He jumped off the counter and bowed to her with a big flourish before pouring himself more wine.

He looked so boyish and carefree that she had to smile at him. "Then I should feed you so we can be sure you don't expire. I know how much fairies love food."

"That we do!" He hurried into the dining room where she had two places already set with intimate candles and her sister's beautiful china, leaving her to carry in the spaghetti and the sauce. He had thought to bring the bottle of wine with him, though.

So they ate, and Ken talked. And talked. And talked.

At first Summer just listened to him, commenting now and then (although his exuberant "conversation" really didn't require much participation on her part), and thinking about how cute he looked in the candlelight. His blond hair was thick and a little shaggy, but it looked good on him, and it glistened with a sparkle of fairy magic when the candlelight caught it just right. His blue eyes were big and expressive, his face completely animated. He really was a cute guy. And the direct opposite of dark and broody and intense and sexy . . .

No! Ken was sexy. She'd always thought he was sexy. After all, she'd had a major crush on him since they were teenagers. And she also—

"Sum, did you hear me? I said that you've really grown all up. It's kind of a surprise. Not that you don't look awesome," he hurried to add. "But it's a grown-up awesome. You've changed."

"Oh, uh, thanks. I think." Summer took a sip of wine. "You haven't changed at all," she said.

"Thanks, Sum! You know how fairies are—young for years. Good thing, too, 'cause the party planning and supply business isn't for the old and serious."

"So you're going into your family's business?"

"Of course! I love parties, and I especially love fireworks." He sat up straighter, clearly proud of himself. "You've been gone, so you probably don't know this, but I've been put in charge of the pyrotechnics for *Fairies 4 Fantastic Festivals, Inc.*"

"That's great, Ken. I'm really proud of you. Your dad must be—"

"Yeah, it's awesome! Just wait till you see what we're planning for Beltane this year. It's gonna be super cool with . . ."

Summer smiled and nodded while Ken talked. And talked. And talked. She also studied him. She hadn't been exaggerating. He really hadn't changed in the four years she'd been gone. He was wearing a T-shirt that said THIS WAY TO THE GUN SHOW with arrows pointing to his biceps. Summer had to stifle a giggle. His biceps were like the rest of his body, young and cute and lean. They were definitely not "guns," loaded or otherwise. And she definitely wasn't comparing them to Colin's muscular arms.

She mentally shook herself while Ken paused in his monologue to jog into the kitchen to snag the bottle of Chardonnay. He came back in the room, still talking about the plans for the "awesome" fireworks show that would be the climactic event of Mysteria's Beltane festival. She saw that his faded, baggy jeans were fashionably shredded over both knees, and he was wearing bright blue Sketchers.

Nope, he definitely hadn't changed since high school.

It was about then that Summer began to wonder if dinner would ever end.

"Dang, Sum, sorry about your headache," Ken said as she handed him his jacket and walked him to the door.

"I guess I'm just tired from teaching all day."

He stopped at the door she'd opened and turned to face her. "It was great to see you again. I'm really glad you're back, Sum." Ken rested an arm over her shoulder nonchalantly as he slouched in the doorway. His blue eyes sparkled with another smile. "Dinner was totally—"

"Awesome?" She provided the word when he hesitated.

"Yeah, it really was. And you're awesome, too." Slowly, Ken bent to her. His kiss was sweet and questioning and very, very gentle. In other words, it was everything Summer believed she'd wanted in a kiss from the man she'd been fantasizing about for years.

She didn't feel a thing in response.

Give him a chance, she chided herself. *This is what you decided you want. He fits in the plan.* Summer leaned into Ken and put her arms around his neck, returning his questioning kiss with an exclamation mark.

She felt the surprise in his body, and then he parted his lips and followed her lead, kissing her deeper, longer. Summer thought he tasted, weirdly, like wine and lemonade. She wondered vaguely why he always reminded her of lemons—not the tart kind, but the supersweet Country Time Lemonade lemons, with lots of sugar. Lots.

Ken was still kissing her, softly and sweetly, while Summer's mind wandered. She was thinking about what she was supposed to teach her sophomores the next day as she absently looked over his shoulder at the dark edge of the forest. She thought she saw something move there, just inside the boundaries of her yard, and wondered what it was. The moon was high and insanely bright and almost about full. Could it be one of the town's many werewolves?

And then it hit her; she was thinking about school, and werewolves, and the moon while Ken was making out with her. That just couldn't be right. When Colin had kissed her, she hadn't been able to think of anything except him. His touch. His mouth. His taste. His kiss. Ken's kisses made her want to compile a shopping list or maybe fold some laundry.

No. This definitely was not going to work. Time to change the plan.

Instantly she pulled away from him. He gave her a sweet, boyish smile. "Sorry, Sum. Did I get carried away?"

"No, Ken, honey." Summer patted his cheek gently. "I got carried away. I think it's best if you and I stay good friends and don't mess that up with trying to be more than that. Do you know what I mean?"

Ken's smile didn't falter. "Sure, whatever. That's fine with me. Hey, do you think I could have some of that awesome spaghetti sauce to take with me so I could snack on it later?"

"Sure Kenny-benny," Summer said and, laughing, made him up a quick to-go package, patted him on his head, and said good night. Before she closed the door, she heard the distinctive giggles of several female fairies who had obviously been waiting to escort their Kenny-benny home. Or wherever.

She was still shaking her head at herself while she cleaned up the dinner dishes. "Jenny was right. I might be insane." Ken was so not the man for her. Actually, if she was being totally honest with herself, Kenny-benny was so not a man yet, and clearly, he might never be. Rinsing the dishes, she laughed out loud. She should be upset at having her fantasy of the Perfect Man blown to pieces and her future plan messed up, or at the very least she should have been disappointed, but she wasn't. She definitely wasn't.

Her hands slid through the warm, soapy water making her think of slick, naked skin sliding against slick, naked skin . . . of heat . . . and passion . . . and a kiss that could seem to stop the world . . .

No! She couldn't want the vampire.

And then, while washing Kenny-benny's very empty plate, she looked up at her reflection in the dark window above the sink. Her face was flushed, and her eyes were big and dark with desire.

"Am I absolutely positive that I can't want the vampire?" she asked herself.

Yes, you're absolutely positive, her reflection seemed to reply.

"But his kiss was—"

Reason one you can't want him, her refection interrupted, *is that he is a carnivore, and that makes you want to throw up a little in the back of your throat.*

"I don't have to eat what he eats. Oh, Goddess, I don't, do I?" Did one share one's blood with a vampire, or did one's vampire eat solo?

Reason two, her reflection continued, *his flesh is cold, dead, hard . . .*

"Well, what's wrong with hard?" she argued with herself. "Plus, he touched me before we were in the painting, and it really wasn't that bad."

Reason three, he's not your type!

"Okay, look," she told herself sternly. "Up until about ten minutes ago, I thought Kenny was my type. Maybe I need to change my type!"

Reason four—her conscience ignored her—*he makes you feel out of control, and you don't like feeling out of control.*

"Well, that's because he was unexpected. He's expected now, so I won't have a control problem. I left my purse at his gallery." Silently she thanked the Goddess for that slip, Freudian or not. "I have to see him one more time."

"Yeah, so, tomorrow I'll just swing by the gallery after school and pick up my purse," she talked around her toothbrush to her reflection in the bathroom mirror. "No big deal. No enormous ulterior motive," she lied. "Just getting my purse, saying a quick hello, then coming home. There won't be any more kissing. None at all. It wouldn't even be appropriate. Really."

Summer crawled into bed, thinking about the difference between Ken's kisses and Colin's kisses. *What a difference . . .*

Why had she ever thought passion and heat were bad things? Okay, she knew the answer to that, even if she didn't like to admit it. She was scared of too much passion, that it would cause her to lose control, and if she lost control, she'd get burned.

Summer had learned that lesson well with her stupid out-of-control magic. Maybe it was smart of her to be scared. Was playing with a vampire like playing with fire? Or ice?

Fire, she decided as her body heated the cool sheets. Colin's passion had been exactly like fire. Her hands touched her lips, remembering Colin's caress, and then slid slowly down her body, pausing to cup her breasts. Her nipples ached. Summer squeezed them, gently at first, and then she craved more, and her touch got rougher as she teased her ultrasensitive nipples. She moaned. Almost as if she couldn't stop the impulse, one of her hands moved down between her legs. Summer gasped at the slick heat she found there. She was liquid with desire. She closed her eyes and stroked herself. As her orgasm built, Summer imagined hands on her body and lips against her skin, and when her release came, it was Colin's intensity that she was thinking of and his touch she yearned for.

Seven

✳

Colin had never felt like such an utter fool. What in all the levels of the underworld was he doing walking through the moonlit forest carrying a purse? *I know exactly what I'm doing. I'm being a gentleman*, he thought. *I may be dead, but chivalry isn't. Summer left her purse at the gallery, and I'm returning it.* A woman's purse was a sacred thing. Goddess knows what all was kept in one; Colin would almost rather take a long walk outside at noon than actually look in the damned thing. Thankfully, it was zipped closed, but he still held it gingerly, like it might explode if he handed it too roughly. There wasn't much he could do except return it. The sooner the better. Sure, he could hang on to it and wait for Summer to realize where she left it and then come claim it. But she'd been through a lot. It might take her a day or two, hell, even three, to get around to it. Until then, what about all that important stuff inside the purse? The only thing he could do with a clear conscience, was to return it to her right away. Or at least that's how he rationalized his overwhelming need to see her again—immediately.

The package carefully wrapped in the gallery's chic, black,

hand-pressed paper was a damn sight tougher to rationalize away.

Or maybe not. Colin shrugged his broad shoulders. Why hide behind rationalizations? He was courting a woman. That was nothing to feel foolish about, even if it meant carrying her purse through the woods while pink love petals fell from the sky and fairies giggled annoyingly as they played naked hide-and-seek among the trees. Goddess, fairies were irritating!

Colin glared at a silver-winged, pink-haired fairy who had frolicked close to him and given the vampire a coquettish smile that was a clear come-hither invitation.

"Not interested," he said firmly, giving the naked creature a dark look.

Not at all offended, she shrugged her smooth shoulders and scampered off.

Colin scowled after her. Fairies had never interested him. Actually, now that he was thinking about it, it had been a long time since any woman had caught his interest. Were he completely honest with himself, he would admit that no woman had affected him as this one had. And it wasn't simply because she was beautiful and interesting. Summer had brought him sunlight!

Summer . . . Colin felt the urge to laugh aloud. The name fit her perfectly. Sure, he knew she'd said the whole sunlight thing had been because of how her magic worked on spells, but she'd been wrong. He'd smelled sunlight on her, felt it in her touch, since the moment he'd taken her hand.

After living in darkness for so long, there was one thing he definitely recognized, and that was the touch of the sun. He had to have more of that touch. So he was going to woo her until he won her.

"You're so different here," she'd said of him on the balcony, and she'd seemed to like the difference. Colin had been different. He'd been himself again—or at least his prevampire self. Unending night had worn on him until he'd become as dark as his surroundings. Even his ranch had become a black place for him. He'd never been able to go out on his land, work his horses, or care for the cattle in the daylight. He hired hands to do that for him. But for decades he'd found solace in roaming his land at night—in chasing the last rays of sunlight

as day reluctantly gave way to night, and then, in turn, giving way to the sun as it inevitably reclaimed the sky. Not so recently. Recently his life had seemed nothing but unending darkness, his beloved ranch not freedom and open space, but just another gilded cage where night continued to imprison him.

Living a life of shadows had worn on him and darkened Colin's personality as well. But that wasn't really *him*. It was what this damn vampire curse had turned him into. Summer could change that; Summer could change everything, and he wanted her to. He wanted to be the Colin who laughed and lived and loved again

So he'd put in an overseas call to his brother who was still sleeping his way around gay Paris, and Barnabas had told him Summer was staying in her sister, Candice's, cabin, which sat in a clearing at the southern edge of the pine forest surrounding Mysteria. Which is why he had just trekked through said forest with Summer's purse and a gift for her and why he was now standing just inside the edge of trees facing the brightly lit little cabin with its homey, wraparound porch.

Colin drew a deep breath. Sunlight and honey —he could scent her from there. She had to be home. He started forward, telling himself that the jittery feeling in his stomach wasn't nerves, it was just anticipation. Which was only natural; it had been decades since he'd been interested enough to actually consider courting a lady. He just needed to remember that he used to be good with the ladies. Charming—that's how they used to describe him. Out of practice he may be, but he'd dig deep and put back on that old charm, and Summer would see that—

The door to her cabin opened, and Colin came to an abrupt halt when a man's body was silhouetted clearly in the doorway. Summer joined the guy, and Colin's gaze focused on her, blocking out the man and the night and everything but this amazing woman who was, to him, a waking dream.

He loved what she was wearing. The skirt was soft and feminine, and coupled with the creamy yellow of her shirt and the gold of her hair, she looked just like she smelled: like a vision of sunlight and sweetness. He wanted to take her in his arms and mold her softness to his body and inhale her fragrance until he had to fight with himself not to explode.

Then the guy moved, blocking his view of Summer. With a growing sense of horror, Colin watched the jerk nonchalantly drape an arm over her shoulder. Another scent came to him then: one of lemons and laughter and . . . and . . . fairies?

The asshole who was trying to steal his sunshine was a fairy? His jaw tightened, and it felt like someone had slammed a sledgehammer into his gut when the Goddess-be-damned fairy bent and began gently kissing Summer. For a moment Colin stood, rooted into place. Then, with a small sound of disgust, he turned and melted back into the darkness of the forest.

Just beyond vision of the cabin, Colin paced . . . and paced . . . and paced. He had the urge to throw her purse into the branches of the nearest pine and break the carefully wrapped package into a million little pieces, but he managed to control himself, although just barely.

Summer had said she had a boyfriend, but he'd scented her then and hadn't smelled even a hint of another male on her. He had most definitely *not* smelled that fucking blond lemon drop! Yet the fairy had been there—in her home—with his lips all over her.

All right. Fine. He should have expected a woman as attractive as Summer to have other suitors. He would just have to step up his game. He was more than a match for the lemon drop. Fairies, even the wingless male variety, were all fickle sluts. Didn't Summer know that? Maybe she didn't. His brother had said she'd just moved back after being away for most of her four years of college. Maybe she didn't have much experience with adult male fairies. Colin's jaw clenched again, and his hands fisted. He'd crush that damn lemon drop into a little yellow speck if he did anything to hurt her.

By the time he'd paced off his temper and returned to Summer's cabin, the lights had been turned out. The scent of lemon fairy had also been extinguished, which helped to calm him. The damn lemon drop hadn't stayed the night. Colin left his offering on the porch just before dawn.

The morning was gorgeous. It was weird how getting rid of an old crush had cleared her vision. Her plan had been flawed, but that didn't mean she shouldn't get busy on a new one . . . a new one that might just be tall and dark and handsome. She really shouldn't obsess so much about being in perfect control. And, anyway, she could handle the vampire. She'd certainly handled the fairy. She was definitely interested in Colin, or at least she thought she might be interested in him. Well, she was going to stop by the gallery on her way home from school to get her purse. She'd see then if there really was any attraction going on with the vamp and take it from there.

Summer felt amazingly alive and happy as she slathered black raspberry jam on a piece of toast and munched on it hurrying out of the cabin on her way to school—and almost tripped and fell face-first over the heap of stuff in front of her door.

"What the—" Summer rubbed the knee she'd landed on, looking back at the pile of . . . "My purse," she murmured. Sure enough, her purse was there. Right in front of the door. Sitting next to it was a package wrapped in expensive black tissue paper. There was a simple ivory card taped to it that just said *For Summer* in an old-fashioned-looking cursive script. Intrigued, she fingered the card and then opened the package carefully, so she didn't mess up the beautiful paper.

Summer gasped and oohed in pleasure. It was a copy of the Romeo and Juliet painting, reproduced in oil on canvas and framed in an exquisite gold-painted wood frame.

"Colin," she whispered and felt a thrill of pleasure thrum through her at the sound of his name.

"That might be the most romantic thing I've ever heard," Jenny said over the barely edible lunch they'd bought from the vomitorium, aka the school cafeteria.

"It has to have come from him. Right?"

Jenny rolled her eyes. "Of course it came from him. Hello! He brought back your purse, and—now, correct me if I'm wrong, but I do believe he's the only vampire you got zapped into the R and J painting with."

"Definitely the only one."

"The vamp is wooing you," Jenny said smugly.

"Wooing? Is that even still a word?"

"Yes. And that's what he's doing. So prepare yourself."

"For what?"

Jenny shook her head sadly. "Oh, you poor child. I would imagine that a rough ballpark on your vampire's age is probably at least two hundred."

Summer blinked. "He's not my vampire."

"Yet," Jenny said.

"Two hundred," Summer said as if she hadn't spoken. "As in years old?"

"Yep."

"Wow."

"And as that very tasteful, expensive, and sexy gift shows, men used to know how to do some wooing."

"Wow." Summer considered Jenny's words as she tried to chew her soyburger. "I'm going over there," she said decisively.

"To the gallery?"

"Yes. I'm going to thank him for the painting. And for returning my purse. Plus, uh, I'd, well, like to make sure there's no misunderstanding about anything he might have accidentally seen last night."

"You lost me on that one."

"Ken kissed me good night last night."

"So? You said you decided you're totally not interested in him."

"I did, and it was his kiss that sealed my decision. But first I thought I should give him a chance, which meant I kissed him back."

"Again, so?"

"Well, I was kissing him and looking over his shoulder and thinking about the moon and lesson plans and stuff, and I thought I saw something—or someone—outside by the edge of the woods. Then the next morning I found my purse and the painting on my front porch."

"Wait, back up. Kenny was kissing you, and you were thinking about lesson plans and crap like that?"

Summer nodded.

"That's a damn shame. I don't know what the hell's wrong with fairies these days. Kenny-benny doesn't ring my bell, but damn! He's a *fairy*, a fey being who practically has sex and frolics for a living. He should be able to hold a woman's attention with a kiss."

"Don't be so hard on him. I'd just been kissed by Colin, and the comparison was not good for Kenny."

Jenny rolled her eyes. "Yet you were going on and on about how you weren't interested in the vamp and how he wasn't your type and how he didn't fit into your control-freak plan."

"I'm not a control freak, or at least not all the time. Anyway, Colin might not be exactly what I've thought of as my type, but he's definitely a better kisser than Ken."

"Big surprise there," Jenny said.

"Be nice," Summer said.

Jenny rolled her eyes again.

"Like I said, I'm going to swing by the gallery after school. This time it'll be just me and not a busload of germs and hormones. Maybe sparks will fly again between us, maybe not. But I'm going to give him a shot."

"Good idea. And speaking of germs and hormones, I'm not done deciding on that damn Purdom kid's detention for that bullshit spell he cast yesterday. I'm still looking into the he-had-an-accomplice angle."

"You might want to interrogate McArter; they're buds. Oh, and remember, don't tell him about my magic," Summer added quickly.

"I got it the first hundred times you told me to keep quiet about it. Don't worry; I think it's hilarious that they don't know about your magic. Makes them think their magic is totally screwed up, which serves them right. They shouldn't be using magic at school or at a school event. Brats," Jenny said, eyes flashing.

The bell rang, and both women sighed. "Back into the fray," Jenny said.

"Do you think it's possible to Shakespeare freshmen to death?" Summer asked.

"One can only hope," Jenny said.

Eight

Summer checked her lipstick in her car's rearview mirror and smoothed her hair, feeling insanely thankful that the day was bright and clear and humidity-free, which meant she was having a good hair day. She glanced at the front of *Dark Shadows*. There were no other cars parked close by, and she mentally crossed her fingers that three o'clock was too early for evening visitors and too late for lunchtime visitors, so it would be empty. Well, except for Colin, that is.

She could do this. She could go inside and smile and thank him for returning her purse and leaving such a great gift. She could figure out a way to let him know that Kenny was history. And maybe, just maybe, she could see if that amazing sizzle that sparked between them yesterday was more than just a magical fluke. Then she could consider revising her future plan to include him.

Before she could chicken out, Summer forced herself to get out of the car and enter the dark, cool gallery.

Her first thought was that her hunch had been right; the gallery appeared deserted. Her second thought was that it was very uncomfortable to be standing there all by herself with only the feeling of being watched to keep her company.

The feeling of being watched?

Definitely. She definitely could feel eyes on her: dark, hungry, intense eyes. Almost as if he drew her gaze, she turned her head and looked deeper into the shadows of the gallery. Sure enough, Colin was standing there, his gaze locked on her.

"Good afternoon, Summer," he said.

His voice reminded her of dark chocolate and wine and sex.

"Hi," she blurted, hating how nervous she sounded. Then she cleared her throat and got control of herself. "I hope you don't mind me just dropping in like this."

His lips tilted up slightly. "It's a gallery. The idea is for people to drop in."

"Then I'm glad I have the right idea," she said, tilting her own lips up.

"And I'm glad you came by. I wanted to see you again. Would you like to come back to my office?"

"Yes, yes, I would."

Summer's smile increased as she followed Colin, getting another excellent view of his tight butt as he led her through the room with the Romeo and Juliet painting, back to an inconspicuous door that opened to an ornate, fussily decorated office.

"This is definitely not you," she said, running her finger down the back of a gilded Louis the Something-or-Other chair. Then her gaze flew up to him as she tried to gauge if she'd just offended him.

He simply shrugged and said, "You're right. This is Barnabas's office, and it's definitely him. He likes pomp and circumstance and lots of gold."

"And what do you like?" Summer heard her voice asking the question that had flitted automatically through her mind. She clamped her mouth shut. She usually had more control than speaking her thoughts aloud, but she found herself being temporarily glad of her lack of control when his gaze went dark and intense as he answered her.

"If you mean what kind of decoration, I like it more masculine, although I don't think a house is really a home without a woman's touch." The vampire blinked, obviously surprised at his response, and then he smiled almost shyly at Summer. "I think that's the first time I've admitted that to myself."

"Admitted that you like a woman's touch?" she asked softly.

His gaze trapped hers. "Admitted that I *need* a woman's touch," he said. "But I shouldn't be surprised. You affect me oddly, Summer."

"Is that a good or a bad thing?" she asked.

"For me, it is a very good thing," he said.

They stared at each other until Summer became uncomfortable under the heat of his scrutiny. "Thank you for returning my purse to me," she said, trying to temper the electricity that was building between them with words. "And I absolutely love the Romeo and Juliet painting. Thank you for it."

"I'm glad you like it. I wanted to give you something that might make you remember what happened yesterday."

"It's been kinda hard for me to forget," Summer said.

"For me, too." Colin moved closer to her. "Yesterday meant a lot to me. I haven't felt the sun on my skin in many decades. It's not something I want to forget."

"You know I didn't do it on purpose. I can't bring you the sun again." Summer was finding it hard to think rationally with him so close, but her mind was working enough that she wanted to make it perfectly clear to him that she couldn't just zap them back into the picture; she couldn't make the sun shine for him.

Colin touched the side of her face. "You're wrong about that."

Summer shivered. His touch was cool, but her skin beneath his fingers came alive with heat.

You are my sunshine.

Summer jumped when his voice sounded inside her head.

"You heard that, didn't you?" he said.

"Yes," she whispered. "I also heard you call to me from across the room yesterday."

That dark intensity was back in his eyes, and he spoke with such emotion, such passion, that Summer's heartbeat quickened, and she felt her breathing deepen.

"You don't know me, and I don't know you, but there is something between us that I've not experienced until I touched you yesterday. You say you can't bring me sunshine again, yet to me your skin, your breath, your hair, even the summer-sky color of your eyes—all of you is light and shining to me. It is as if, somehow, magically, you are literally *my* summer, *my* sunlight."

"I—I don't know how that could be. I'm just me." Summer couldn't help leaning her cheek into his hand. His scent and touch were intoxicating, and she wanted nothing more at that instant than to get closer to him.

"I don't know how it could be either, but you are an unexpected gift that I plan to cherish. If you'll let me. Will you give me a chance, Summer?" Colin lifted her chin. "I realize I'm not what you're used to—not the kind of man you would consider a *boyfriend*." He ground the word out. "And yesterday you said you were already seeing someone."

"I'm not," she said.

"Not?"

"Not seeing anyone." She stared up into his dark eyes, utterly mesmerized by his closeness.

"But last night . . ."

"Was nothing. There's nothing between us. Ken isn't my boyfriend."

"I saw—" he began.

"You saw him kissing me. It was just, well, basically a test. I wanted to see if he could make me feel what you made me feel."

"And did he?"

"No," Summer said, staring into the vampire's eyes. "Not even maybe. That's one of the reasons I'm here. I had to see if it was still there," she said softly.

"It?"

"The sizzle between us."

Colin smiled. "It's still there. Let me taste you, sunshine, and I'll prove it to you."

"Yes," she whispered, already leaning into him.

Colin didn't claim her mouth right away. Instead, he drank in her scent and touch, mingling breath with breath. "I want you more than you can know." He spoke the words against her skin. "When I touch you I'm alive again. I can feel the sunlight on my face." He nuzzled her neck and then buried his hand in her thick blond hair and breathed in the scent of sunlight and honey that clung to her.

"Kiss me, Colin," she murmured.

With a strangled sound, his mouth finally met hers, easily erasing any lingering memory of Ken's soft, sweet, boring kisses. His skin didn't have the heat it had the day before, but it didn't matter. It was still *him*, and Summer craved his taste and touch like she'd never wanted anyone or anything before in her life.

When they finally broke apart, it was only to stare dazedly at each other. "What is it between us?" Summer said. "It's crazy. It's like you're my human version of catnip."

His smile took away what was left of her breath. "I'm your catnip; you're my sunshine. I think we make an excellent pair."

"But I don't even know you. You're practically a stranger."

Colin took her hand, threading his cool fingers through her warm ones. "Can you say we're strangers when we're touching?"

Summer looked down at their linked hands. His was so pale and large and strong, and hers was tan from working in her sister's flower beds. They seemed direct opposites. He was the opposite of everything she'd believed she wanted for so many years. Yet he was right; when they touched, something was there, and it was something that hadn't been there with any man before him.

"Colin, we have to slow down. I have to think about—"

The buzzer that signaled the opening of the front door of the gallery made both of them jump. Colin threw a dark look over his shoulder. "I'll get rid of them and close the gallery; then we can talk." Like an amazing old-time gentleman, he kissed her hand before he started out of the room, but he stopped in the doorway, glancing back at her. "You were right, Summer. You don't really know me, and I don't know you. But what I do know is there is something special between us. I've walked this earth longer than you—a couple hundred and some odd years longer." She gaped at him. Was everyone a zillion years older than her? Colin's smile was sad and his eyes haunted with loneliness as he continued. "I can promise you that in all the long years of my life I haven't ever felt what I do when I so much as breathe in the scent of your skin. If you feel even a fraction of what I feel, how can you not give us a chance?"

"What if this is all just because of my messed-up magic?" she asked.

"What if it isn't?" Colin said.

Then he turned and left the room.

Summer's knees felt wobbly, and she dropped down into the closest gilded chair. What was going on with them? One thing was sure; the attraction between them was still there, in spades! She wiped a shaky hand over her brow. He was right. She'd never felt anything like what Colin made her feel just with the touch of his hand on her face, let alone his lips against hers. What would happen if their naked bodies pressed together? A thrill of anticipation sang through her. Could she handle such passion, and if she couldn't, what happened then? Was it worth taking a chance on? What was it the ancient Greek playwright, Euripides, said about too much passion . . . something about a lion loose in a cattle pen?

Plus, she really didn't want to be in love with a vampire. Besides the whole vegetarian/carnivore issue there was the day/night issue. She loved daylight and sunshine and all that went with it. Wouldn't she have to give that up to be with Colin?

Her head was starting to ache when the voices that had been drifting to her from the outer gallery began to register.

"Yeah, man, we didn't mean for nothin' bad to happen," said one male voice.

"For real. We were gonna come by today and say sorry, even if Ms. Sullivan hadn't made us," added another.

Summer snorted a little laugh. That had to be Purdom and one of his partners in crime. Jenny had been right. There was more power behind that spell than one kid could have conjured.

"That Ms. Sullivan is one mean woman," said the first voice.

Summer smiled. Yep, Jenny had definitely known it.

"Yeah, but she's so fiiine," said the second, she now recognized as her student and Purdom's bud, Blake McArter.

She heard Colin's deep voice answering them but couldn't quite make out what he was saying. She attempted to sit still for a minute more, then curiosity killed discretion, and she walked quietly to the doorway of the office.

"We thought we'd make up a little thang for ya," said Purdom.

"Like, to make up for what we did," said McArter. "Okay with you if we bust out with it?"

"Sounds fine with me," Colin said.

This time she could hear Colin's voice more clearly, and the good humor in his tone made her smile. Her feet seemed to move of their own accord as she continued walking soundlessly down the hall. After all, she'd been a victim of Purdom's magical stunt. He should apologize to her, too. Well, again, that is. Naturally, Jenny had made him grovel appropriately at school earlier that day. But still, more groveling never hurt, plus the other kid was here, too, this time. She crept slowly into the gallery until she came to the room that held the Romeo and Juliet painting, aka the scene of the crime. The two boys were standing in front of the painting with their backs to her. Colin was facing them, so he could have spotted her, but his attention was focused, with an amused lift of one of his dark brows, on the boys as they started making the ridiculous rap noises that always reminded Summer of a mixture of farts and messed-up engine sounds. As McArter did the sound effects, Purdon rapped their song.

We come to apologize 'bout the other day.
See, we didn't know you and Miss S. would go away.
We was just tryin' to get in some play.
We sorry you had ta dress all gay.
And then Miss S. and you almost went all the way.

Those brats! They did know Colin and I had been in the painting! At that point there was a "musical" interlude in the rap, and both boys mouth farted and popped around looking silly and semicharming at the same time. Summer had just decided she'd been entertained enough and had started forward again when her eyes went to Colin, and she froze in place. He was watching the boys and laughing with the youthful joy of a man filled with light and promise. And Summer once again saw the happy, open man who had shared the painting, and his passion, with her.

He was completely and utterly captivating.

It was then that the question of whether she should risk getting entangled in a life of passion and darkness became moot. She *was* entangled with him already. Somehow within this dark, brooding vampire there lay the man she'd fantasized about and longed for all these years. It wasn't a question of fitting him into her future. Colin was her future.

Summer must have made an involuntary sound, because Colin's gaze instantly went from the boys to her. The smile didn't leave his face; on the contrary, when their eyes met, his joy seemed to blaze from him to her.

"So we be here to make yestaday okay," rapped Purdom.

"Yea, we got to give you somethin' 'cause Sullivan says we got to pay," intoned McArter.

"And she's scary—even though I'd like to tap that play."

The fart noises came to a crescendo, then Purdom went into the closing lines of the rap.

"We thought 'bout what we could do that would stay.

And come up with a magic spell to melt our dissin' ya away."

Magic spell? Those words broke through the smoldering look she was sharing with Colin at the same time she noticed that the little shivers going up and down her spine weren't just because she was hot for the vampire. *The rap was really a spell the boys were casting!* Then four things happened simultaneously.

Summer opened her mouth to scream at the kids to stop.

Colin moved toward her with an inhuman speed that blurred his body.

Purdom finished the rap/spell with the line, "Dude, we give you a future bright as the sun's ray!"

And as the vampire's body slammed into Summer, she

realized the magic catastrophe was unavoidable, so she closed her eyes and braced herself, sending out one concentrated desire: *This will not mess up Colin and me.* Then the area around her exploded with light.

Nine

✳

When Summer opened her eyes, she was in a strange bed in a room she didn't recognize. It was nice—she noticed that right away. Actually, it was freakishly like her dream room: huge, antique iron bed piled with rich linens in soft blues and yellows. The furniture was simply carved oak, well made and expensive but not fussy. The floor was glossy pine wood, dotted here and there with thick butter-colored area rugs. The walls told her she was in a log cabin—a damn big one at that. There was a fireplace along one wall. The others held several incredible original watercolor paintings of landscapes that all had one thing in common: they were bright and beautiful and painted in the full flush of summer days.

Then her eyes caught something on top of the long, low dresser. Was that her jewelry box? She climbed down from the mountain of a bed and realized two things: One, she was wearing her favorite style of pajamas: men's boxer shorts and a little matching tank top. Two, it was, indeed, her jewelry box sitting on top of the dresser. Actually, as she looked around the room more carefully, she saw that the jewelry box was just one of several items that belonged to her. Over the ornate beveled mirror hung one of her favorite scarves. The Kresley Cole book she'd been reading was on the nightstand beside the bed, as was her favorite honeydew-scented candle. Feeling surreal and very *Twilight Zone*–ish she opened the top drawer of the nearest dresser and, sure enough, inside was a neat row of her bras and panties.

"What the hell is going on?" She cried, and then, wondering how she could have been stupid enough to forget, memory flashed back to her, and she recalled the two boys and their rap that had become a spell and the terrible light that exploded just as Colin had grabbed her.

Light? Colin?

Light! Colin! The two definitely didn't mix. Where was she, and where was Colin? Summer hurried to the window and peeked out. The sun was setting into the mountains, painting the lovely landscape around the cabin in hues of evening. She was definitely in a cabin, out in the woods. But it wasn't her sister's cabin. She tried to calm her freaked-out mind. *Think—I have to think! The kids' spell finished with something about Colin having a bright future. Goddess! Did that mean he was trapped in the dark somewhere? And if so, why was she here in this pretty cabin?* It didn't make one bit of sense.

"Okay. Okay. You're a college graduate. You can figure this out," she told herself. "This room looks like it could belong to you, so . . ." With sudden inspiration, Summer went back to the bedside table and, sure enough, plugged into the charger, just as it was in the bedroom in her sister's cabin, was Summer's cell phone. She grabbed it and dialed the first number that came to mind.

"Summer! Where are you? Are you okay?" Jenny's voice was uncharacteristically frantic.

"I'm fine, I think, and I don't know where the hell I am. Where's Colin? Is he okay?"

"Other than having lost his damn mind worrying about you, your vamp's fine. And what do you mean you don't know where you are?"

"What do you mean he's lost his mind?" Summer and Jenny spoke their questions together.

"I can't tell—" Summer began.

"He's freaked completely—" Jenny said.

Both women paused. "You start," Jenny said. "Why don't you know where you are?"

"'Cause I've never been here before. I'm at a gorgeous cabin and, weirdly enough, it's not just decorated exactly how I would have decorated it, but a bunch of my stuff's here. Now tell me what's up with Colin."

There was some unintelligible noise in the background and then Jenny said, "I'll do better than that. I'll let Colin tell you himself."

Summer could hear her passing off the phone, and then Colin's deep voice was in her ear. "Summer? Are you hurt? Where are you?"

"Colin! Are you okay? What happened?"

"I'm fine; don't worry about me. Are you okay?" he said.

"Other than not understanding what happened, I'm fine. Especially now that I know you're okay."

"I am okay, sunshine." She could hear the smile in his voice. "Now that I'm not scared into my second death. Don't ever disappear like that on me again."

"Disappear? Is that what happened? All I remember is a bright light. Are you sure you're okay? I know the whole light thing isn't good for you."

"I didn't see a light. The kid finished the spell just as I grabbed you, and then an instant later my arms were empty, and you were nowhere." His voice lowered. "I don't like my arms being empty of you."

His words made warm, fluttering things happen in the pit of her stomach. "Yeah, I know," she said.

"Where are you? The sun's setting. I'll come to you."

"I wish you could. I don't have any idea where I am. I woke up in this beautiful iron bed in an amazing room that, weirdly, has a bunch of my stuff in it." Summer walked to the bedroom door while she kept talking. "I peeked out the window, and I'm somewhere in the mountains—great view, by the by—in a big cabin. You should see this place. Your brother would definitely appreciate the quality of the watercolors on the walls, and they're all of summer landscapes. I haven't gone out into the rest of the house yet, though."

"Does the bedroom have a large, wood burning fireplace in it?"

Summer nodded. "Yeah, it does."

"Go out into the rest of the cabin, and tell me what you see." His voice had a strangely excited tone to it.

"What's going on, Colin?"

"I have a hunch. Just leave the bedroom, and I'll know if I'm right."

She took a deep breath and opened the door. "Okay, this is definitely my dream home," Summer said.

"Describe it to me, Sunshine," Colin said.

"I'm on a landing looking down at an incredible living room. The furniture is all leather, but it's not too testosteroney because it's mixed with antique end tables and thick, furry rugs. Oh, Goddess! I hope it's fake fur."

Colin's deep laugh was in her ear. "I'll bet it is now."

"Now? What do you mean?"

"First, go down the stairs and into the living room and describe to me the painting over the fireplace."

"Okay, it's kinda freaking me out that you know this place."

"Don't be scared, Sunshine. Trust me. All will be well."

She loved the tone of happy excitement that filled his voice and hurried down the stairs. Sure enough, there was a huge painting over the fireplace, and when Summer realized what it was, she laughed aloud. "It's the Romeo and Juliet! Goddess, it looks like it's the original."

"It is, sweet Sunshine. Stay right where you are; I will come to you."

"You know where I am?"

"I do, indeed. You're home, Summer."

"You're home, Summer" was all that Colin would say before he hung up. What did that mean? But she didn't have time to worry and wonder, because all of a sudden a dark mist began to spill into the room. Wordlessly, Summer watched it surround her and thicken and then change, elongate, and solidify until Colin was standing in front of her.

He looked around them, and his handsome face blazed with a triumphant smile. "I knew it! Makes me really glad I didn't eviscerate those boys."

"Colin, would you please explain to me what's happened?"

"*We've* happened," he said, still smiling. "This"—he swept his arm around them in a smooth motion—"is my home. Only it's been changed. A woman's touch has been added. *You've* been added to my home, Summer."

Summer stared around her in amazement. "This is your home?"

"It is."

"How did this happen?"

"The boy said that he was giving me a bright future. His spell, mixed with your magic, has gifted me with you." Colin closed the space between them and took her in his arms, inhaling her scent and touch. "Let me show you how much we belong together."

"Colin." She spoke his name like a prayer and reached up to touch his face. The instant her hand met his cheek, the vampire gasped and jerked as if she'd zapped him with a jolt of electricity. Summer pulled back, afraid she'd hurt him, but what was reflected in his dark eyes wasn't pain, but wonder.

"Touch me again, Summer."

Before she could respond, Colin took her hand and pressed it back against his cheek, and this time Summer saw the glow of light that came from her hand and felt what was happening beneath her palm. The vampire's cool flesh shivered and then flushed and warmed.

"What's happened?" she whispered.

"You're bringing light to me again, my darling. Only this time your magic is calling alive my flesh." He turned his face so that his lips pressed against the palm of her hand. She felt a tingle of heat pass through her hand, and then his lips were on hers. They were warm and insistent and very much alive. Speaking only her name, Colin lifted her into his arms and strode from the living room up the stairs, kicking open the bedroom door and gently placing her on the bed.

When he bent to kiss her again, she pressed him gently away from her. "Wait, I have to see . . . I have to touch you and know . . ." she murmured.

Slowly, carefully, she unbuttoned his shirt, pulling it apart so his muscular chest was bared to her. Then she lifted her hands and, pressing her palms against his skin, began at his shoulders, sliding her hands down his chest in a slow, thorough caress that spread light down his body. Against her glowing skin his flesh warmed, and she watched in awe as his carved marble skin and muscles shivered and then, as long as she touched him, flushed with health and life. When her hand reached the place over his heart, Colin moaned—a sound part pain, part pleasure—and he pressed his hand over hers, stilling her caress.

"Ah, Goddess!" Colin said. "My heart beats again!"

"I can feel it. Oh, Colin! I can feel it beating."

"Don't stop touching me, Summer. Don't ever stop touching me."

Light-headed with the swirling emotions of passion and awe and desire, Summer looked into Colin's dark eyes and saw love and life and her future there. And then she closed her eyes and bowed her head, breathing deeply while she tried to calm her turbulent emotions. *I will not lose control and cause this to end! I will not!*

Ten

"Summer, what is it?" Colin's voice was filled with worry.

She opened her eyes and met his gaze. "I'll never stop touching you, Colin. I promise, but you have to let me be with you on my own terms."

His expression only became more confused, and mixed with that confusion Summer saw hurt and withdrawal. "I know that my being a vampire is hard for you. I understand you might not want to bind yourself to someone like me."

"No, no I didn't mean that," she explained quickly. "It has to do with my magic. I have to maintain control of my emotions, because if they surge too much and I lose control, the spell will be broken and the messed-up magic, along with all of this, will end."

"Sunshine, *this* isn't as simple as a spell or magic. What's happening between us is real."

"I hope so," she said. And then she drew her hand down his arm again, watching as the glow under her palm warmed his cool flesh. "But *this* is definitely magic, and I don't want this to end for you."

"As long as I have you, I'll have sunlight—magic or no."

"You have me, Colin," she said, but still Summer controlled her breathing and kept a firm hold on her emotions as, never taking her hands from his skin, she undressed him. First she pushed off his shirt, skimming her hands down his arms until she threaded her fingers through his, staring into his eyes as her touch brought his skin alive.

"Summer," he moaned her name. "I never imagined I could feel like this again."

"How do you feel, Colin?" Summer asked breathlessly as her mouth moved down his naked chest.

"Like a man, Sunshine. You make me feel like a man again."

His words sent a thrill through her body. Summer caressed Colin's waist, reveling in her ability to give him such pleasure. She unzipped his jeans, and he stepped out of them. She stared at his naked body and imaged that she knew what Pygmalion felt as his sculpture of Galatea came to life.

Calm and slow, Summer reminded herself as she pulled him down beside her on the bed. *Focus on giving him pleasure.* When his eager hands reached for her, she allowed Colin to pull her into his arms. Her mouth met his as she pressed her body against his nakedness. Separated by only the thin cotton of her boxers and tank, it was an exquisite sensation to feel her heat warming him, her flesh bringing him alive.

His hardness pressed low and insistent against the softness of her stomach, and while their tongues met her hips shifted, bringing him fully against her core. He moaned against her mouth as she thrust against him, sliding him the length of her wetness.

When her head started to spin, she broke the kiss. Concentrating on controlling her breathing and trying to find calmness within her again, she rolled over on top of Colin and held his wrists, stilling his roving hands, which had been kneading her aching breasts. "Let *me* touch *you,*" she said, regaining her breath. When he started to protest, she stilled his words with a kiss, then whispered against his mouth, "I don't want the magic to go away, Colin. Help me keep the magic."

"Sunshine, I've been trying to tell you that you *are* the magic." His voice was deep and rich with desire.

"Humor me," Summer said with a smile and then began to

move down his body, kissing and caressing. When she reached his cock, she took him in both of her hands, loving the textures of him, the hardness sheathed in such soft skin. Still stroking him, she glanced up and met his gaze. "You're wrong, Colin. It's you who's magic." And then she bent and let her tongue flick out around the engorged head of his cock. He moaned her name as she licked the length of his shaft, discovering how exciting it was to be able to bring him such intense pleasure so easily.

"Do you want me to take you in my mouth?" she asked huskily.

"Oh, Goddess, yes!" he gasped.

Summer swallowed him. He was too large for her to take all of him in her mouth, but she stroked his shaft with her hand, squeezing while she tasted him, loving how his cock heated and pulsed beneath her touch. She cupped his heavy testicles, and another moan was torn from his throat as his hips lifted to give her better access to him.

"Your body is so beautiful," she murmured against his skin, teasing the head of his cock with her tongue. "I never knew a man's body could be so beautiful."

Then she swallowed him again. "Summer!" Colin gasped her name, his voice rough with barely controlled lust. "I can't stand much more. If you don't stop, I'm going to come in your mouth."

Summer loved that *she* was evoking this response in him. She felt gorgeous and sexy and very much in control. "Then give in to it," she purred, imagining for the first time in her life that she was the Marilyn Monroe type, the kind of woman men dreamed about. "Give in to me." She laved his engorged head with her tongue while she ran her hands down his thighs, feeling his muscles tremble and warm under her hands.

Summer heard a ripping sound as his hands gripped the thick comforter while he struggled to maintain control, and then he moved with a vampire's preternatural swiftness, and suddenly his hands were lifting her, and she was on her back looking up at him.

"Colin, wait, I need to do this my way!"

"Sunshine, lovemaking is something best done together, rather than controlled by one. And I have to have my turn."

She started to protest again, but the dark intensity of his gaze caught her. "Trust me, Summer. Trust that I'm telling you the truth when I say that what's happening between us is more than an accident of magic."

"I trust you," she said softly, *but I'm still going to stay in control,* she added silently to herself.

His smile had a sexy, feral glint as, with one flick of his powerful hands, he ripped the cotton tank off her. Colin cupped her breasts, running his thumb lightly over her already sensitized nipples. She gasped and bit her bottom lip.

"Since I saw these beautiful nipples, aroused and pressing against that sweet teacher's blouse you had on yesterday, I've thought about doing this over and over again. His head dipped down, and he took her nipple into his mouth, sucking and licking gently. She threaded her fingers through his thick, dark hair and pressed him more firmly against her. "Harder," she whispered, and then all her breath left her body in a rush as he went from gentle to forceful, pulling on the nipple with his teeth while he lifted his hard thigh between her legs so that her hips could lift and grind against him.

Control . . . control . . . she reminded herself frantically. Summer breathed deeply, letting the pleasure wash in waves over her but not allowing herself to drown in it.

Colin shifted his attention to her other breast, and she closed her eyes, feeling the desire that was building inside of her but keeping it banked just enough that it didn't engulf her.

Then his mouth followed the edge of her rib cage down to the soft indentation of her waist. He hooked his fingers in her shorts and quickly skimmed them down her body, leaving her naked before him. She felt a moment of embarrassment, but it passed when she saw the expression on his face and heard his husky, "Sunshine, you're even more exquisite than I dreamed you would be." He kissed her stomach reverently, gently, before letting his hands glide down her body to cup her buttocks. He positioned himself between her legs as he lifted her to his mouth.

Summer stopped breathing completely when his tongue parted her folds and dipped within.

"You taste just like you smell: like sunlight and honey," he murmured against her intimately.

When his tongue found her clit, her hips buckled against him. She squeezed her eyes closed, fighting against the cascade of pleasure. She wanted too badly to let loose, to allow him to make her come against his mouth. But what would happen then? How could she bear it if she was suddenly transported, midorgasm, back to her cabin—alone?

"Colin, come here to me," she said, reaching to pull him up to her. When he only intensified his caresses, she added, "I have to feel you inside me."

That got through to him, and he raised himself over her. She took him in her hand again, lifting her hips so that she could position the throbbing head of his cock against her wet opening. Summer was already getting her breathing back under control, and she'd keep that control while he spent himself inside her—at least she hoped she could. That Colin could turn her on was abundantly apparent, but being turned on and actually orgasming were two very different things.

This would be for Colin. She'd bring him light and life and love. She'd let him bring her to completion another time, when she was sure her emotions wouldn't cause their whole world to disappear. So her plan was to take him inside her and just maintain her sanity this once. She'd worry about next time the next time. Everything would work out in the future when she—

"Look at me, Summer."

His voice brought her attention back to the present. She looked up into his expressive, dark eyes.

"I want to look into your eyes while I love you, while I make you mine," he said. He thrust into her with one powerful plunge, filling her completely.

Summer gasped as the pleasure spiked through her. Her hips lifted to meet his as her legs wrapped around him. Colin braced himself on one arm, raising up so that he could continue to look into her eyes. The vampire impaled her. They moved together, slick and hot.

Summer felt her body gathering itself, and she fought against it, even though the pleasure was so intense that it bordered on pain. But she maintained control—she did it. Until Colin reached between them and began rubbing his thumb rhythmically against her swollen, slick clit.

"Colin!" she gasped. "Oh, Goddess, I can't—"

"Shhh," he whispered. "What we have is beyond magic. If you trust me, give yourself completely to me. I can prove it to you. Will you trust me?"

"Yes," she said without hesitation. "I trust you, Colin."

"Then I make you mine, truly and completely." He bent his head to her neck. Summer felt his lips, his tongue, and finally his teeth. At first they just grazed her, then she felt him gather himself, and Colin bit her, puncturing through the soft skin above her pulsing vein.

The pleasure she felt at his claiming was as sharp as the bite, and she couldn't fight against her desire any longer. Summer felt the wave begin within her and knew it would utterly, completely overwhelm her. She grasped Colin's shoulders and, for once in her life, completely gave up control to a man, body and soul. As her body shuddered in orgasm, and he joined her in release, she felt the familiar tingle of her magic becoming active. This time instead of running, or bracing herself against it, or fighting it, Summer released her magic, instead choosing to hold on to Colin and his promise that there was more between them than smoke and mirrors.

The flash of light against her closed lids had Summer opening her eyes in surprise. Colin jerked back from her neck as if her blood suddenly burned. And then *he* was burning as the light that had been focused in Summer's hands surged from her into him.

"Colin!" Summer cried, trying to pull away from him, trying to stop the transfer of light.

"Trust me, sunshine," Colin ground the words out between teeth clenched in pain. "I accept any price I have to pay to be with you, and it will not separate us." At his words the light intensified until it bowed his body. The vampire screamed, and then he was knocked from the bed. He landed on the floor, limp and unconscious.

Summer was sobbing when she rushed to him, touching his face, calling his name, praying to the Goddess to please let him wake up . . . please, she'd do anything . . . just please . . . please . . .

Colin drew a deep breath and then exhaled, coughing painfully. Summer helped him sit up. "Colin! Goddess, are you okay?"

"I'm fine," his voice was raw, as if he hadn't spoken in centuries. "I'm fine," he repeated, after clearing his throat. He started to take her in his arms but suddenly froze. "Blessed Goddess!" He sounded utterly shocked.

"What is it? Maybe I should call someone. A vampire doctor?"

Then Colin completely surprised Summer by jumping to his feet, throwing back his head, and laughing with uninhibited joy.

Still on the floor, Summer looked up at him, utterly confused. "Colin?" Was he hysterical? Is this how vampires acted when they'd been mortally wounded?

"I don't need a vampire doctor, Summer, my sunshine, my dream, my love. Somehow, someway, you and your magic have made me human again!"

She stared at him, this time really seeing him. He was still a tall, handsome man, but the marble cast of his skin was gone. It had been replaced by the healthy flush of a living, breathing man.

And she wasn't touching him at all. He was truly alive.

"It'll go away," she whispered. "It won't last."

"I think you're wrong, Sunshine," he said, pulling her to her feet. "Have you ever given up trying to control your magic before tonight?"

"No," she said slowly. "I've always fought it or run from it. And it's not just my magic I gave up control of tonight, Colin. It's my life. When I trusted you, I had to give up being in total control of myself."

"I think there was something about your decision to trust me that drastically affected your magic." Colin cupped her face. "All these years you've believed your magic was flawed, messed up. I don't think it was. I think it was pure light—the pure energy of sunshine—and when you gave me your complete trust, when you relinquished control, you also gave your magic to me."

"It should have killed you. You're a vampire; you can't stand the light."

"Perhaps, but I've never loved the light until I loved you. I desired it, coveted it, yearned for it, but never really loved it until you."

"So my light didn't kill you."

"No, Sunshine. Your light burned away the darkness of my past and saved me."

"So now you think we can make love and I can orgasm without worrying about us being zapped apart."

"Over and over again, Sunshine," he said, smiling.

"Sounds like a perfect happily ever after to me."

"Me, too, Sunshine. Me, too."

Colin took her back to bed and, as the Certified Discipline Nymph Jenny would say, ravished her thoroughly for many passion-filled, out-of-control years.

MYSTERIA

By

MaryJanice Davidson

Susan Grant

P. C. Cast

Gena Showalter

Hundreds of years ago, in the mountains of Colorado (just close enough to Denver for great shoe shopping), the small town of Mysteria was "accidentally" founded by a random act of demonic kindness. Over time, it has become a veritable magnet for the supernatural—a place where magic has quietly coexisted with the mundane world.

But now the ladies of Mysteria are about to unleash a tempest of seduction that will have tongues wagging for centuries to come.

penguin.com

New in hardcover from

MaryJanice Davidson

the author whose novels are
"delightful, wicked fun!"
(*New York Times* Bestselling Author Christine Feehan)

Undead and Unworthy

Betsy Taylor thought entering the world of the
Undead was a big adjustment. Being a new bride
isn't much easier. Betsy's husband, Sinclair, has been
perusing The Book of the Dead, and Betsy's visited
by a ghost who's even more insufferable, stubborn,
and annoying in death than she was in life. She not
only blames Betsy for her condition, but insists she
fix it. It's all just a prelude to the fun and games
awaiting Betsy and Sinclair when a pack of ancient
vampires, hungry for blood and power, pays a visit
to the happy couple.

Welcome to married life, Betsy!

penguin.com